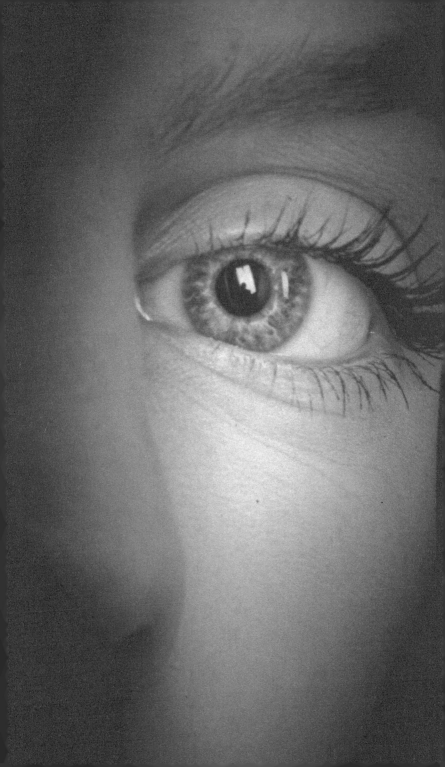

# THE HOUSEMAID

SARAH A. DENZIL

## Also by the author:

Harborside Hatred (A Liars Island novella)

A Quiet Wife

"He says unloved women have no biographies—they have histories."
    F. Scott Fitzgerald, *The Beautiful and Damned*

"Look like the innocent flower,
    But be the serpent under it."
    William Shakespeare, *Macbeth*

# THE MUSIC ROOM

Ghost is another name for housemaid. An unseen entity that slips through each room, straightening, wiping, dusting, rummaging. The eye does not linger on the maid in the corridor. The heart does not feel for her. There was a time I convinced myself otherwise, but no matter what you are to your house—a confidante, an ally, a lover—a ghost is what you will transform into. A ghost is what I became.

I thought I was someone to him—to *them* even—but in the end, I was nothing.

I don't dream anymore, but if I did, I would imagine myself back in the music room, sitting on the piano stool with him next to me. His long fingers caressing the white and black keys and the swell of the music filling up the large space inside that room. *Emily, what would you like me to play?* He would grin because he knew I always picked my favourite piece—the Debussy. He would perform it for me diligently. But what he didn't know was that I loved the way he said my name more than any music he played for me. It made me feel noticed, appreciated even, and for a maid, that's important.

When a man, a powerful, rich man, looks at you and says your name, well, let's just say it can elicit an adrenaline rush that chases away common sense.

Inside the music room, I went to another place. He and I were from two different worlds, but in that room it didn't matter. I forgot about everything I'd left behind when he started to play. Perhaps I forgot too many things. Perhaps I forgot myself.

The mistakes I made are my own, and I will never forgive myself for them and for becoming the very thing I'd tried so hard not to be: another ghost.

# CHAPTER ONE

I was twenty-one years old, broke, homeless, and desperate for a job. Lost, both literally and metaphorically. I realised, once I hopped down from the bus in Paxby village, that I couldn't afford a taxi to the house. There'd been an unexpected cost along the way. The bus company no longer sold their day saver, and I had to buy a full-price ticket. It left me with three pounds in my wallet and a debit card that belonged to an empty bank account.

Luckily, I'd arrived in Paxby over an hour early because of my own anxieties about being late. The maid job at Highwood Hall was one I'd coveted for a long time. Highwood Hall provided living accommodation for their maids, and I needed somewhere to live.

The decision was made for me. I had to walk to the house now that I couldn't afford an alternative. So I set off at a steady pace, mindful of the warm weather. Not wanting to turn up to my interview soggy from perspiration.

The ramparts and turrets of Highwood Hall peeked out from above a canopy of sloping green. All I needed to do was walk towards those slate-grey walls. And as I crossed the road, my heart pitter-pattered. In truth, the promise of accommodation was part of the reason for my application. I had to admit that it thrilled me to think of working in that stately home, one of the largest estates in Yorkshire and possibly the last one of its size that hadn't yet been opened to the public. The Howards had held on to their privacy, able to pay for the upkeep of the Hall through Lord Bertie's successful finance company. At least, I'd read that he liked to be called Lord Bertie; his actual name was Reginald Peregrine Charles Howard.

It was late May, and peroxide sunrays exploded through the clouds. As I made my way out of the village, away from the limestone walls and identical rows of cottages, I rolled up my shirtsleeves and pulled my hair back into what I hoped was a tidy bun. Fortunately, I'd had the foresight to wear tennis shoes and carry a pair of—borrowed—smart pumps in my tote bag. Looking at the steep hill up to Highwood Hall, it was the right decision.

All in all, it took me around thirty minutes to reach the forest, walking slowly so as not to sweat too much. The sudden shade from the canopy above was a welcome respite from the sun, and I allowed myself a moment to drink some water and let my legs rest. I wondered whether any of the other candidates had walked up from the village. It was possible. This interview was for a low-paying job, and I couldn't be the first interviewee without the means to drive myself there. I couldn't be the only maid living day by day, sofa surfing through the contacts on my phone, queuing up at closing time in Tesco to get the best discounts on the food they were about to discard. No, there would be others like me, I felt sure of it. I stretched out my legs and kept going, sticking to the road that snaked its way up through the woods.

I decided I'd go walking in the woods if I got the job. Maybe I'd get up early, just before dawn, and walk them alone. But what drew me to this spot, I don't know. There was no beauty here. I saw no grandeur, simply a wildness that I liked. I peeked through the trees at the thorns, weeds and long stretches of nettles. Every tree was twisted, branches malformed, the trunks growing at awkward angles, roots zigzagging down the sloping earth. Cool air spread over my skin. I unrolled my sleeves. I wrapped my arms around my body, hugging my ribs, and I quickened my step, thinking that perhaps I wouldn't go walking in the woods after all, that I wouldn't be brave enough.

Then the hall came into view. A set of wrought iron gates cut the building in half, the metal curving across the front facade of the house, and with each step, those curling bars of iron loomed taller above me. I brushed stray hairs out of my eyes and tucked the strands into my bun. I smoothed my wrinkled shirtsleeves and straightened the collar. Before I reached the gate, I ducked to the side of the road to change my shoes, checked in my compact mirror for smudged make-up, and hoped that no one would notice I'd walked a mile up a hill. Then I went back to the gate and pressed a buzzer that had definitely not been around when the house was built during the Tudor period.

A voice crackled through the speaker. Whose voice? I wondered. A security guard? A servant? When the agency organised the interview, they didn't tell me how many members of staff the Howards employed, but I guessed there must be a team. I leaned closer to the speaker and relayed why I was there. I was ten minutes early, despite the walk, but the gate opened for me anyway, and when I stepped through, I saw what the wrought iron had blocked. I saw the stained-glass windows, the rambling magenta roses extending across the bricks, clumps of green leaves dangling over the arch of the great wooden doorway. The house, or rather estate, stretched down towards the forest, running adjacent with a manicured lawn, stone pots of bright flowers, hedgerows of tufty reeds and neat privet hedges. Where I had seen a wild nature in the woods, I saw it repeated here amongst the beauty of the hall. Yes, the hedges were trimmed and no moss dwelt within the cracks of the path-ways, but I saw ivy strangling the roses, flaws running along the panes of glass, tall fern fronds leaning over the path and the light dusting of crumbling stone on the doorstep. I felt an immediate kinship with this house. I understood what it was like to be worn down. But unlike me, the house had help to rebuild itself. It had a team.

I stepped beneath arched stone and grasped the door knocker, an iron circle around a Tudor rose. I cleared my throat as I waited, worried that my first words would be a croak. Silence stretched for several long seconds. But when I lifted my hand to knock again, the door opened and the scent of old paper, wood fires, and pastry spilled out of the house. A woman stood on the threshold. She was wearing a simple burgundy dress with slightly puffed sleeves and buttons on the cuff. The neckline was high but not severe. From the square cut of her dress rose a slender neck and a chin lifted like a ballerina's. The woman had high cheekbones that gave her face a skeletal structure, and from within her narrow eyes gleamed two black marbles. Her russet skin was slightly looser around the jaw, and a couple of small, wiry grey hairs poked out from her hairline. I put her age at mid to late forties. No hint of a smile came from her full lips.

"Come to the servants' entrance around the east side of the house," she said and then closed the door in my face.

# CHAPTER TWO

What an idiot. There I was, striding boldly up to the front door of *Highwood Hall*. The Howards didn't want their maids wandering into the house. I needed to learn my place, and that place was around the east side of the house with the rest of the servants. As I hurried, the heels of my borrowed shoes caught on the flagstones. A lock of hair came loose. A woman so tidily dressed as whoever had opened the door would not appreciate messy hair or sweat patches. Perspiration formed on my upper lip, but I didn't want to keep her waiting, so I made haste rather than stopping to arrange myself.

The woman at the door had to be the housekeeper, I supposed. She would be more my employer than Lord Bertie and the rest of the Howards. The thought of her straight back and sharp cheekbones brought discipline and order to mind. Nerves tickled in the pit of my stomach.

She was waiting for me by the time I reached the door, which was flung open, ready. She stood in the entrance, again on the edge of the threshold, my roadblock to overcome if I wanted somewhere to live. One thin raised eyebrow lifted her eyelid and revealed the dark iris within, as shadowy as the woodland around the hall.

"Come with me," she said, turning abruptly on her heel. She hadn't even introduced herself or allowed me to introduce myself.

I closed the heavy wooden door behind me and rushed to keep up with her stride. Her dress wasn't particularly tight, but it was fitted snugly to her mid-calf, and yet she walked as fast as any man. In time, I would learn to keep up, but I struggled then, especially after my uphill walk from Paxby. The borrowed pumps were already beginning to rub.

Once we'd made our way through a stone hallway, she walked me into a kitchen and gestured for me to sit at a long wooden table. I knew immediately that it was old, centuries maybe. The wood was thicker than the width of my hand, and the surface was beaten and scratched from years of domestic work—chopping, peeling, scrubbing, polishing. I imagined this place the heart of the house where the staff pumped and bled and kept everything alive.

At the other end of the long room, the cooks were preparing lunch, whistling along to the radio as they chopped and stirred. The scent of baking pastries wafted over from the oven, making my mouth water. I'd skipped breakfast and now feared that my stomach would betray me with a thunderous rumble.

"My name is Mrs Huxley," she said, drawing my attention away from the cooks.

Still with that straight back, she pulled out a chair and took her seat on the other side of the table. Behind her, I noticed an old clock on the wall next to a row of bells. It was ten a.m.

"I'm the housekeeper here, and that's exactly what I do. I keep the house running smoothly."

I nodded my head, imagining that Highwood Hall ran like clockwork under the watchful gaze of Mrs Huxley.

"I believe I have your credentials. You've been a maid before?"

"Yes," I said. "For about five years now. I started cleaning part-time when I was sixteen. That was at a hotel in York. Since then, I've worked for various households and one agency. I think there were three references included in the application."

"I read them." Again, she did not smile. She did nothing to put me at ease. There had been no pleasantries, no chat about the weather, not even a quick history of the room, which was clearly teeming with antiques. Even the hanging pots and pans seemed old. "Highwood Hall is not going to be what you're used to. Every part of this building must be preserved. You cannot spill. You cannot break. If you break anything at Highwood Hall, it is irreplaceable. Every plate, every vase, every ornament has a place in this house and in its history. You will have to follow my schedule in order to clean this house, and you must follow the rules when you clean. There will be a method. Is that clear?"

"Yes."

"The family will have other tasks for you," she continued. "You will be on hand to help them with whatever they ask. We run on an enthusiastic skeleton staff here at Highwood." She lifted her chin haughtily as though to counter the admission. As though ashamed that the grandeur of Highwood faded as time went on. "And that means part of your job as maid is the role of an assistant. A little of everything. Do you understand?"

"I do."

"Because you will be required to work whenever the Howards need you, there will be a room provided for you. It's a perfectly adequate, comfortable room. You will have meals here, in the kitchen, made by the kitchen staff." Mrs Huxley's eyes briefly flicked across to the cooks humming and chatting, breathing life into the house. Huxley was the opposite, cold and still, like the ornaments she so prized. "This is a generously paid position, which reflects the expectations on you. This is not an easy job, and I have seen many young women such as you who have tried and failed to keep this job."

I noticed the sweat forming on my lip again as she tapped the tabletop.

"I'm aware of your background and the difficulties you've faced. Lord Bertie has a soft spot for helping those in need. I do not. I believe a strong nature is required for this position. Frankly, I don't know if you're up to the job, and I suggest that if you have any concerns, you turn around and walk away now. You know where the door is."

I was taken aback. It seemed that she was trying to get rid of me already, and I hadn't even completed the interview. "I have a very strong will," I said. "And I'm determined to do well. This is a fresh start for me." Somehow I managed to not stutter my way through the words.

Mrs Huxley sighed as though in defeat. "Very well. I'll take you to Lord Bertie. He likes to talk to our new recruits."

# Chapter Three

S he moved like a dancer, gliding across the floorboards so that I had to scurry along next to her in my ungainly stride. Even though we walked beneath centuries-old painted ceilings and between luxurious wood panelling, Mrs Huxley did not offer up any history. She remained silent and stiff, eyes always ahead. I, however, craned my neck to see the murals above and twisted my torso to catch glimpses of the courtyard outside. I greedily drank in the faded furniture placed as an Elizabethan or a Jacobean might sit. I caught flashes of stern-faced portraits of Cavalier men atop their horses, feathers in their caps, long ringlets of hair cascading down their necks. I occasionally stared at my own feet, imagining the people who had walked where I was walking. The many maids, some of them no doubt as young and desperate as I was then.

The ground floor of the house stood eerily still, and the place seemed more like a museum than a family home. Despite the light streaming in from long windows all the way down the hallway, there was a coldness to Highwood Hall that reminded me of its boundary forest.

"You won't walk through the main part of the house. This doesn't belong to us." Mrs Huxley turned sharply, and we made our way up a carpeted, central staircase. "Today is an exception because you've never been here before. But once you start, I'll show you the servants' corridor." At the top of the stairs, she stopped and placed a hand on the wood panelling. "Behind most of these panels is a second corridor hidden from the rest of the house. The servants at Highwood Hall have used these corridors for centuries. We have our own set of stairs too at the back of the house. It'll take some time to get used to the layout." She eyeballed me as though unconvinced I'd ever manage to traverse this sprawling estate. I began to think she was right.

Nothing at Highwood put me at ease. Mrs Huxley was as welcoming as a guard dog. The place felt empty and uninviting, despite its obvious beauty. I was about to meet the family who owned their very own mansion, who had titles and mixed with royalty and came from a bloodline so far removed from my own that I might as well be a rat in the cellar. As we continued down the hall, I had an irresistible urge to turn back and hightail it out of there, and if it hadn't been for the blisters forming on my heels, I wondered whether I might have done just that.

Finally, we reached a walnut door with a gilded handle, and Mrs Huxley knocked quietly. I barely heard the "come in", but Mrs Huxley, finely tuned to the Howards, caught it immediately and led me through to an expansive study. Lord Bertie was sitting behind a mahogany desk, his feet resting on the surface, his chair pushed back into a reclining position. He was staring at his phone and not paying attention to us. I managed to get a good look at him before Mrs Huxley cleared her throat to announce our arrival. He was older, in his fifties, with salt-and-pepper hair combed neatly into a side parting. He wore high-quality jeans, a striped shirt tucked into the waistband, and tartan slippers. When he saw us, he smiled—it was my first smile of the day—and beckoned me forth. He didn't seem in the slightest bit embarrassed to be seen lounging.

"Ah, the new maid. Wonderful. Do take a seat."

*The new maid* gave me pause. Did I already have the job? I'd considered this an interview.

"Thank you, Huxley." He grabbed a piece of paper from his desk, and behind me I heard the slight swish of a skirt and the soft closing of a door. The housekeeper had left. "Lovely, lovely," he said, staring at a sheet of A4 paper, piercing blue eyes trailing back and forth as he read my CV. "Fantastic experience here. And you can start right away?"

"Yes," I said. "Whenever you like. I just need to go back to York and get my things—"

"Good, good." He placed my CV back on the desk. "Has Huxley told you what we need?"

I faltered for a moment, somewhat wrapped up in the surroundings, a sense of realisation hitting me. I would be working at *Highwood Hall*. I noticed framed photographs behind the desk. Lord Bertie shaking hands with Prince Charles, standing next to several politicians, a few prime ministers. So many grey-haired men in suits. "Y-yes. A maid and an assistant rolled into one."

He pointed at me. "Exactly. And how are you doing with your troubles?" He picked at a fingernail. Some movement next to the desk caught my eye, and I realised that there'd been a dog stretched out along the width of it. A black Labrador whose glossy coat had blended in with the dark mahogany floorboards.

"I've moved on from that period of my life," I said. "I've been clean and sober for a year."

"Well done, you." He dropped his feet to the ground with a *thump*, and the dog lifted its head. "I don't know if you know this, but I tend to hire staff from the Providence programme. Like you. I believe in second chances. We all need to get behind a worthy cause, don't we?"

I nodded, not sure what kind of cause I could get behind when I *was* the cause.

"Do you need to give notice at your current address?" he asked.

"No. I'm staying at a friend's right now."

"In that case, when can you move into the maids' quarters?" He bent down and scratched the dog's ear.

"Tomorrow?"

"Excellent. Go and tell Mrs Huxley, would you?" He raised his head and winked at me, a grin spreading across his face. His eyes twinkled, as though surprising me with the positive news had been part of a grander plan to make him feel superior about his charitable gesture.

I sensed the need to be thankful. "Thank you so much," I said, getting to my feet. "I'll go and do that now."

"I think you'll fit in well here at Highwood." He placed his hands on the desk. I noticed that he was handsome and had probably been even more so when young, his large eyes framed by a set of thick lashes. "We're very happy you'll be joining our team here."

"Thank you so much for this opportunity," I said, before slipping out of the office. A bolt of electricity shivered down my spine. I couldn't work out if it represented pleasant nerves, the kind you get in anticipation of a new beginning, or the bad jitters, the kind that warn you that turning back is your best option.

# CHAPTER FOUR

As it turned out, I hadn't needed to inform Mrs Huxley of Lord Bertie's decision. She seemed to know as soon as I approached her outside the study. Perhaps she'd been listening in.

"I'll walk you out," she said in an unemotional voice. Almost morose. "Go home, pack your things, and arrive back at the hall at nine a.m. sharp tomorrow morning."

"Okay," I said, still somewhat taken aback by how fast everything had gone. "Thanks again for..."

"Don't thank me," she said. "Lord Bertie makes the decisions here."

The unspoken words hung between us, her implication clear. Given the choice, Mrs Huxley would not have hired me.

"So, do you live at Highwood too?" I asked.

"Yes."

"What about your husband?"

We were close to the stairs at that point. She simply turned to me and frowned. Over her shoulder, one of the portraits frowned down on me too; it was like both the house and its keeper rejected me in the same breath. "I like to keep my private life just that. Private."

I said nothing out loud, but in my head, I thought *wow*. Privacy was one thing, but not even talking about partners was another. Perhaps I'd made a mistake saying the word husband. What if Mrs Huxley was a lesbian and defensive around new people who could potentially judge her? We descended the stairs, and I didn't press. And then she showed me out of the hall via the servants' entrance. By that point, I was practically limping, my poor feet ached so badly.

"I'll see you tomorrow," I said as the door swung closed. "Wow." This time I said it out loud. I couldn't help it. My first meeting with Mrs Huxley had been bizarre to say the least. She'd been nothing short of hostile.

Once out on the driveway, I crouched down to retrieve the trainers from my tote bag and eased the high-heeled pumps from my sore feet. Slipping into those cushioned shoes felt like stepping onto clouds. I squatted near the house, running a finger between the back of the trainers and my heels to check for blisters, when I heard a burst of crunching gravel and the skid of tyres. A red Ferrari hurtled up to the front of the house, spraying stones as it went. I immediately stood, self-conscious of my unladylike squat, fingers wrapped tightly around the handle of my canvas bag. Music filtered out from the car as it came to a halt next to a cherubic water fountain. The door didn't open, but I could see the sports car top down, revealing a man with dark hair, sitting in the driver's seat. He reached forward, turning the music up even louder.

I suppose you would expect a rich, young owner of a Ferrari to listen to some sort of contemporary music. Personally, I would have put money on the soulless electro-pop music played by overpaid DJs at festivals. But no, it was classical. I didn't know the composer then, but now I could recognise Liszt's *Hungarian Rhapsody* from the first bar. Bold, bombastic and fast. I took a step closer and saw his arms flailing from behind the steering wheel as he mimed playing the notes. Dark hair moved with the soft breeze, and when he turned his head slightly, I saw his profile. Alex Howard, it had to be. Despite the mere glimpse I caught of him, Lord Bertie's features were evident in his own. That same square jaw, the dark hair. His movements were stiff, controlled, and serious. But he was clearly enjoying himself, and it made me smile.

The music stopped, and the smile faded from my face. If this was Lord Bertie's son, I didn't want him to see me hiding behind a fountain with old trainers on my feet. I attempted to scuttle away, keeping myself tucked behind the fountain. Even worse than him seeing me like that, he might suspect I'd been spying on him, which I had. I know I wouldn't want a stranger to see me in a private moment. From there, I saw him bound up the steps to the house, his swinging stride brimming with natural confidence. He was slim, tall, and just as handsome as his father. An imperceptible shiver of electricity travelled down my spine as I watched him, knowing that he couldn't see me there, that I had the first glimpse of the heir to this mansion. And then he was inside the house, out of sight, and I walked away, towards those great iron gates, about to make my way back to the bus stop.

I allowed myself one last glance back at the house, and from there, I saw Mrs Huxley in the ground-floor window. Perhaps she'd been there the entire time, watching me scurry around the fountain like a crab, spying on Alex Howard. Her expression was grave, as it had been when I'd arrived. I had no evidence to believe Mrs Huxley ever smiled at that point. Her hardness gave me a jolt of fear and uncertainty. I didn't know why, but I was convinced her solemn attitude revealed some sort of personal issue with me. Lord Bertie had hired me, not Huxley. For some reason, that housekeeper already didn't like me at all, and I had no idea why. But it made me hesitant for the future. I had a feeling deep down in my bones that Mrs Huxley was not going to make my life at Highwood Hall an easy one.

But I *had* to work here. No one else knew how much the interview meant to me. While finding somewhere to live was obviously very important to me, I had another reason for applying to Highwood Hall of all places. As unlikely as it seemed, I had a connection to this grand mansion. It and I were tied to one another with history. My mother once worked as a maid... at Highwood Hall. Twenty-one years ago. Right before she abandoned me as a baby.

## CHAPTER FIVE

On the way back to Paxby, I decided to meander through the woods. Amidst the twisted trees, I could've sworn I heard my name on the wind, and for the briefest of moments, I contemplated veering from the footpath to wander into the dense thicket of silver birches. It was a strange sensation, like the call of the void. I had to calm my heart as I carried on down the slope back to the village. It'd been the breeze, nothing more. The breeze and my overactive imagination.

By the time I reached Paxby, I'd missed the bus by five minutes and my hands were shaking. I spent an hour browsing the gift shops and annoying the staff by not buying anything, all the time wondering if I'd made the right decision taking the job. When I caught the next bus, I spent the journey back to Annabel's house chewing my thumbnail down to the quick. What would I learn about my mother at Highwood Hall? Maybe nothing. Maybe everything.

Annabel wasn't home, but I found a note on the fridge, letting me know she'd gone to stay over at her boyfriend's place. That would make things a lot easier, I thought, because then I wouldn't have to say thank you. I'd never found it easy to express those kinds of emotions.

My aunt Josephine brought me up after my mother left. While she did the best she could, single parenthood was not an event she'd prepared herself for, and it was not a role she was particularly skilled at.

I moved out of Aunt Josephine's home when I was sixteen and lived in a shared flat with two other cleaners. We were constantly competing for jobs, falling out and making up on a daily basis. Our collective income was so low that we even competed with each other for food, queuing up at food banks and soup kitchens. In our tiny flat, we labelled our food and measured the milk because even a sneaky cup of tea could throw a person out of sync for the rest of the week.

And then I found myself drowning out my problems in the worst, most expensive of ways. Drink and drugs. Eventually I managed to get a place in the Providence programme, a local drug rehabilitation centre, which was where I met Annabel and she helped me get back on my feet. But growing up the way I did with an aunt who didn't want me there, expecting me to be grateful for the meagre scraps of affection she threw in my direction, made it hard for me to show that gratitude to anyone else even though I truly did appreciate everything Annabel had done for me.

That night, I ate leftover macaroni and cheese, put the radio on as I packed my belongings, and set an alarm for six a.m. the next morning. My last night on Annabel's sofa resulted in twisting and turning in borrowed sheets. I tried to sleep. I tried hard. All I could think about was Mrs Huxley watching me from the window. When I pictured her face with those high cheekbones and the pursed lips, I dreaded going back there. In fact, I tried to talk myself out of it several times in between restless snoozes and unsettled dreams.

In the end, I finally drifted into a deeper sleep, and my alarm blared unexpectedly, breaking the settled silence around me. It took a moment to allow it all to sink in. The interview, Highwood Hall, Lord Bertie and his son. Mrs Huxley. A young woman who had left her baby behind to be a live-in maid two decades ago. I sat up, stretched and rubbed sleep from my eyes, still deathly tired. Annabel wouldn't be here to see me leave, and I was sorry for that. I was sorrier for what I was about to do, but I saw no way of getting around it. After a shower and a cup of coffee, I opened up the cereal cupboard, took out a purple biscuit tin, and removed forty pounds from Annabel's emergency fund. Then I scribbled her a note explaining what I'd done, where I was going, how sorry I was and how grateful I was. It was easier to write than say to her face. I placed the note on top of the one she left me the day before, and then I backed away, tears gathering in my eyes.

Annabel and I met in the programme, both achieving sobriety at around the same time. She, however, had a family to help her rebuild her life. She'd taken me in—a stray with nowhere to go, Josephine had given up on me by that point—and let me stay with her until I found a job. This was how I thanked her, by stealing one last time. But if I didn't, I wouldn't be able to afford my bus fare to Paxby.

I was halfway to the door when I stopped and turned around. She'd put up with a lot from me. She'd seen me at my most desperate and listened to every sorry story I'd told her. She'd been so happy for me when I got the interview for Highwood Hall. I slipped the gold ring from my finger—the one present I treasured from my aunt—and left it in the middle of the kitchen table. Then, finally, I left.

# CHAPTER SIX

This time I caught a taxi from the bus stop with the money I took from Annabel's house. When the driver pulled up to the gates, I paid him, slung the rucksack over my shoulder, and pressed the buzzer. I noticed that the disembodied voice belonged to Mrs Huxley. Before opening the gates, she reminded me to use the servants' entrance, and I tried to bite my tongue. As if I would be stupid enough to make that mistake twice.

"Is that all you have?" she asked as she waited for me with the door swung open.

I nodded, not wanting to explain my circumstances to her. She backed away from the doorway to let me in, trapping me within the walls of my new home. My new sanctuary. I wondered how long I would be here.

Mrs Huxley did not slow down her stride as she talked. The woman seemed to have an endless supply of breath. "You'll be sharing a room with Roisin, our second maid."

That wasn't surprising to me. I'd assumed that the servants' accommodation would mean sharing with at least one other girl.

"You'll meet her at breakfast in thirty minutes," Huxley continued. "And then, I'll take you through your tasks for the day. It'll take time"—she glanced at me sideways—"plenty of time, I'm sure, but you will slip into the routine."

We walked through the kitchen as we had the previous day, but the kitchen staff were too busy to do any more than nod a hello to me. Then we entered a much more austere corridor of plain walls—a deep green shade like ivy leaves—with several black doors on the right.

"This is your room." Huxley came to a halt. She removed a key from her pocket and handed it to me. "I suggest you unpack and come to the kitchen right away. There is a uniform set out for you on the bed." Her lips twitched as though she was attempting a smile. I was so shocked that I failed to return it.

But as she started to move away, I suddenly felt an urge to keep her talking to me. God knows when I'd get another opportunity to spend time with her, and there was so much I wanted to know.

"Mrs Huxley."

She raised an eyebrow. "Yes? Are you confused already?"

"No," I said, a prickle of annoyance at the back of my neck. "I just wondered how long you'd worked here."

She frowned, and a line emerged between her eyebrows. She could frown at least, if she couldn't smile. "Twenty-three years."

"Oh," I said. "Wow, that's a long time to work in one place."

"Yes, it is."

"Do you like it here?"

Huxley's lips pursed together. "You'd best unpack. We don't have much time for chit-chat at Highwood."

Before I opened my mouth once more, she turned away and walked back down the bare corridor. But at least now I knew she'd worked here at the same time as my mother. I placed a hand on the door, hesitating. It was a small sliver of knowledge that I had to chew on and decide what to do with. I could be upfront with Huxley and mention the connection right away. Or I could keep it to myself.

I pulled in a deep breath, opened the door and entered my new bedroom, not sure what to expect. In this servants' wing, a damp odour —like a cellar or a bathroom that hasn't been aired—permeated the space. I placed my palm on the wall and felt a chill.

Still, it was a spacious room. The walls were the same dark shade of bottle green as in the corridor, and a window overlooked the stables behind the house. There were no horses inside the stables, which was a disappointment. They seemed to have been converted into yet more rooms. What the Howards needed more rooms for, I had no idea. I dumped my bag next to the bed with the uniform folded neatly on top of the duvet. Then I lifted the clothes and examined them. I'd dreaded a formal uniform, one of those French affairs with the frilly apron and the short skirt, the kind parodied by Halloween costumes and farcical pornography. To my utmost relief, I unfolded a sensible pair of elasticated black trousers and a loose-fitting black tunic. I stripped to my underwear and pulled them on. Despite me not giving Mrs Huxley my measurements, they actually fit fairly well.

Another slim single bed had been pushed up against the opposite wall with a bedside table, lamp, wardrobe and drawers. I saw a pair of sparkly silver shoes kicked under the bed and a book on the table. Curiosity got the best of me, and I picked up the book. Love poems.

The other maid had spent little time decorating her space, but there were some touches. A red cushion on the plain white bedspread, photographs tacked to a corkboard. Two short people stood next to a waiflike girl with strawberry blonde hair and red lips. Parents, I presumed, from the ages and a likeness around the eyes and mouth. I picked up a lipstick from the top of a chest of drawers and read the shade: *Cherry Kiss*.

Fearing that my new roommate would walk in and see me snooping, I quickly filled the drawers of the cabinet with my clothes, slipped my phone into the pocket of the trousers, and paused. I had a thin bundle of letters in my hand. Letters that mentioned Highwood Hall. I threw them underneath my underwear and then tucked the empty bag under my bed. It was an easy walk, following the bleak walls back to the kitchen. Perhaps it was the darker shadows in that part of Highwood and the cool chill that none of the many fireplaces in the hall could touch, but goosebumps spread along my arms despite the long sleeves of my top.

In the kitchen, a small team had gathered around the table. Mrs Huxley sat at the head, her heavy-lidded eyes watching me approach. A girl around my age laughed along with one of the cooks. My gaze immediately went straight to her because she moved and breathed life into the room with that musical laugh and a smile that stretched from ear to ear. She tilted her chin towards me and immediately jumped to her feet.

"Roomie!" she declared with a little squeal at the end. Then she threw Huxley a worried glance and sat down, nodding at me to make sure I followed suit.

The owner of the *Cherry Kiss* lipstick, the slim, strawberry blonde girl from the photograph. Her smile was as infectious as it'd seemed in the picture, and I found myself returning her grin. But before I could say anything, Mrs Huxley shushed us.

"Yes, thank you, Roisin," Huxley said. "Perhaps we can maintain decorum." The taciturn housekeeper sipped tea from a porcelain teacup.

As I sat down, Roisin leaned across the table, her hands reaching my arm between a teapot and a stack of cups. I noticed there wasn't any breakfast food on the table.

"It's so nice to meet you. I've been positively lonely these past few weeks since—"

"Roisin, we're on a schedule," Huxley snapped. She turned to me. "I've allowed us ten minutes to have a cup of tea. Then Roisin and I will lay out breakfast for the Howards." She shifted a large ring binder across to me. "While we do that, you can make a start on this reading material. And then after the Howards are catered for, we have our own breakfast before getting on with the cleaning. Is that clear? Both of you?"

Roisin retracted her hand and stared down at the tabletop in dejection. "Yes, Mrs Huxley."

That was the first time my temper rose up. I recognised that look. It was the expression of a scolded child. Worse, a child who had grown accustomed to their scolding, and I wondered how many maids Huxley had snapped at, berated and bullied during her time at Highwood. But I didn't say anything. I poured myself a cup of tea, craving the caffeine.

Roisin and I managed to talk quietly while Mrs Huxley turned her attention to the cooks. Roisin was just eighteen, a couple of years younger than me. She'd moved away from her family in Sligo and ran out of money while working as a waitress in London. This job was a way for her to earn a living without going back to her family.

"It's not that I'm too proud," she said. "We just don't get on."

I decided not to pry.

As Mrs Huxley and Roisin cleared away the teacups, I opened the ring binder and began thumbing through it. My mind was already drifting from the extensive lists of which cabinets in which rooms I should dust and which I was never to touch. Then there was the schedule, a long, boring timeline of weekly tasks. The Howards would keep out of certain rooms at certain times so we could clean them. All I wanted to do was go exploring. I forced myself back to the binder. How was I ever supposed to remember this?

A printed map caught my attention. I ran my fingers along the corridors, wishing I had a pen and paper to replicate them. I wanted to know each hidden passageway, each nook, cranny and secret. This was an old house, and I was sure there would be many.

After Mrs Huxley and Roisin carried breakfasts up to the Howards, the cooks drifted out of the kitchen, presumably for a break. I was alone in that old room. After a minute or two, I heard the sound of footsteps travelling along the hallway outside the kitchen. Dainty, short strides that almost sounded as though someone was skipping. And then someone began to hum.

When the door opened, a blonde-haired young woman strode in, carrying a small box in her arms. It was about the size of a generous box of chocolates, but taller.

"Hello," she said brightly. "You must be the new maid."

I nodded cautiously, aware of the fact that this person was definitely not one of the staff. She was wearing casual clothes, shoes with a short heel, and had her hair pulled into an untidy bun. The shoes were leather, expensive, and the clothes were high quality too. She wore them like her expensive clothes meant nothing, slung over her body, slightly crumpled, slightly lopsided, and yet clearly luxurious.

"Our postie delivered this," she said. "I got to the door before Huxley, so I thought I'd pop it down here. It seems it's for you." She placed the box on the table next to the folder. "Oh, I see Huxley has the binder out. Lucky you. I'm Lottie, by the way, the youngest Howard." She rolled her eyes as though being the youngest was a bore. "Go on then, open it. If you have a secret admirer, I want to be the first to know." She grinned, rubbing her hands together. I got the impression I was this morning's entertainment.

A flush of heat worked its way up from my collarbone to my cheeks. "It can't possibly be for me."

"Check the label," Lottie said, pointing towards an envelope tucked into a red bow.

I pried the envelope from under the ribbon. She was right. It had my name on it.

"This box came inside packaging, but the label had nothing but our address on it, so I opened it up, I'm afraid," Lottie said. "I figured it was for you because I know everyone else's name, you see." She lifted her hand, palm up, towards the box. "Go on then."

Tentatively I reached across the table and tugged at the thick ribbon, which *swooshed* as it slowly unspooled. As the bow melted away, the front of the box fell open and the last coils of the ribbon shivered down to the tabletop. I spun the box to face me so that I could see what was inside.

At first I thought I was looking at a doll's house. The box had been transformed into the walls of one room. The first element of the scene that caught my eye was a cleverly constructed spiral staircase that travelled down from the roof of the box to the floor, made out of some sort of fine wood, like matchsticks, and painted black. The bottom of the box had been painted to look like wooden floorboards. Wainscoting ran along the "walls" of the box, and actual wallpaper stuck to the sides. It was blue with golden feathers.

"Oh how funny. That's the back staircase," Lottie said. She leaned in, close to my shoulder, and then gasped and leaned back.

I'd seen it before her, but I hadn't quite processed what I was looking at, it was so strange and out of place. The entire scene was unnerving, the situation quite bizarre. Someone had sent me a diorama in the post, and I had no idea why or even who knew I would be working here. In the centre of the scene was a little doll with brown hair, like mine, dressed in the uniform I was currently wearing. The parcel had been addressed to me. The doll, surely, had to be me.

And it was dead. It lay in a pool of blood at the bottom of the staircase.

# CHAPTER SEVEN

The idea of someone sitting down to create this scene and then
send it to me was preposterous, and I think for that reason, I
sat there dumbfounded for several seconds, just staring at the
box. Why would someone go to so much effort for an utter nobody like
me? Lottie was speechless too, hovering somewhere behind me after
she'd manoeuvred around the table for a better look. We remained like
that until the silence was finally broken by Mrs Huxley and Roisin
walking back to the kitchen.

"Miss Howard!" Mrs Huxley stopped in her tracks next to the table.
"Is there a problem I can help you with?" Her eyes drifted over to the
table and the small box on top of it.

I saw Huxley and Roisin out of the corner of my eye because I
couldn't pull myself away from the diorama. It was so *intricate*. This
person had taken the time to measure and cut little treads for the staircase. They'd painted knots on the "wooden" floorboards and arranged
the hair around the doll's shoulders. It was exquisite and grotesque and
baffling.

"I'm afraid something odd has happened." Behind me, Lottie must
have gestured for Mrs Huxley to come around the table. I watched the
housekeeper glide towards me. Both her and Roisin stood behind my
chair to see what the diorama depicted.

"Christ!" Roisin said. "That's the staircase in the servants' quarters."

"Yes," Lottie said. "I noticed that too."

"Why would someone send this?" Roisin said.

Mrs Huxley was quiet until she added, "What would you like to do with it?"

It was a moment or two before I realised she was talking to me. I wanted to burn it. I wanted to see flames destroying it, tearing through the paint, melting the doll, reducing the wallpaper to ash. But when I didn't answer, Roisin reached over my shoulder, lifted the front of the box and retied the ribbon so that I didn't have to look at the gruesome scene anymore. Then she pushed it to the other side of the table, and the others filtered away from behind me so I could see them without turning around.

"Perhaps it was a joke," Lottie offered, her voice light and playful. "A rather bad one, obviously."

Mrs Huxley nodded. "I'm sure that's exactly what it is." She smiled warmly at the girl, and the sight was almost as jarring as the diorama. But an understanding washed over me—Mrs Huxley was always going to agree with whatever one of the Howards said. She was a sycophant. "It's a bad joke, that's all. Nothing to get too upset about."

But from whom? One of the Howards? One of the staff?

"Do you have any friends who would find this funny?" Roisin asked gently.

"No one would find this funny," I said, finally able to find my voice. "No one."

"Perhaps you should contact the police," Roisin suggested. I saw her glance at Lottie and then back at me. "Whoever sent this knows what the inside of Highwood Hall looks like."

"That's true," Lottie said. "But there are some photos of the interior online. We had the photo shoot a few years ago."

"A three-page spread in *Tatler*," Mrs Huxley said proudly.

Lottie Howard stepped forward and placed a hand on my shoulder. It was a strange first meeting with her. I wasn't quite sure what to make of the gesture, whether it was genuine or patronising or designed to keep me in line. "Daddy will take care of this. He knows people. Shall I take it to him?"

In hindsight, it was a bad idea to let her take the evidence away. I should have kept an eye on it myself to ensure no one else touched it. There would be DNA evidence, wouldn't there? Would the police use such resources for someone like me? Would they care? It wasn't as though I'd been physically attacked. It was one strange parcel. That was it.

I watched slack-jawed as Lottie carried the box out of the kitchen. Something unusual and downright surreal had just happened to me, and I wasn't sure how to process any of it.

"Look, you can sit around and cry about it, or you can get to work and take your mind off it," Mrs Huxley said.

Her tone wasn't completely cold, but it wasn't exactly warm either. She was right though. I wasn't one to wallow, and I needed a distraction. Plus, it felt like an appropriate opportunity to show the inimitable housekeeper my mettle.

"What do you want me to do first?" I asked, straightening my back.

Roisin smiled and nodded encouragingly. Mrs Huxley's eyes narrowed as though she was trying to suss me out. Inside, I thought I might crumble. This wasn't how I imagined my first day at Highwood Hall. I'd had other plans. I'd hoped to be the one in control, the one with a hidden agenda. But that power had ebbed away from me as soon as I'd opened the box, and now my legs shook with fear.

# CHAPTER EIGHT

I followed the housekeeper back through the servants' quarters in a daze. She rambled on about my routine. Mopping hallways, scrubbing bathrooms, hoovering carpets and making beds. In the afternoon, I might be asked to run errands for the Howards or help with the laundry. There were many tasks for two young maids to complete in one day.

I managed to take in maybe half of what she was saying and hardly noticed the corridors around us. I'd told myself to pay attention to everything in order to learn quickly, but of course that was before the parcel showed up. When we turned a corner and came to a spiral staircase, it took my mind a moment to understand what I was looking at, but as soon as it hit me, I gasped.

I stood before the dollhouse room only without the dead maid at the bottom of the stairs. I craned my neck up, following the track of the ornately carved wood as it travelled up to the next level. As I looked up and up, I imagined my body plummeting down the steps, face smashing against the balustrades, nose bursting, shoulder cracking against the treads, my body landing crumpled and broken by the time I reached the floor below my feet.

"Are you coming?" Mrs Huxley asked. She stood halfway between me and the staircase. For a heartbeat, I stared stupidly at her, confused as to what she wanted. Then I realised she wanted me to walk up those stairs, and I was appalled. How could I possibly do that after what had happened this morning? "You'll have to get used to them eventually. This is the servants' staircase, and we use it every day. You'll be taking tea up to Lady Margot soon."

I rubbed my upper arms and took a moment to compose myself. While I was building up the courage to use the steps, I noted that the diorama had depicted this part of the house perfectly. How did the artist know what the staircase looked like? Surely the photo shoot featured in *Tatler* focused on the grand living room and the wood-panelled hallways with the painted ceilings.

Of course, Mrs Huxley flew up the stairs with ease, her back straight, her hand never once veering to the rail. When I followed her, I tried to block the image of the doll out of my mind. It was just a doll. One of the kitchen staff probably sent it to haze me. Maybe they were all in on it and it was supposed to make me so nervous I didn't want to stay. Well, if that was the intention, I'd show them that I'm made of tougher stuff than that.

Even though the stairs were much sturdier than I thought they would be, my hand gripped the support the entire way up. Ever since I was a child, I'd had the strangest worry that one day I'd throw myself over the side of an escalator or tall staircase. Whenever my aunt took me to a department store, I would cling on, my eyes trained on my feet. But that wasn't an option when traversing the servants' stairs. I needed to keep my attention focused on both the steps and where I was going because it was easy to bump into the rail and throw yourself off balance.

"Wasn't so hard, was it?" The corner of Mrs Huxley's lip twitched upwards. Perhaps she was attempting a smile to reassure me, but it seemed more like a smirk. "I'm going to set you up in the library. It's a large room, but it's one of the easiest to clean." She led me through what I assumed was the servants' corridor from its bare walls, until we arrived at a door.

To my surprise, we came out of one of the wood panels into an upstairs hallway. She turned back and closed the door with a click. It completely melted into the background.

"How do I find these doors?" I asked.

Mrs Huxley ran her finger down a barely visible crack in the wood. "You'll get used to it." She bustled off, her heels thudding dully against the deep red carpet. And then she stopped next to a narrow door, taking a key from the bunch hanging from her thin belt. "Supplies cupboard. I'll get you a key tomorrow."

Once I had dusters, cleaning products and cloths, she opened a wide wooden door and took me into the library. For one glorious moment, the nasty surprise from the morning faded out of my mind and I was just a girl looking at a beautiful room filled with precious books, inhaling the scent of dry paper, wood and leather. On the far side of the room, three large windows let the sunlight stream in from the front lawns. My movements disturbed the dust, and the golden sunlight illuminated floating lint in the air.

There were several portraits on the walls, all of serious men in uniforms, then a few horses with beautiful long necks, and one woman staring down at me with soulful eyes in the middle of a round, pale face. The rest of the walls were covered in books. Nothing but leather-bound volumes with gilded titles on the spines filled the space from floor to ceiling. New and old. Faded and fresh.

"Do not touch the books inside the glass cabinets." Huxley gestured across to the three glass cases tucked away in a shadowed corner of the room. "Those are the most precious antiques."

For the next thirty minutes, Mrs Huxley showed me how to clean the library. From the careful dusting of the books to the wood cleaner used on the floor to the leather cleaner on the chairs and glass cleaner for the cabinets and windows. There was a lot to take in, but it was an effective distraction from the diorama. When she left, I wished for a set of headphones and some music to play as I worked, but I settled for the creaks and groans of the old house.

I was slow that first time. I know I was. I spent nearly all morning on that room, and I think had Mrs Huxley not been busy, I would've received a warning. But I was enjoying myself. I loved reading the spines along the books. From Shakespeare to Milton to the Brontës. My fingers trailed them, walking over each bump and crack in the leather, but I did not dare remove any from their resting places. My aunt Josephine had her faults, but she'd always given me books, and it was books that had comforted me in my deepest, darkest moments of addiction and loneliness. They were more than paper, ink and glue, they were old friends.

Once finished, I placed my products back in the supply cupboard— which Mrs Huxley had left open for me—and tried to find the door leading back to the servants' corridor. My fingers groped along the wood panelling, but for some reason I couldn't find that tiny crack of light that Mrs Huxley had shown me. I went back and forth for a few minutes until I decided to follow the hallway along to the main staircase and quietly slip down it. From there I intended to get to the kitchen, but I realised I'd come down a completely different set of stairs. This one had the same carpet, which confused me, but landed on the other side of the house looking out across many acres of lush green fields. I stepped across the floorboards, putting my hand on the thick stone window ledge and staring out, trying to get my bearings. It seemed that if I went left, I'd be following the direction of the garden and hopefully come back out to the front of the house.

Luckily, the Howards were nowhere to be seen. Perhaps they were in their many private rooms: bedrooms, offices, cosy snugs, or the pool house on the other side of the estate. No one stopped me in my tracks and shouted at me to get out. And when I walked past a particularly unusual room, there was no one around to stop me from snooping.

It was the dining room. A long, windowless room brightened by the exquisite chandelier hanging above the vast table and the open double doors allowing light from the rest of the house to seep in. I couldn't help myself. I flipped the switch and turned on the chandelier, watching as reflected light speckled the walls. I'm glad I did turn on the light, because otherwise I wouldn't have seen the mural painted across the wood panels. Every single part of the wall had been painted in warm browns, peachy-pinks and sweet pastels. The mural was made up of Renaissance women with cherubic features, dancing and lounging across the walls. A bright-eyed young girl fed grapes to a dark-haired beauty. What surprised me about the mural was the variation of skin tones. I suppose we're conditioned to think of historic art depicting white women with perky, apple-sized breasts and curved hips. On this mural, however, were women of all shapes, sizes and ethnicities. It was extraordinary.

I made my way around the room, taking in every face. One in particular made the air inside my lungs freeze. The woman on the wall lounged on the grass, her back resting against a tree. A young beauty, her dark hair curled around the olive flesh of her shoulders. Her figure was noticeably slim, her face almost gaunt. It made her eyes stand out. Two deep pools of chocolate brown. She looked like me. Or I looked like her. I shook my head and laughed a little. It was simply the dark hair and eyes and the thin face. It could be a portrait of any skinny twenty-something.

Enamoured, I leaned closer, lifting a finger to trace the lines of the paint, and at that moment, I heard the strangest of creaking sounds. At first I thought it was the house settling, the expanding and contracting of wood as the house heated and cooled throughout the day. But it was followed by a click. I cocked my head in the direction of the sound when a winged angel suddenly opened up and swung out into the room. A man emerged from inside the wall. I had to clamp my hand over my mouth to stop myself from screaming.

# CHAPTER NINE

He was tall enough that he bent his head as he stepped through the panel into the room. And when he stretched to full height, he leaned over me slightly. I realised that I was rooted to the spot, not far from where he'd entered, and that I should take a step back to allow him room to manoeuvre. To my surprise, as I was stepping away, he placed his finger on his lips and grinned. I gave him a quizzical expression in response.

"I'm trying to escape my father," he said in a low voice. "He wants to talk *business*." He made a face, stretching his lips into a grimace, and then his eyes sparkled.

When he began to laugh, I found myself laughing with him, as though I was in on the joke. Perhaps I could explain it away by nerves or those bright blue eyes as clear as deep water.

"I'm Alex," he said, sticking out his hand. "Are you our new maid?"

"I am." And then I realised that I was standing in the dining room for no real reason, and I blushed. "I don't think I'm supposed to be in here. Sorry. I got lost."

"Oh, don't worry," he said. "I still get lost. This place is a labyrinth, and half the corridors are hidden behind the walls. A lot of fun when you're ten and your little sister is afraid of the dark though." He flashed me a grin. He swung the hidden door open again. "This little corridor leads to the servants' hallway. We have them in lots of rooms. If you follow it, you'll end up back at the kitchen so fast that Mrs Huxley won't even notice you were gone."

He'd correctly guessed that I was worried about Mrs Huxley's wrath, and I thanked him for the tip. But before I ducked into the hidden passageway, I had to address the mural.

"This room is so unusual," I said, nodding to the painted women.

Alex leaned against the wood and let his gaze travel lazily around the room. It was as though he just now saw the room through my eyes, taking in the splendour for the first time. And while he was still, I noticed again that his face in profile was a beautiful thing. He was how I imagined Lord Bertie to have been in his youth, angular and yet soft, boyish but still deeply masculine.

"It's new," he said. "It's not ancient like most of the things in this house. My mother commissioned it before she died. We still add to it sometimes. A nymph or an angel, whatever takes our fancy. It's a work in progress." When he moved, it took me by surprise and I physically started. Then he strode across the room, stepping around the head of the table to one of the painted women. She was pictured in a flowing dress, her eyes lifted as though she were staring at the sky. Her hair flowed down to her waist in caramel waves. "This is my mother. We added her to the wall after she died."

I couldn't help myself. I walked over to him and stood by his side. I saw her close up for the first time. Her features weren't quite accessible to me because of the movement in the painting, from the flowing hair and rippling dress. She danced away from the painter, shielding herself like a person who didn't want to have their photograph taken. Half her face was in shadow, which seemed like a strange choice considering she was Lady Howard, the former mistress of the house.

"I'm so sorry for your loss." They were empty words, but they filled an awkward silence.

He rested two fingertips on the side of her face. He had strong hands, I noticed, and for some reason that surprised me. "I'm sorry we lost her." He allowed his hand to drop and turned to me. "But that's life, isn't it?"

I gazed up at him, in his shadow, feeling tinier than ever. Looking back, I believe it was probably the uniform that made me feel that way. I decided that it was time for me to go, so I stepped away, about to make my excuses and return to the kitchen, but he opened his mouth to speak.

"I saw the package you were sent this morning. I can't believe anyone would be so cruel."

The truth is, I'd forgotten about it for a moment, and then all the fear came creeping back in. I wrapped my arms around my torso for comfort. "I don't know who knew I was coming here. Apart from the friend I shared a house with." A generous way of describing my sofa surfing.

"We won't stand for it," he said. "There's no bullying at Highwood. If we find out it was someone here, we'll deal with it." Then he frowned. "Daddy will anyway."

"Thank you. That's good to know. I should probably be..." I jabbed my thumb towards the hidden passageway.

"Yes, you don't want to keep Huxley waiting." He let out a sharp exhale through his nose. "To be honest, she even scares *me* a little bit."

I knew he was being kind, so I smiled in return. "Thanks for showing me the way."

"I'll give you a tour one day. I'll show you the other hidden doors and the north wing if you like. There's a secret peephole above the main staircase too."

"Seriously?"

"Oh yes. You can see through the big portrait of the duke."

"That is insanely cool. Do you use it often?"

"I used to use it on Lottie quite a bit. She used to play with her Barbies on the stairs. She didn't know it existed until she was ten, so I managed to make her think I had psychic powers until then." He grinned. "By the way, I wanted to ask you a favour."

"Me?"

He laughed. "Yes, you. I don't know if you know this, but I'm a trained pianist and I play a little when I'm not working in the business."

I thought back to the first time I saw Alex in the convertible, fingers moving along to the music. Now it made more sense. I just shook my head.

"I have to practise an awful lot, and I need a page turner to help me learn the music."

"Oh."

"It'd be every Friday at seven. Would that be okay for you?"

I had nowhere else to go, nowhere else to be. I didn't have friends to visit, pubs to drink in or nightclubs to dance in. "That's fine."

"Great," he said. "Wait for me outside the music room just before seven. I'll clear it with Huxley, and she'll show you where to go."

"Okay."

"I look forward to it." He smiled. It was a pleasant smile, an easy one, but it didn't seem warm. I thought perhaps that he was still thinking about his mother and that sadness crept into his expression. And then, he said my name before he left. For the first time in as long as I could remember, I felt seen.

# CHAPTER TEN

To my surprise, I didn't receive a tongue-lashing when I returned. Instead, she glared at me with cold, dark eyes until I mumbled an apology and stared at my shoes. Out of the corner of my eye, I saw Roisin hovering next to a supply cupboard, biting her lip, eyebrows scrunched together. What was she concerned about? The diorama? Or Mrs Huxley's clear dislike of me.

"Perhaps I'd best have Roisin supervise you for the rest of the day." She sighed wearily, taking a key from a hook on the wall. "You can do the laundry together. The bed sheets need washing."

As the housekeeper left, Roisin passed me a large tub of detergent and beckoned for me to follow her down to the cellar. We were met by two large industrial washers, a tumble dryer and three baskets over-flowing with white sheets. I bent down to collect an armful of sheets and stuffed them into one of the machines. Cloying air made my hair stick to the back of my neck each time I bent and lifted, but despite the hard work, it was nice to finally be alone with Roisin.

"So I guess my first day has been a bit of a disaster," I said.

"I'm so sorry about the box. I don't understand it." She huffed and puffed while bundling the sheets, but I could still tell that she meant it.

"Me neither. I mean, what a welcome." I shook my head. "And Mrs Huxley."

Roisin rested against the machine. "Oh, I know. She's not the friendliest woman in the world. But you get used to her, you know. Or, rather, she gets used to you." I noticed her easy smile and the way her cheeks dimpled. The cellar was lit dimly, but her light copper hair stood out against the shadows, brightened by the naked light bulb above us.

"She hates me. Lord Bertie hired me, not her. I think I'll be out of here in less than a week." Saying the words lifted a weight from my chest, letting the fear out. "Maybe she sent me that... thing."

"She wouldn't."

"How do you know?"

"She's not like that." Roisin dropped an empty basket to the ground and straightened up. "Her bark is worse than her bite."

"You know that for sure, do you?"

She shrugged. "I choose to believe it."

We slammed down the machine lid, and it echoed through the cellar, like the rumbling of thunder on a stormy day.

"The more I think about that... *box*, the weirder I think it is. Someone took the trouble to create this... this intricate piece of art just to tell me I'm going to die. By falling down the stairs apparently. Maybe it's God telling me to keep off that bloody staircase."

Roisin laughed. "Maybe. Listen, I'm sure Bertie will get to the bottom of it. He knows everyone. MPs, other rich bastards, police officers probably."

"Must be nice to have connections," I said. "The only people I know are in prison or rehab." It was supposed to be a joke, but it fell flat. The washing machine churned, water and white cotton spinning and mixing. "Someone doesn't want me to be here, and I don't know why."

"That seems unlikely," Roisin said.

"It was addressed to me. It depicted me dead."

"I know," she said softly. "I'm so sorry. It was awful." She bit her lip. "Look, I probably shouldn't be telling you this, but..."

Next to us the machine clanged and whirred. I leaned closer to her, eager to discover what she knew. "What?"

"The girl you replaced. Well, she left quite abruptly. She didn't give notice or even say goodbye to anyone. We shared a room, and I got back after a long day to find all her things gone. Not that she had much to begin with. I think she had an argument with Mrs Huxley, because I saw them near the staircase, the spiral one, and Chloe—that was her name—

walked away crying. I tried to catch up with her, but she didn't want to talk."

"Oh," I said. "Do you think it was her? Do you think she sent me the box?"

"I don't know. But she was troubled. She came from the Providence programme."

"I did too."

"I know," she replied. "Sorry, I didn't mean it like that. Chloe had this stubborn streak that didn't go down well with Mrs Huxley. She was independent and hated being told what to do. They had this battle of wills thing going on that no one was going to win. If Huxley told Chloe to clean the library first, she'd dust the stairs instead. If she was asked to clean the floors, she cleaned the chandeliers. She'd do whatever the Howards wanted, but with Huxley it was a whole other story. Chloe used to say how that woman had too much power and she wanted to take her down a peg."

"I can relate to that feeling," I said.

Roisin laughed. But then the smile faded from her lips. "Look, it's best not to go there with Huxley because you aren't going to win. It's pointless. It's like getting your horns locked with a bull and both of you are going at it with the same strength." She mimed two fighting bulls with her fingers that made me laugh out loud. "Like, I don't know if I should tell you this, but there's more. It's a secret though, so keep it to yourself, all right?"

"What?" I asked, intrigued.

"Chloe and Alex Howard were having an affair."

# CHAPTER ELEVEN

Getting ditched by your own mother strips away the safety net and never truly allows you to be naive. It had always been hard to shock me with outrageous gossip. I didn't go to sleep with a comfort blanket. I slept with one eye open, wondering what could happen to me next. It certainly didn't surprise me to learn that the attractive, rich, young heir to Highwood Hall had been sleeping with the maid. But I did find it interesting. Firstly, because now I knew Alex had a thing for maids, and secondly, because it seemed the girl I'd replaced left under a storm cloud. Perhaps the diorama was her strange way of telling me to get out. It was either a warning or a threat. I wasn't sure which.

My first day had been strange, to say the least. Frightening even. I used the spiral stairs just once that day and wondered whether I'd ever feel comfortable moving up and down the steep wooden treads. I couldn't imagine being on those stairs without picturing the doll lying on the ground, the floor painted red.

I thought of Chloe, this faceless maid, scurrying up and down the staircase five, ten, maybe fifteen times a day, forever at the beck and call of the Howards and Mrs Huxley. And all the time she was keeping that secret, an illicit affair with the boss's son. It was a story I could imagine ending unhappily, perhaps doused in the sort of bitterness that made you resent the person who came after you. My head was spinning. I'd come here for a job, yes, and also to perhaps learn more about the mother I never knew, but I hadn't anticipated this.

We finished up the laundry and headed back to the kitchen. Mrs Huxley waited for us at the top of the stairs.

"Lord Bertie has reported the suspicious parcel to the police," she said. Her hands were clasped together in front of her body. "Now, let that be the end of it. You can put it out of your mind by helping the kitchen staff prepare the silverware for the Howards' dinner. Come along."

Roisin imitated Huxley's abrupt heel turn as we went back into the servants' corridor and followed the housekeeper through the house, ending up back in the dining room. At least this time I had an official reason for being there.

Huxley gestured to a tray of cutlery in the centre of the table that we were to set. "You'll set the tables for an informal dinner. No starter, just main course and dessert. Then you'll carry the food on trays and serve them. I stay for the duration of the meal, topping up drinks and serving vegetables, but you can then go back to the kitchen for your evening meal."

Roisin and I worked methodically around the table, setting knives and forks on place mats. Then we headed back to the kitchen where Pawel and the kitchen staff passed us trays of sea bass in samphire sauce, grilled asparagus and buttery potatoes. I had a sudden urge to rebel, like sneeze on the food or steal a potato, anything naughty. But I didn't. Instead, I concentrated on walking through the corridors without spilling anything. When we arrived back in the room, most of the Howards were ready and waiting for their food.

Lottie, her petite, upturned nose catching the light of the chandelier, sat playing with her phone, her shoulders slumped and a waterfall of blonde tresses caressed the tablecloth. Lord Bertie drummed his fingers against the base of his wine glass, short, stubby nails creating a metallic ring. I couldn't help notice that his hands were just as strong as his son's, though around twice as old.

Alex looked at me with an open, pleasant face. He smiled and thanked me as I placed the fish in front of him, and a waft of his citrus aftershave hit me. When I moved back to stand with Roisin, I found my gaze reaching for his, as though it were magnetised. I was sure Mrs

Huxley would notice, which was why I then forced myself to look elsewhere.

The last to enter the dining room was Margot Pemberton, Lord Bertie's mother-in-law and the woman whose dead daughter was painted onto the dining room wall. She staggered in, wearing an enormous fur coat wrapped around her shoulders, a pair of Jackie O sunglasses sliding down her narrow nose, and a bright purple turban atop her head. She was clearly inebriated, with a slim cigarette hanging out of the corner of her mouth. I hung back away from the table, waiting for Mrs Huxley to let us leave, completely transfixed by this woman. When she sat, she hung the fur on the back of her chair to show off her little black dress and the slightly drooping skin it revealed. And then her head turned towards me. To my surprise, she slipped the sunglasses from her face and narrowed her eyes at me.

"So, you're the replacement, are you? Come here, girl."

I felt like I was in a period movie from the 1920s. I walked over to her, avoiding Alex's eyes, vaguely noticing Lottie pull her attention away from her phone, and stood before Margot Pemberton.

She then beckoned for me to lean closer and grasped my face between her pale, bony fingers. Once she'd examined me, she tutted.

"A pretty one, Bertie? Again." She pulled my face close to hers and whispered in my ear. "Don't take any shit from these pissers. Especially not my son-in-law and *especially* not that godawful housekeeper." And then she released me and addressed the table. "What is it tonight anyway? I hope it's not fucking fish again. We eat so much goddamn fish I'm afraid of growing gills."

Lottie leaned across the table and touched her grandmother's hand. "It's good for you, Mo-mo."

Margot rolled her eyes. "Oh, whoop-de-do. Maybe I'll make it to my eighty-fifth birthday. Wouldn't that be a delight for you all?"

"Margot dear, please shut up," Lord Bertie said, barely even moving his eyes away from his plate. "Can we just get on with dinner? Huxley wants to send the maids away. If you've finished inspecting them of course."

The matriarch glanced in my direction once more. "One moment." She hooked a finger at me, and I approached again. "What's all this about threatening mail? Has someone got it in for you?"

"I don't know," I muttered, feeling stupid. I found myself fiddling with the bare finger where I usually wear my ring.

"Stop fidgeting, girl. Well, if someone does have it in for you, you'd best start growing a spine. My mother knew Al Capone, you know. I grew up around some interesting Hollywood types who could get you anything. Have you got a pistol?"

"Mo-mo—" Alex started.

"Margot, really." Lord Bertie let out a weary sigh.

Mrs Huxley stepped forward. "I'll get the girls back to the kitchen. Is there anything else you need, sir?"

"English mustard would be wonderful." Bertie continued to stare at his mother-in-law.

I backed away from them, my skin vibrating with excitement. The burgeoning of a giggle fit built in my stomach, and every time I imagined Margot's dark brown eyes widening as she said the word pistol, a little laugh escaped from between my lips. Once we were a few feet down the servants' corridor, Roisin grabbed my arm, and we couldn't contain the laughter any longer. Luckily, Huxley was still in the dining room and not there to chastise us.

"Are they always like that?" I asked.

"Oh, yes, absolutely. Margot once told me I'd never find a husband because my ankles were too fat. They broke the mould with that one, I tell you."

The release of laughter made my shoulders lighter. Being with Roisin tended to do that. Finally, I relaxed for long enough to take in the strange dark walls of our private corridor. A place so many other ghosts had tread. The nameless, faceless servants lost to history. We would forever remember a stone trodden on by Anne Boleyn, but who remembered the maid scuttling along by her side?

"A lot of people have lived here," I mused.

Roisin made an *mm-hmm* in agreement.

"There must be stories. Are there any stories about the maids that came before us?" I asked.

"What do you mean?"

I shrugged. "I don't know. I just thought there might be tales of maids from years ago. Affairs and disappearances, that sort of thing. Like Chloe and Alex."

Roisin raised her eyebrows. "I think Chloe and Alex are probably the biggest story right now. But she didn't tell me much. She kept to herself mostly. She was a bit scary, to be honest. She had mood swings."

"What sort of mood swings?"

Roisin shook her head. "One day she'd be fine, the next she'd be in the worst mood. I could never work her out."

I thought of the psychological struggles that came with addiction and wasn't surprised. None of it meant Chloe was unstable; it just meant she was struggling. Guilt gnawed at my stomach. I had no right to assume Chloe sent me the diorama because of her affair with Alex. I'd need a lot of questions to be answered before I made any assumptions. But I was too tired to even think about it. I decided to change the subject.

"Is Highwood haunted?" I asked.

The smile faded from Roisin's lips. "I hear things at night."

That stopped me in my tracks. The expression on my face must've been one of terror because Roisin backtracked slightly.

"It's the house, I suppose. It's so old, and it settles at night. Sometimes those sounds mimic other sounds, like footsteps or voices."

"Voices?"

She shrugged.

"I guess with all these corridors and passageways, voices must carry in unusual ways."

"Well, I'll tell you what I heard, but don't tell Mrs Huxley, will you? The thing is, I'd stayed up late with"—she blushed—"with Pawel. The cook. We'd been drinking, and then he told me he wanted to show me a painting he said looked like me near the north wing. It was like two a.m. or something, so we walked through the house super quietly and he showed me the painting."

"Did it look like you?"

Roisin rolled her eyes. "It was of Lady Godiva with her tits out and hair all over the place. Looked nothing like me at all, but I think he wanted to see *my* tits, judging by the way his hand kept travelling down my back. Anyway, I told him to feck off, and we started walking back to the kitchen. That was when I heard a door slam, and I don't know... whispering." She leaned against the wall. "The north wing is empty. It's not in great shape, and the Howards don't want us in there because it's a safety hazard. I guess there's a draft somewhere near there and the wind came through. It sounded so much like a voice." She shuddered. "I don't mind admitting that it scared the crap out of me."

I felt the coldness of the wall behind my back, the stillness in the air. "What about Pawel?"

"The bastard ran away." She laughed and shook her head. "I guess that killed any illusions I had of finding a decent man at Highwood." She blushed then, turning away. I wondered if there was more to the story. "I saw Alex looking at you tonight."

It was time for us to head back to the kitchen. I started walking, ignoring her prompt.

"I'd be careful there," she said. "In fact, I'd be careful about everything at Highwood."

"Is there anything you're not telling me about this place?" We were close to the kitchen, but I slowed to keep her there in the hallway. "Is it about Chloe?"

Roisin glanced around her to make sure we were alone even though it was clear we were. Then she leaned closer to me and whispered what she wanted to tell me. "I tried to call her once, after she left, and her phone was disconnected. I guess she might've not paid her bill, but I worry about it. I checked her Instagram account, and she hasn't posted for weeks. She was pretty. She used to post selfies of herself in the beautiful gardens here, and she had a small following, you know. Why would she abandon five thousand followers?"

"Maybe if she couldn't afford to pay her phone bill, she can't access the app."

"I guess that makes sense," Roisin said. "I just wish I could get in touch with her. I'm worried about her."

"Did she and Alex break up?"

Roisin gave me a long stare. "Oh, undoubtedly. He obviously used her and threw her away. That's what rich arseholes do to us lot, isn't it? Chloe thought they were in love. Sometimes he bought her jewellery, and for that, she thought he loved her. She thought she'd be Lady Howard one day. How could she be so stupid?"

I wondered the same thing. It was my first moment of true naivety.

# CHAPTER TWELVE

After wolfing down a stew Pawel made for us, I left Roisin to flirt with the cook and went to bed. But I had an ulterior motive for slipping away from the others. I'd seen Mrs Huxley leave, and I wanted to see where she went in the evenings.

Mrs Huxley hadn't shown us to her office or room or wherever it was she spent time away from us. I knew she lived in the house just like we did, but I didn't know where. Instead, she seemed to mostly remain in the kitchen if we needed her. But I was curious, so I followed her along the hallway and stood outside my bedroom, watching her. She continued on to a room at the end of the hall, and there she removed a key from her pocket and entered. I frowned, wondering whether she always kept the room locked.

There would be records in Mrs Huxley's office, I was sure of it. Perhaps evidence of my mother's employment here. But I wasn't going to find them tonight, and I was exhausted from the long, strange day I'd had. I opened the bedroom door and went inside, grateful for the quiet and even more grateful for the soft bed. I kicked off my shoes and plopped down.

I'd decided not to tell anyone about my connections here. I had my own reasons. It was partly because I didn't want Mrs Huxley looking over her shoulder at me, constantly suspicious of a hidden agenda. No, I just wanted to do my job and maybe uncover some secrets at the same time. Which meant staying sharp, being smart. My plan was no plan at all; it was to roll with the punches and see where the job took me. However, the arrival of the diorama had thrown me an unexpected curveball, and now I had two things to worry about.

My mind didn't settle easy that evening, but I shed the uniform, checked on the letters I'd hidden in my underwear drawer, and slipped between the bedsheets, my body so tired I didn't even have the energy to wash my face. Uneasy thoughts moved through my mind as though on a conveyor belt, but one stood out to me. I remembered a few lines from the letters in my drawer. I had them memorised. *I think there's something wrong with Highwood Hall.* That line went around and around in my mind. Somehow, despite everything, I fell into a deep, dreamless sleep.

The second day went relatively smoothly compared to the first. Mrs Huxley gave me a written schedule and map along with a key to the various supply cupboards hidden around the house. I spent most of my time with Roisin, which helped keep the anxiety at bay, but it made exploring Highwood tricky.

I'd heard nothing from Lord Bertie about the strange parcel I received in the post. I spent most of my time cleaning and washing clothes. It was a Thursday, and Lord Bertie was in his office most of the day. I often heard soft classical piano music playing on his sound system and his voice on the telephone.

The warmth of the late May day made my uniform stick to my back as I walked around the hall. At around eleven a.m., I made my way to the living room to dust the ornaments and Roisin had gone to vacuum the upstairs bedrooms. I saw Margot walking through the entryway, her hair pulled up into one of her turbans, wearing nothing but a swimming costume and heels. A cigarette hung from her red lips, skin the shade and texture of leather. She didn't notice me as I hurried past, duster gripped in my fist. She walked surprisingly well in her high heels, like a model on the catwalk, but with that mid-century cool shoulder slump. I assumed, or rather hoped, that she was on her way to the pool.

When I reached the Howard's living quarters, I expected it to be empty, but Lottie smiled at me as I entered.

"Good morning," she said brightly.

"Morning," I said, wondering if I was supposed to give her a title, like Miss or Lady. "Do you want me to come back later?"

She swiped the air with a relaxed hand. "No, just ignore me."

Her long, slender legs dangled over the arm of an ornate, floral sofa. Half-closed hazel eyes watched me as I worked, one foot bobbing up and down as though to music. A book lay on her lap, splayed out and page down.

"God, I'm bored." She sighed dramatically. "This book is bloody awful. Have you read it?"

She lifted the cover and I squinted to read the title. I'd never seen it before, but it looked like an old cosy mystery, something in the same vein of Agatha Christie. I shook my head, and she dropped the book to her lap.

"So, where are you from?" she asked. "I like to get to know the maids. You lot are always much more interesting than books."

"I grew up just outside York." I didn't mind her asking questions so much, but I was quite concerned about losing concentration as I dusted the priceless antiques dotted around the mansion.

"Was it a council estate?"

"No, but it wasn't the nicest area."

She nodded solemnly and tugged at a skinny gold chain around her neck. "What's it like being a junkie?" The necklace slid between her lips, and I saw her tongue slink out and back in, twisting the metal. "Sorry, I like to run my mouth off. That was terribly rude."

Before I answered, I carefully replaced a porcelain horse on top of its plinth. The word she'd used had taken me by surprise, and I hadn't had a chance to react. Resentment, anger, and annoyance bubbled up inside, but I pushed it down. "It's a lot more boring than you'd think. Most of the time you're just out of it, sleepwalking through everything. You don't live. You exist. There's a high, but it doesn't last. Then there's just... numbness and this feeling that you want the high back." I shook away a thought, a feeling, a remnant from my past, not wanting to dwell on those times. And I certainly didn't want to look at her, smiling sympathetically, if not genuinely, with her head tilted to one side. I gritted my teeth and tried not to think about pills and powder and the blurring of a dirty room as the world drifted away.

"You don't talk like... someone with your background."

By that, I assumed she meant I didn't have a broad accent. My patience began to wear thin. The Howards liked to look at me as though

I were a rare specimen. I wondered if Lottie had been like this with every maid who came from the Providence programme.

"My aunt raised me. And she was old-fashioned. She thought I'd have a better life if I didn't pick up an accent, so she used to teach me received pronunciation. She gave me a lot of books to read too." There were hackles standing up on my neck, the edge of a defence mechanism, the weariness of being presumed to be one way because of where you happened to be born.

Lottie swung her legs back over the arm of the sofa and dumped the book on one of the mahogany tables. Her unbrushed hair bunched around her shoulders. She leaned forward, watching me, her hands gripping the sofa cushion. I wondered what she did day in and day out. She was about my age, maybe a year or two younger, and yet she didn't appear to be a student or have a job. What kind of existence was that? Then I glanced at my duster, wondering the same about my own.

"Aren't these figurines frightful?" She wandered over to a glass cabinet and took out a porcelain monkey head with large black eyes and bared teeth. "It's a Meissen from the seventeen hundreds. Ugly thing." She picked up a large dinner plate decorated with vines and cherubs and fruit. "This is Italian. Very expensive. Stupid things really. What's the point?"

My heart was beating hard as she put the porcelain back in place. I'd been told not to touch any of the antiques behind glass. If Lottie broke a figurine, would I be blamed? Would I be assumed to be the culprit? Would Lottie own up to her own misdemeanour, or would she throw me under the bus?

"There's so much around this house that makes no sense whatso-ever. I keep telling Daddy to at least send it to a museum or gallery, but he never listens to me. It's rather obscene, don't you think? Us owning all this." The glass door rattled as it closed.

I couldn't quite make out what she was saying to me. Perhaps she thought she was on my side because she saw her family's riches as unfair, or perhaps she wanted to remind me of my position in the world. Either way, I saw no correct answer to her question without committing to some sort of an opinion about it. She could be testing me.

"I wonder why someone sent you that box," she said out of the blue.

"I don't know," I replied, wanting nothing more than to leave. "It doesn't make sense to me."

"No," she said, dragging out the word. "I suppose it doesn't. If anyone's going to be threatened in this house, I'd imagine it would be Daddy."

"Oh, why is that?" I tried to hide the interest in my voice.

"Well, because he's rich of course. We're hated for it, you know. I mean, I don't blame some people; life is rather unfair at times. But all the same, we're hated for a part of us that we can't change." She sighed and closed the cabinet.

"I'm sorry."

She waved a hand as though it was nothing. Soon after, I made an excuse to leave. Perhaps the arrival of the diorama had made me paranoid, but her toying questions made me wonder: Did Lottie send me the box? She'd brought it down to the kitchen after all.

# CHAPTER THIRTEEN

A fter lunch, Roisin made a start on the bathrooms. There were seven altogether, but we regularly cleaned three—the down-stairs powder room, Lord Bertie's en suite and Margot's en suite. The weekend cleaners tackled the rest. But for some reason Alex requested my assistance in his office. He wanted me to help him file documents. Mrs Huxley said the words between her teeth. When I asked her where his office was, she told me to look at the map.

It turned out that Alex worked in the converted stable block outside the main house. I folded up the map and stuck it in my trouser pocket on my way to the servants' door, but before I reached it, Alex appeared from around the corner, a devious grin stretching his full lips. He lowered his chin and raised his eyebrows as though he'd put some sort of cunning plan in action.

"We're not going to my office," he said. "I wanted to get you away from Huxley for an hour." He leaned against the wall, the shadows of the dark servants' corridor transforming his blue eyes into charcoal pools.

"Oh. Then what—?"

He beckoned me away, and we strode past the kitchen towards the main part of the house. "I wanted to give you a tour. The thing is, I know our housekeeper pretty well—I was a toddler when she joined us —and I know she doesn't tend to show anyone around. Therefore, I've taken it upon myself to treat any new staff to a personal excursion with someone who knows this place like they grew up here. Come on."

He skipped up the main staircase, and I hurried along behind, not quite mustering the same energy. I caught up with him halfway up the stairs where he stopped and pointed to an oil painting. "Look, I'm not the best historian. Daddy would eat me for breakfast if he knew I couldn't remember which duke is which and which ancestor died of syphilis, but I can tell you the nicknames Lottie and I made up when we were younger. This is Oleg the Vampire. Lottie decided that he was a friendly vampire, but I told her he ate children. Look at the teeth. That's a killer if ever I've seen one."

The toothy, stern man frowned down at us from the wall. "I suppose only a murderer would frown and show teeth in a portrait."

Alex waggled his eyebrows. "Oh, most definitely. And this rather strapping young woman"—he gestured to a portly older woman in a powdered wig—"is clearly Catherine the Countess of Cats. Lottie made that one up I'm afraid. Not quite as scary. Unless she had a scary number of cats."

"How many cats would it take to reach frightening proportions?" I asked.

"Oh, at least a hundred."

"A hundred cats would be terrifying," I agreed, aware of the sardonic smile forming on my lips. Alex noticed it too, and his own twitched at the corners. "That's over a thousand claws and many, many teeth."

"Indeed it is," he replied. He leaned closer, and I could've sworn a jolt of static electricity bounced from his blazer to the bare skin of my collarbone. Frazzled air filled the space between us, and I held my breath. "This way." He bounded up the stairs two by two until we reached the landing.

Then we took a right and walked a few paces along the corridor. Alex rapped his knuckles on a panel. "This is where you can spy on Mrs Huxley." He pressed the wood, and a mechanism sprung it back towards us. I gasped in surprise. The door was tiny, about half the size of a regular door. You had to bend down practically on your knees to get into the opening. Alex gestured for me to go first.

"You want me to go in there?" I gave him my best dumbfounded expression, slightly mocking but also genuine. I'd never considered myself claustrophobic, but even I balked at the tiny space.

"Are you scared?"

"No."

He leaned closer again. "Are you sure?"

"I'm sure."

"You're lying to me," he said, lifting a finger and tracing the shape of my eyes in the air. "I can see it, the fear. Your eyes just changed colour from brown to deep maroon. I think it's because you're scared. But it's also very... becoming."

My instincts told me to take a step away from him, but I didn't, and we stayed there, staring at each other, breathing a little deeper, lost somehow.

"I'm not scared," I said, proving it by stepping into the hole.

He squeezed in beside me. The warmth of his breath caressed my neck. Sage and bergamot—the scent of his expensive aftershave—lingered in the air between us. Everything around us smelled of wood and varnish, like we'd been transported to another time. He reached across my body, his gaze penetrating, and gently slid a peephole cover to one side. The movement was slow, like he wanted to drag the moment out, like he wanted to be there with me, close to me, for longer than necessary or appropriate.

"If you peek through the hole, you're actually looking through the large portrait hanging over the stairs. The one of the duke in the wig."

I leaned forward and pressed my face closer, intoxicated with the thought of observing people without them knowing.

"The thing about voyeurism is you don't know how powerful it makes you feel until you try it," Alex said.

His words took me by surprise. They were intense, private. A confession. Again, I wasn't sure how to feel. I turned to him in that tiny space where our noses almost touched. He wasn't smiling any longer. Instead, he breathed heavier, his lips parted, the barest gap between them.

"Do you watch people a lot?" I asked. It was bold. Everything about it stepped over a line. Alex was my boss, at least part of the boss's family, and I shouldn't have been in that cupboard with him at all. I waited for an answer, not moving, not daring to.

"Sometimes." His blue eyes were in shadow again, dark pond water, murky and opaque. Time stretched as we held each other's gaze. I didn't breathe for several heartbeats.

A door slammed and the moment was broken. Alex glanced behind us before easing himself back into the hallway. He was gentlemanly enough to reach through to help me out.

"I'm so sorry, but I actually do have to do some work now. Would you mind if I showed you the rest of the hall another time?"

"Of course not," I said, baffled by his sudden change of heart.

"I'll see you tomorrow anyway," he said. "At the music room."

"That's right," I replied. "I'll see you then."

As he walked away, I noticed that he held himself somewhat oddly. His back and gait were stiff, and his head was lowered. He held something within himself, I thought, something he'd been keen to let out when we were pushed together in that tiny viewing area. But now he repressed it, folded it, tucked it away. If I was right, and if that were true, then I knew all about folding up a desire and ignoring it. I did the same thing every day. In that quiet corridor, I watched him walk down the stairs, open the front door and leave, and then I noticed that my hands were shaking.

# CHAPTER FOURTEEN

I waited for Alex outside the music room at seven p.m. as he'd asked. He was wearing a blue shirt with the sleeves rolled up to his elbows. I felt as small as a child as he came closer, sinking down into the sensible shoes that went with my maid's uniform, gazing up at the easy smile on his face. He was slightly breathless when he said hello to me and unlocked the door. There was one thing I'd noticed about the Howards and rich people in general—the confidence. The ease. The way they moved, talked and existed was different. They looked like nothing could touch them, they were invincible, and this world was made for them.

"I thought I'd play for about an hour, if that's all right," he said, swinging the door wide open to let us both through. "That way I should be able to get through the whole piece. Can you play an instrument?"

I shook my head as we entered yet another large room tucked in the folds of Highwood Hall. It was clear that this one had hardly been touched since the house was built, with a faded fresco of salmon-pink flowers running along the ceiling. Someone had added striped wallpaper to the walls that seemed out of sync with the intricate roses painted above our heads. In the middle of the room stood a grand piano, nothing like the chipped upright my old primary teacher had used for nursery rhymes. The walnut curves gleamed beneath the chandelier, polished to a mirror shine. I heard a thud behind me and turned to see the door close.

"You'll soon pick it up," he said. "Don't worry. I'll show you the ropes. Would you like a drink?"

I hesitated. Was it a test? I'd ask for an alcoholic drink, and he'd fire me for drinking. If I don't ask for a drink at all, I'm being rude. "No, thank you."

He strode over to a cupboard and pulled out a bottle of Scotch and a crystal glass. "I find it helps loosen me up. But don't tell Daddy." He grinned again.

"I won't. Don't worry," I said, sensing my own anxiety in the tremor of my voice.

We walked together towards the piano, and I stood behind him while he arranged the music, hovering like a person who doesn't know what to do with themselves. Finally, his papers were in order and he lifted the lid to reveal the ivory keys. When he sat down on the piano stool, he gestured for me to sit next to him.

"It might be a bit of a squeeze," he warned, "but it's the best place for you to see the music."

He was right about both. Our hips grazed when I took a seat next to him. I thought about the way we'd been pressed close together in the cupboard above the stairs. The bergamot aroma swelled around me, intoxicating, along with the whisky providing that edge, the slightly sour note.

It felt wrong, and yet right, to be so close to him, to this man, this heir. I couldn't speak, I was so nervous. I crossed one leg over the other and then dropped it back to the floor. I placed my hands on my lap and then on the stool and then held them together, squeezing the flesh between my thumb and forefinger. I wondered if he could smell the bleach on me. He placed his Scotch on top of the piano, and I worried about condensation on such a beautiful instrument. My fingers twitched, longing to remove it or fetch a coaster.

"I'll nod to you when you need to turn the page. It'll be easy." He flexed his fingers over the keys, hesitating. "I need to warm up first. I'll play a few simple pieces, and we'll move on to the sonata later. There's a fiddly bit I haven't got the better of yet." He smiled. Was he nervous too? It seemed unlikely, but he appeared to be rambling slightly.

The moment between him talking and his fingers hitting the keys stretched. My breath caught in my chest, waiting, anticipating what would come. And then he began to play.

I couldn't pull my gaze from his fingers. His strokes were soft, quiet, and the music rose from the piano, spreading out until every note resonated throughout the room. It was a melody that built from devastatingly quiet to powerful, resounding chords, gradually sweeping me away with every bar. I could be standing in the ocean, pulled by the tide, my chest swelling to double the size as the music filled my lungs. He stopped abruptly, and I gathered myself, not wanting to let my feelings show.

"That wasn't the sonata?" I asked.

"No," he said. "A Chopin waltz to start things off."

"Wow. But that was so beautiful. And... fast."

He laughed. "You haven't heard much classical music, have you?"

My cheeks warmed with embarrassment. "I'm a philistine."

"No," he said. "You're just not used to it, that's all."

"Taylor Swift's more my thing," I admitted.

He laughed and then played a few bars of *Love Story* with a smile.

"Seriously?" I said, the nerves finally ebbing away.

"All right, I'm going to start for real now." He stretched his arms out, examining the page before him. And then he began to play again.

The piece had a melancholic tone. It was more complex too. He reached past me to hit the high notes before nimbly working his way down to the low notes. I stumbled on the first nod, and it meant he had to slow down his playing, but he took the time to flash me a smile to let me know that it was all right. And then we carried on. He played for longer than an hour, but I didn't notice at all.

I'd slipped into another world. A world with no dioramas dressed up inside a white box with a red ribbon. A world where I hadn't been left by a young mother two decades ago. I forgot about her, about her history with Highwood. The music room became another world to me. It was me and him here, with no one else. I watched Alex play, and I convinced myself he would always be like this, talented, amusing, and someone who truly *saw* me.

When I got back to my room and climbed into bed, Roisin whispered, "What was it like?"

"Everything I'd hoped for," I replied.

We laughed at my corny answer and talked about ex-boyfriends until the late hours. She had an ex back in Sligo who'd hit on her mum. I'd spent a year getting high on uppers with a guy who dumped me when he got sober and went to university. I was his past, he'd told me. The dirty past. The magic of the music room slipped away. Reality hit hard. Whatever Alex had made me feel in there, I didn't deserve it.

# CHAPTER FIFTEEN

The next morning, the pandemonium of breakfast time echoed down the corridor. An unusually frazzled Huxley threw an apron at me and informed us that Pawel was off sick. A clamber of bodies and limbs hurried to scramble eggs and fry bacon. Oven doors opened and slammed. Hot oil hissed. One of the assistant cooks yelled that Margot would throw eggs out the window if they over-cooked them.

In an attempt to be useful, I tried to pass utensils around, but still groggy from the late night, a heavy-bottomed pan slipped from my fingers. Someone yelped behind me, and I turned to find a man hopping on one leg, clutching his foot.

"Oh, I'm so sorry! I didn't see you."

"Bloody hell, what's that pan made out of? Concrete?"

"Sorry!"

"Will you please get out of the way," Mrs Huxley snapped, forcing herself clutching a bowl of chopped tomatoes.

I helped him limp over to the table to rest his foot. He had a London accent, slightly cockney but softer, and a deep, velvety voice to go with it. When he sat down and glanced up at me, two dark brown eyes caught mine. They were lined by thick eyelashes, his eyebrows heavy too. "I guess that'll teach me to be in the kitchen. I brought some radicchio in from the vegetable patch."

That was when I realised he was Ade, the gardener. For some reason

I'd expected someone older. Ade was no older than thirty, his skin a rich umber brown and kept his black hair in tight cornrows close to the scalp. I stepped away as he pulled off a Wellington boot, wanting to give him some space. Even in a sitting position I noticed how tall he was, and broad, presumably from the gardening.

"I'm so sorry about the pan. It just slipped out of my hand when I wasn't paying attention. Is everything all right? Nothing's broken is it?" I gripped my hands together, the sinking sensation of guilt tugging at my abdomen. Ade needed his legs to work. If someone broke my wrist or sprained my ankle, I'd lose out on income. I felt sick.

"Just a bruise," he said. "Hurts like a bitch, but I'll live." He pulled his sock back on and pushed his foot into his boot. "I'd better get back to the garden before you throw any knives at me, new maid." He grinned, but I saw steel in his big brown eyes.

"At least I wasn't carrying the meat cleaver," I replied. "Though at least you'd have more room in those boots."

He stuck out a hand and introduced himself. "Maybe next time we can avoid physical violence. The radicchio is excellent, by the way. Make sure they add a balsamic glaze and serve it with the fish tonight."

"Will do."

Ade stood up opposite me, ready to leave, when his eyes widened and his lips pulled together in an exaggerated grimace that made me think he was about to give me a warning. And then I heard a throat clearing behind me.

"Have you finished flirting?"

My skin flushed hot. I turned abruptly. "I'm—"

Mrs Huxley's demeanour showed no humour whatsoever. Her face remained as strict as a school mistress in a Dickens novel. I added the cane in my mind, slapping down on the palm of her hand as she leered at me. Her, Miss Trunchbull, me Matilda.

"Then it's time to serve breakfast." She thrust a silver tray into my hands and turned sharply on her heel.

When I glanced over my shoulder, Ade was gone. Perhaps he wanted me to avoid the embarrassment of being scolded in public.

WE WERE RUNNING SLIGHTLY LATE, and Margot slid a pair of glasses down her nose as we arrived through the servants' door to set up breakfast. Lord Bertie was sipping tea, an open newspaper by his coffee cup. Lottie was reading her phone, and next to her sat Alex, also looking at his phone. He didn't raise his eyes to meet mine when I walked in the room. He did nothing. Despite the hot food I carried in my arms, a chill washed over my skin. Silently, I placed the tray down in the centre of the table and began lifting the plates from it. They rattled in my shaking hands.

"I'm so sorry we're late, sir." Huxley's voice was sickly sweet. She let her sycophantic side reign whenever we were even a few minutes behind schedule. It made the scrambled eggs seem completely unappetising to me. "Pawel let us down this morning. He has a stomach bug apparently."

Lottie grimaced. "Well, at least he's not making our food."

"Not to worry," Bertie said. "These things happen."

As I backed away from the table, I couldn't help but watch Alex. However, he still hadn't so much as nodded in my direction. Instead, he buttered his toast, avoiding me altogether. I moved over to Roisin by the hot plates set up along the far wall. She gave me a sympathetic smile, and I realised she'd noticed too. I hadn't told her about Alex taking me to look through the peephole above the stairs, but she was intuitive enough to know something was going on between us.

We stood there waiting for Mrs Huxley to finish and let us go. We should've started the linens at that point. When the doorbell rang and Huxley hurried out of the room, I wondered whether we could make our excuses and leave. It'd be an opportune moment to try Mrs Huxley's office door, though I expected that she kept it locked at all times.

"Coffee." Margot lifted an arm, clicking her fingers.

Roisin rushed over to the coffee pot. I backed up closer to the hidden door, dropping a not-so-subtle hint.

"This is barely lukewarm, girl," Margot complained.

"S-sorry, Mrs—"

"Don't be silly, just go and warm it up."

Now Alex's eyes finally met mine. I expected to find amusement in them, but they were penetrating, cold. He quickly glanced away. I noticed his leg dancing up and down beneath the table. Was he upset?

I'd known him barely a week, and yet it already felt as though he had two personalities. Alex, who was eager to give me a tour of Highwood, who told me about the silly names he'd given the portraits as a child, and then Alex, crammed up next to me in the cupboard, revealing intimate thoughts, an aura of intensity surrounding him.

"Miss Howard, you have a parcel." Mrs Huxley glided back into the room, carrying a cardboard box around the size of a tub of biscuits with a bright scarlet bow tied on top.

A prickling sensation spread over my scalp, and I inhaled sharply as the walls of the room seemed to close in around me. My diorama had arrived in an almost identical box. Lottie had clearly forgotten, as she clapped her hands together and let out a squeak of excitement. Mrs Huxley's expression remained grim while she placed the box down on the table, and my heart hammered against my ribs. I wanted to look away, or flee. My eyes flicked over to Alex, who stared intensely at the box, frowning so sternly that tiny dimples of tension appeared on his chin. Everyone in the room stayed quiet and still, apart from Margot, who slurped on her lukewarm coffee. I instinctively took a step closer, wondering what sort of threat poor Lottie was about to receive.

When Lottie untied the ribbon, the front of the box dropped, just like it had when I'd received mine. I slowly began making my way around the table, hoping no one noticed me moving to get a better look. I needed to see the scene for myself.

"Well, is there a note?" Margot asked, not sensing the tension in the room or completely ignoring it.

"No, Mo-mo," Lottie said.

She was moved by the gift—I could see that—but not by happiness. It was more like fear. Any trace of the little-girl act she liked to play faded away, and for once she appeared older than her years. Her eyebrows were drawn together, creating a skinny crevice between them. She chewed on her bottom lip; eyes fixated on the box. I continued edging around the table until I stood behind her shoulder, dangerously close to Alex. He stared at the box, not saying a word.

Another diorama. This time without any blood and no broken doll at the bottom of a staircase. The depiction showed a child sitting cross-legged in the middle of a large room. I recognised the library at a glance. Every detail had been re-created with care, from the ladders that leaned against the shelves to the glowing fire painted onto the back wall of the box. The little girl had her face resting on her hands as though she was in deep concentration, reading the book on her lap. It was pretty and not at all sinister like the scene I'd received.

The rug beneath the child was covered in tiny torn pages scattered around her like confetti. The child hadn't been reading the book at all. She'd been destroying it. I glanced at Lottie's profile and saw a shadow of pain move across her features.

"This is getting ridiculous now." Lord Bertie lifted the box flap to conceal the scene. He picked it up, cradling it against his chest. "If the police won't do anything this time, I'll find out what's going on myself."

# CHAPTER SIXTEEN

Two dioramas had turned up at Highwood Hall in my first week. But I wasn't the only target. Whoever sent these strange, creative threats had decided to terrorise Lottie, too. But why? I couldn't figure it out.

Back in the kitchen, as we ate leftover pastries and toast from the Howards' breakfast, we suffered through a silence enforced by Mrs Huxley's presence. I saw the strain on Roisin's face, the furtive glances between the kitchen staff, and the unsmiling expression of the house-keeper daring us to gossip. That was one of Mrs Huxley's greatest flaws —she couldn't read people. She didn't understand what her staff needed. We needed to blow off steam, but her ramrod posture and pursed lips prevented us from it.

"Do you know why Lottie received that scene?" I asked the house-keeper, breaking the silence.

I hadn't realised how lost in thought she was. She jerked sharply in my direction and appeared to pull herself back to reality. "Why would I know?"

"Alex— Mr Howard mentioned that you started working here when he was a toddler, so you must have been here when Lottie was born." I shrugged, ignoring Roisin's wide eyes. "I just assumed you might know what event it referred to."

"No," Huxley muttered. "No doubt I was too busy with work."

"Who delivered it? Was it in a separate box? Was it the postman?"

"It was on the front doorstep," Huxley said. "No outer box." She stood, her chair scraping back, and left the room without another word.

Roisin shushed me when I opened my mouth to speak. Instead, we listened to Mrs Huxley walking up the stairs.

"She's gone up to his office," she said.

"Lord Bertie's office?"

She nodded. "Do you think it's to talk about the... thing?"

"The diorama?"

"Is that what it's called?"

"I think so."

Roisin replaced a spoon. "I wonder who's going to get one next. Maybe it'll be me. Maybe they'll send me a pale-faced doll dead on the kitchen table or hanging from the rafters."

I tutted. "Don't."

"Sorry." Her guilty smile flashed shyly. "Well, I suppose we should clean the silverware."

I helped her tidy away the breakfast dishes and collect the three large carriers of silverware we needed to polish. I folded my legs underneath me on my chair and picked up a fork.

"Did you see it?" I asked.

She shook her head. "I didn't get a decent view of it."

"It wasn't scary like the one sent to me. At least there wasn't a bloody murder scene or anything. It's of a little girl sitting on the floor in the library with pages of a book scattered all around her. Do you know what that means?"

Roisin frowned deeply and put down her rag. "I don't know. Maybe it was Lottie when she was a child. It had to be personal to her; otherwise, she wouldn't have gone so white."

I thought of Lottie's frozen expression, the wariness in her eyes. Yes, she'd been afraid. And perhaps it meant the diorama was more threatening than it seemed. What was the history there?

"Whoever sent the dioramas must've been involved with the Howards for a long time, right?"

Roisin shrugged. "Unless they heard about whatever happened secondhand. What if Lottie told them a secret?"

"You mean someone like a maid. Someone who worked with her." I thought about Chloe again, the maid I replaced. "Or... think about it.

Apparently the parcel turned up on the front step, with no outer packaging. That means they got through the gate, unless..."

"Huxley."

I nodded. "Huxley."

"What about me?"

I dropped the fork to the table and winced as it clattered noisily against the rest of the silverware. In the doorway she stood, tall enough to fill the space, her shoulders hunched because she clenched her hands together in front of her torso. Roisin let out a gasp.

"I... um..." I sat there floundering, mouth flapping open stupidly. How had she come down the spiral staircase without either one of us hearing? How had she appeared so quickly? I took a deep breath before changing the subject entirely. "Has Lord Howard managed to find anything out about the mystery gifts?"

Inside I prayed that she hadn't heard the first half of our conversation in which I accused her of being the mysterious sender. I couldn't think of anything worse. I wanted to sink into a hole in the ground and never emerge. Someone could bury me in it as long as I didn't have to stare into Mrs Huxley's jet-black eyes ever again.

"That's none of your business. I suggest you get back to work, girls."

Despite everything, I couldn't help myself. I stood. "Wait a minute. It is my business. Someone sent *me* one of those packages."

"Yes, I'm aware of that," she snapped. "The answer is no; Lord Howard doesn't have any news for you. Is that better? Are you happy now?"

"Not particularly."

She took a step into the room and clasped her hands together. "I'm not sure what you were expecting. Did you think that the world's best detectives would flock together to uncover the mysterious case of the creepy dolls? Did you think that Lord Howard, a man with much better things to do, would be able to find the culprit within forty-eight hours? Do you honestly believe you are special enough for all these things to happen because someone sent you a Barbie doll at the bottom of some stairs? Now, I suggest you distract your overactive little mind and get on with your job, unless you would like to work elsewhere. Would you like to work elsewhere?"

My cheeks burned red-hot. I hadn't felt such embarrassment for a long time. And yet all I could do was shake my head as I sat back down.

"Good."

Roisin didn't dare look at me until she'd left.

I picked up the fork with trembling fingers. As I carried on with my work, I kept glancing back at the door as though expecting her to appear again, but she didn't. Neither I nor Roisin dared to speak, but inside, my thoughts were loud enough to drown out the silence. I felt an infinitesimal shift that day in my attitude, in the way I regarded Mrs Huxley. A new, burgeoning anger budged my embarrassment out of the way because I didn't want to be spoken to like that ever again. And more importantly, I realised I didn't trust her. Not one little bit.

# CHAPTER SEVENTEEN

**H**ighwood Hall fizzed with subdued excitement for the rest of the day as we dusted and hoovered and polished. I held more money in my hand when I dusted an ornament than I'd ever earned in my entire life. It made my heart skip a beat, but Roisin was much less nervous as she manoeuvred around the hall with her vacuum cleaner.

I was surprised when Lottie pulled me out of the dining room to ask me to help her organise her closet. She sniffed a lot as we walked up the stairs to her room, and along with the red-rimmed eyes, I realised she'd been crying. But when I asked if she was all right, she glanced upwards at me from beneath her pale eyelashes and said, "Just peachy." It felt like an attempt to shut down the conversation. I closed my mouth and didn't speak again until she initiated the conversation.

Her bedroom was messy enough with discarded books strewn across the floor, candy-coloured underwear dangling out of open drawers like a boudoir in a film noir, and her dressing table covered in half-empty bottles of make-up. An abandoned mascara wand lay on the surface of the table amongst black and tan smudges I'd cleaned away just a few days ago.

She led me into a separate room I could easily use as a bedroom on its own. It wasn't huge, but it was certainly enormous for a glorified wardrobe. But the place was chaos. Dresses, shoes, jewellery, jeans, blouses, coats and more had been piled on top of each other, almost every hanger, drawer or shelf was either empty or stuffed full of screwed-up clothing. Despite trying not to react, an "oh dear" slipped from my lips.

"That bad?" Lottie grimaced. "I've always been a tad untidy. Daddy says I should live in the stables."

"No, no, it's fine. We'll just need to work systematically, that's all."

She clutched my arm dramatically. "Oh, thank God you're here. I wouldn't have a clue where to even start."

For the first hour, she was smiley and sweet, working just as hard as I did to bring order to the chaos. We filtered out all the dirty washing first and then started folding her woollens. She had so many cashmere cardigans it made my head spin.

"I guess we have something in common now," she said. "We both have a secret admirer."

I let out a hollow laugh. "Yeah, I guess so." My heartbeat quickened. I'd wanted to bring up the subject of the diorama, but held back in case I overstepped my role as a servant. Now that she'd broached the subject herself, I wondered if I could get some information out of her that might help me piece together what happened.

"Not a very flattering admirer," she said, sniffing again.

"No," I replied, wanting to tread carefully. "It felt awful, opening that box and seeing what was inside. It was... disturbing. I can't think of any other way to describe it."

She nodded.

"Look, Miss... Lottie. What you saw inside the box is your business, obviously, but I suppose if it is the same person, maybe the two are linked in some way. And perhaps we should talk about it. Help each other."

She gestured for me to sit with her on the floor, and we crossed our legs and faced each other like two girls bonding at boarding school. A mound of colourful scarves lay between us, a mountain made from silk.

"Was yours personal to you?" she asked.

"I think it was more of a threat," I said. "The doll on the floor looked like me."

"Does it connect back to anything that's happened to you? In the past I mean. Like... I don't know, an event from your childhood?"

Gently I shook my head. She hoped that it did. I could see that. She needed comfort from me, a reassurance that we'd both been targeted for the same reason.

"Okay," she said, staring down at the scarves. "Nevermind then."

When she climbed to her feet, I hesitated for a second and then decided not to let this moment pass. "Did you want to talk to me?"

She sat back down and sighed. With one hand cradling her chin, she stared up at me with her large, shining eyes, and I remained patient, sensing that she was working up to a confession. I imagined Lottie getting her own way often by utilising those big, soulful eyes. Perhaps they were the reason for her childlike persona. The slight lisp, the way she said daddy, the lack of focus and direction. Had Lottie been shaped by those who treated her like a child? Or was it the other way around?

"Not many people know about this, which is why I'm so *confounded* by it all," she said. "I was ten years old, and it was all so silly." She flapped a hand. "It was nothing more than a big misunderstanding, but I've felt terribly guilty about it all these years." She picked up a silk scarf, pulling at the corner. "Alex is the genius in the family. He's the one who's going to carry on the family business and make Daddy proud, of course. I'm not like him at all. I'm the opposite, the idiot."

"I'm sure that's not true."

"Well, maybe I'm not an idiot, but I was never a fast learner like Alex, and it took me a shamefully long time to learn how to read. Mummy hired my first tutor when I was five, and I was so naughty that I went through a string of them until she found one that stuck. The one that stuck was the one I hated. Imagine Huxley, but psychotic."

"Wow," I said, and she laughed.

"I called her Lumpy behind her back. Not terribly original, I know. She heard me, of course, and then she was even stricter. She'd have me in the library every day for hours during the school holidays. I'd tried to run away, and that was when she started locking me in." She smiled sardonically. "We had a maid then—I forget her name—but she was kind, and she sneaked my favourite sandwiches into the library through the servants' door. Sometimes she'd even stay with me and let me listen to her CD player. But I was furious with Lumpy. You know the kind of angry you get as a child, the kind when you feel like everything is unfair and grownups are horrible? I was so mad that I took the one thing she loved more than anything in the world. It was a first edition of *Little*

*Women* that my father had given her as a thank you for torturing me until I could read as well as any other ten year old. In my head she didn't deserve it. She was mean. A monster who yelled at me and made me write the same sentence three hundred times.

"I used the servants' corridor, and I snuck into her room and stole the book. I went into the library, pulled the pages out and burned them in the fire. Then I left. I did it specifically at the same time I knew the maid was about to clean the library." She swallowed thickly, still tugging at the scarf in her hands.

"What happened?"

"Well, as you can imagine, Lumpy went straight to Daddy and told him I'd done it. Who else would it be? I was a naughty child who hated her tutor. It was obviously me. But I insisted it wasn't me. I insisted until I was blue in the face and Mummy and Daddy were exasperated with me. Instead, I blamed the maid."

I stared uncomfortably down at the shoes on my feet. I'm not sure why it affected me so much. She was just a child. But it did affect me because I thought of that maid and her low wages. I thought of the toilets she'd cleaned and the ornaments she'd dusted. No one aspires to be a maid. You are one because you're desperate. And then I wondered… But no. If Lottie was ten, the timeline didn't match with my mother's time at Highwood.

"It was an awful thing to do, because of her kindness. She'd even helped me escape one day and then smuggled me back into the library before Lumpy came back. It meant I could go out and play in the sun. She was such a lovely woman."

When Lottie's expression changed, a sense of dread washed over me.

"What happened?" I asked.

"Daddy fired her. I know he didn't believe me, but he was too full of pride to admit it in front of my tutor. So he fired the maid. He fired them both actually, and that was the end of my tutoring. I don't know what happened to the maid, but I never saw her again. I guess she went on to work somewhere else."

"Not as a maid," I said quietly. She wouldn't have known this, but references are important, and once a maid has been fired, it'd be unlikely that she'd find another job like this. A cleaner somewhere else maybe. Scrubbing toilets in offices and restaurants.

"That's it, I suppose. That's the story the diorama depicted. Maybe it was her, after all these years, coming back to torture me."

"Do you remember the names?"

She shook her head. "I've told Daddy. He'll have the names on files somewhere I suppose. Maybe Huxley has it all written down. I'm sure he'll find them. It'd be odd though, wouldn't it? After all these years." She glanced down at the scarf between her fingers, and then she thrust it towards me. "I don't want this. Do you want it?"

I thought about turning it down, but if I took it, it'd be the prettiest item I owned by far. Tentatively, I held out my hand and accepted the gift.

# CHAPTER EIGHTEEN

On the way out of Lottie's room, I heard a swish and caught a glimpse of Mrs Huxley's maroon skirt disappearing around a corner. Before I had time to think—and talk myself out of a decision—I quickly pulled off my shoes and tiptoed after her. At the corner I heard a knock and a door open. Once I rounded the corner, she was gone. But I knew where. She was in Lord Bertie's office.

Silently, I made my way down the hall and stood outside the room, pressing my ear against the wood. My heart pounded so hard that I had to force it to calm with slow, steady, *silent* breaths. Their voices carried through the wood. Faint but clear enough to make out their words.

"The thing is, Huxley, quite frankly I have better things to do than chase up some stupid gifts. But I suppose now Lottie has one this matter needs resolving."

"Are you going to the police?" Huxley's voice sounded different. Relaxed, informal. It took me by surprise. She was always such a fawning minion to the Howards in public.

"No," he said. "I have a friend who runs an investigation company. He'll get to the bottom of it and sort things out."

"When you find out who it is, what will you do?"

"Threaten them, pay them off. Whatever it takes to stop them sending those ridiculous scenes. Whoever it is knew about that business with Lottie and whatsername."

"Susan Cole. The nanny."

"Right. Maybe it's her."

"Maybe," Huxley said. "What do you think of the new maid?"

I trembled, pressed harder, felt a pitter-patter against my ribs.

"I think she's perfectly adequate."

Mrs Huxley waited for a long pause before responding. "Yes, so do I. Feistier than expected though."

"Well, that doesn't bother me. As long as you can keep her in line."

"Of course."

There was a shuffle inside the room and footsteps approached. I moved away from the door, hurrying quietly down the hall. Once I passed Lottie's bedroom, I broke into a sprint towards the servants' corridor, slipped in through the hidden panel and made my way along the hallway. The spiral staircase shivered as I ran down the steps, and when I reached the bottom, I took a moment to catch my breath. The diorama scene flashed through my mind again. I saw myself broken and bruised on the floorboards, blood trickling from a gaping wound.

Stop it, I told myself, angrily stuffing my feet back into my shoes. I made my way past the kitchen and back to my bedroom when Mrs Huxley emerged from her office.

"Did you help Miss Howard?"

I froze. "What?"

"I said, did you help Miss Howard with her closet?"

My voice came out like a crackled whisper as I replied. "Yes."

"Good."

Gliding as always, Mrs Huxley passed me, making her way through to the kitchen while I remained rooted to the spot, still staring in her direction.

How had she reached her office before I'd reached my bedroom? I'd run all the way back here from Lottie's room. It made no sense. I let myself in, pulled the map out of my pocket, spread it out on the bed and examined it for secret passages. This map didn't have the secret cupboard above the stairs marked, which meant there could be other corridors, cubby holes or even rooms hidden within the walls. Mrs Huxley obviously knew one or more of these secrets and hadn't told me about their existence. But had she told anyone?

The silk scarf was still in my pocket. Slightly ashamed that I'd accepted a gift and somewhat nervous that Lottie might go back on her generosity, I stuffed it in my underwear drawer where my finger caught the edge of thin, worn-down paper. My mother's letters. Over two decades old. Perhaps she'd written them sitting on this bed in this very room. I thought about reading them again, but what was the point? I knew them by heart. *I think there's something wrong with Highwood Hall. Things are strange here. All the staff say the north wing is haunted, and sometimes I could honestly swear that I hear noises coming from that part of the house.*

Roisin had said the same thing.

There were secrets within these walls, but was I ever going to be able to uncover them? Who could I trust? Who could I ask? The answer was no one. I closed my mind to the constant questions there because of the unpleasant scratching at the back of my mind. The one telling me I was in over my head.

Nerves tightly wound, feeling skittish and breathless, I made my way back to the kitchen. But just as I was about to step through the doorway, I heard someone whisper my name. When I turned, Alex was leaning against the wall, head casually resting on the door jamb. The light bounced across the dark green paint, giving his skin a sallow tone, deepening the shadows beneath his eyes. He grinned, grabbing my hand and hauling me away.

I protested, not wanting to be late for Mrs Huxley, pulling my weight away from him, but his grin stretched, and he breathed, "Come with me," as his surprising strength tugged me along the hall. The fingers I'd seen expertly playing the piano pressed deep into my flesh until it turned white as milk.

"I can't. Mrs Huxley—"

He reversed his step, moving quickly towards me with such sudden ferocity that I ended up backed against the wall. His face moved close enough to mine that I smelled cigarette smoke on his breath.

"Who's your boss?" His eyes flashed. The mischievous grin was lost, replaced by lips pulled away from his teeth like an aggressive animal. But it was not a threat. Somehow I knew that. It was a test.

I didn't tremble. I didn't look away. "You are."

He let go of my arm. I'd passed the test. His smile returned. "Come on then."

# CHAPTER NINETEEN

For an hour, Alex showed me Highwood. He took me through the Howards' personal spaces that felt lived-in and cosy, and he showed me the formal rooms they didn't use. He pointed out all the paintings of his ancestors and the weapons pinned to the walls. As we walked around the hall, he kept a distance from me the entire time, ensuring that our bodies never touched. It was like taking a museum tour with a guide and a complete contrast to how he'd grabbed me outside the kitchen. For almost the entire time, he kept his hands behind his back while I imagined those fingers locked around my wrist. The more I thought about it, the more the skin tingled where he'd touched it.

Since I'd started working at Highwood Hall, I'd been too afraid to open the bathroom cabinets. It wasn't because I had a goody-two-shoes nature preventing me from snooping. Far from it. The reason I didn't open the cabinets was because I didn't want to see what the Howards had been prescribed. Vicodin. Adderall. Tranquillisers. Even cough medicine. Bit by bit, I'd applied a tough, outer layer to my willpower, clad in steel, but that didn't mean I wasn't cautious. I kept myself away from temptation.

But as I looked at Alex, a realisation hit me. These tests, these power plays, were as tempting to me as whatever barbiturates or opioids were hidden in the Howards' bathrooms. He'd quickly become my new addiction. But what I couldn't figure out was why.

For the last part of the tour, Alex showed me two more secrets. He took me to those tiny, confined spaces reserved for the clandestine happenings of the past. First was the dumb waiter, which I'd seen in the kitchens. It wasn't often used because it needed maintenance, and instead Roisin and I carried most of the food around the hall.

"You could fit in there," he mused. "You're quite petite, aren't you?"

"Yes," I said. "I've skipped a lot of meals."

"We don't feed you?"

"Not now, in the past."

He gave me a strange look. Not sympathetic. Not concerned. Not cruel. I could've sworn that he was aroused.

Then he led me through to another wood-panelled room with a large fireplace and several comfortable sofas arranged in a semi-circle. In this room, I noticed the one and only large flat-screen TV fitted above the fireplace. The kind of warm and cosy snug that makes you fall in love with a house. One you could imagine children playing in the corner and a cat curled up a sheepskin rug. Alex, on the other hand, seemed out of place in this room. He was too formal, too upright. His blazer and striped shirt made it look like he was about to watch a polo match.

"I want to show you something. But before I show you, I want to ask you a question."

"Okay."

"Do you trust me?"

I hesitated for a moment. This felt like another test. The easy answer would be yes. It would be the placating answer, the pandering one. It was the kind of answer an employee should give to an employer, or at least the son of the employer. But it would be a lie.

"No."

He lifted his chin. "Why not?"

"I don't give my trust to people I hardly know," I replied.

"Your trust is a prize to be earned? You hold it dearly."

"I suppose you could put it like that. I think of it as being screwed over too many times."

He smiled at that. "Let's test your ability to trust. Shall we?" He stepped closer to the fireplace, ran his fingers down a panel, and then thumped the wood with the side of his fist. I heard a clunk, and the panel popped out. "It's a priest hole. They used to hide—"

"I know what a priest hole is."

"Do you now?" The grin was back.

"Yes," I said. And then to prove myself, I offered up an explanation. "When Catholics were persecuted, some families hid priests in secret compartments in their homes." I stepped closer to him and the hole, both of which made my stomach flutter with nerves. "It's tiny."

The entrance to the priest hole was so small I'd have to bend double to get into it. I leaned my head and shoulders into it, observing the way the hole then fed into a space behind the fireplace. The brick walls offered no sense of comfort.

While I leaned inside the hole, Alex came closer, his lips a hair's breadth from my ear. "Will you get in?"

When I turned my head, we were so close we almost bumped noses. Tension ran all the way through me. I didn't want him to see that I was nervous. "Why?"

He shrugged.

I knew it was a game. I knew right then and there exactly who he was. It made my heart pound and my stomach churn. It was dangerous to encourage him. I knew it was. But the truth is—I wanted to play. I could dress up the push and pull of the dynamic between Alex and me by saying I was afraid of losing my job, but it'd be a lie. No, I was curious, and I wanted to see how far it would go. I went in backwards with my fingers groping the ceiling of the hole so that I didn't bang my head. I went in blind because I wanted him to see that I would. He watched, his eyes cold, his teeth clenched together, bloodless fingers gripping the wood panel. Once I was inside, I turned to continue deeper into the hole, and then I tucked myself into it.

He closed the door, trapping me in darkness.

He wanted to see me stuck, to know he was the only one who could let me out. I didn't move while I was in that hole. My pulse quickened, but I didn't panic. I closed my eyes and imagined I was in my room, in bed, with the light off. For some reason my thoughts drifted back to my childhood, to the day my aunt told me about my abandonment. I was three, maybe four. I'm not sure now. She'd always been Aunty Josephine to me, and I wanted to know why I didn't call her Mummy like the other children called their mothers.

She wasn't cruel, and she hadn't said anything mean to me. In fact, she gave me a chocolate Freddo frog, my favourite even now, and explained that my mum had left when I was six months old.

"But you have me to look after you," she'd said. "And... Well, I'll do my best."

"That's okay," I'd replied, thinking of nothing but the Freddo. I'd loved her for the chocolate alone.

Later, when I was eighteen, she sat me down and told me that my father was still alive. And then she told me where I could find him.

The door opened. Alex was flushed pink, his skin glowing with perspiration. He reached in and helped me out of the hole, his hands guiding me with a gentleness I hadn't felt from him in the corridor. When he closed the door to the hole, he pushed me and pressed his body against mine. Our noses touched now because he leaned over. But instead of kissing me, he lifted both my arms and pinned them behind my head, and then he watched with curiosity when I didn't protest or struggle.

He released me. Silently he walked away.

I made my way back to the kitchen alone.

"Where have you been? You're late!" Huxley snapped, thrusting a tray of cutlery into my hands. "Set the dining room table."

It wasn't the reprimand I'd anticipated. She didn't even wait for an explanation. I couldn't help wondering, as I carried the tray up to the dining room, whether she knew exactly where I'd been.

In the dining room, Alex never acknowledged or even looked at me as I served food. However, I sensed the presence of Mrs Huxley in the background, like she was watching me as well as watching Alex, silent disapproval seeping from every one of her pores.

Huxley dismissed Roisin and me after the starters had been served, and we walked back down to the kitchen arm in arm. Roisin's gaze skittered up the walls and across the ceiling before it fell onto me. She hesitated before she spoke.

"Were you with Alex again? Is that why you were late?"

I didn't need to respond because she read the truth from the expression on my face.

She stopped dead, and her hold of my arm tightened to stop me too. "If Mrs Huxley finds out—"

I sensed myself bristling. "She can't do anything. It's none of her business."

"She can. You don't know the kind of influence she has over Lord Bertie. She basically runs everything since Lady Laura died."

It was the first time I'd heard her name. Alex had pointed her out to me in the dining room, but I'd not known her name before.

"Alex's mother?"

Roisin nodded. "Do you know how she died?"

I shook my head.

"She fell down the stairs."

I gasped. "The spiral stairs?"

"No, the main ones. By the entranceway. It was the middle of the day. Lord Bertie found her first, apparently. I wasn't working here then, but Pawel told me all about it. He said it was awful. Blood everywhere. Her face was all smashed up."

"What about Alex? Did he see his mother like that?"

To my surprise, Roisin grimaced, as though reacting to a memory or perhaps the mental image of someone else's memory. She removed her arm from mine and placed it on her hip. "What happened with Alex is really strange. Like, fucking weird."

The servants' corridor seemed to cool around us. A faint breeze caressed the nape of my neck, and I wondered whether someone had opened a door in a different part of the house.

Roisin continued. "Pawel said no one could find Alex. He wasn't answering his phone, but his car was in the garage, so they knew he hadn't left. While everyone was waiting for the ambulance to arrive, the staff, and in particular Mrs Huxley, searched everywhere for him but couldn't find him. It was Lottie who found him in the end."

"Where was he?"

"He was in the little cupboard above the stairs. The one with the peephole." She shook her head. "Don't you think that's strange? I could imagine a child hiding away after seeing such a terrible thing. But an adult?"

"Did he see his mother fall down the stairs?"

"I don't know," Roisin said. "Pawel didn't tell me that."

I thought of Alex and me squashed up tight in the cupboard, our bodies almost pressed together. I thought about what he'd said. The voyeurism. The power of watching. I folded my arms around my body, trying to warm myself from the cold chill. It was then that I wondered whether I'd started to play a game I could never win, but was too addicted to stop.

# THE MUSIC ROOM

For some reason, when I waited for him, I tucked my arms behind my back and drew my shoulders up, straightened my spine, lifting my chin. Perhaps I wanted him to see that I had discipline, that my excellent posture was an indication of excellent character. He always walked tall, his strides long but not loping and ungainly, rather contained and controlled. He would sit at the piano with perfect posture. I saw the years of disciplined practice paying off when he touched the black and white keys.

My heart fluttered with excitement when he placed the key into the lock and opened the door. This was my favourite part of the week, and sometimes I spent hours daydreaming about it while dusting the library or folding linens. Beethoven, Debussy and Chopin were reflective earworms that resonated through my mind. His playing made me feel smart. The way he talked to me made me feel like someone who mattered, someone who had a brain.

"We're going to do things a little differently tonight," he said.

"Okay."

I'd felt some anticipation about meeting him here again. The rest of the week had gone by in a blur. I'd ended up working on Sunday rather than taking the day off and found myself in a fog, amazed that it was Friday already.

He told me to sit down on the stool, and he took the seat next to me. "This is middle C," he said, playing a note almost perfectly in the centre of the piano. Then he pointed to a black squiggle on the music paper. "That is the mark for middle C."

At first, I wondered why he was teaching me this. Why would I need to know? But he continued on, showing me several of the notes and their symbols on the paper. He lifted my hands, placed my fingers against the notes and told me to press the keys.

"Not like that," he chastised. "Gently."

He wasn't a patient teacher, but he didn't sigh in frustration or shake his head. He placed my hands where they needed to go. He barked out directions for a while, and then he began to test me. He'd play one note and ask me what it was. He'd point to the squiggles on the paper and make me tell him what they were.

"If you keep getting these wrong, I'll have to punish you."

His eyelids drooped down, obscuring the irises. His lips pulled tightly at the edges. Even under the bright lights, I saw darkness in the contours of his face. I wanted to please him. I longed to be a fast learner who made him proud, but I was clumsy, and my hands never went to the right places. I shivered down to the piano stool, every touch sending electricity up and down my spine.

"That's enough for one day," he said suddenly. And with that, he launched into the sonata.

For some reason I wanted to cry. I didn't cry often, but the most robust sensation of inadequacy ran through me that the little girl inside pounded at my rib cage, begging for me to allow her heart to ache. Instead, I cleared my throat and waited for him to indicate when to turn the page. Then I did it right on cue. Again. And again. And again. I turned the page. This I could do, I thought. I'd never become a pianist because I was too clumsy with my fingers sore and red from cleaning all day. But this I could manage.

At least, so I thought. My concentration lapsed when he began the sonata for the second time. We'd been in the music room for at least two hours by that point, much longer than the hour he'd promised our sessions would take. When I missed his direction, he stopped playing and the silence fell so quickly it was like a heavy curtain dropping around us.

He turned to face me. "Give me your hand, Emily."

I shuddered when he said my name with that soft but firm voice, peppermint on his breath. I could hear my ragged breaths in the quiet, echoing room. Reluctantly, but with a modicum of curiosity, I reached out and placed my palm in his.

"This is for your own benefit, because I want you to learn. What's the point of life if you're not learning to be better?" His long fingers encased my small hand. He held me firmly, but not hard enough to hurt me. And then he pinched me on the forearm. It made me gasp because I wasn't expecting it. And then he did it again, just below the elbow. It smarted, but I wouldn't call it painful. That didn't make it less wrong, but I suppose it made it easier to dismiss. Of course, I knew that an employer shouldn't be doing this to his maid, but it happened so fast that I didn't know how to react. I simply sat there and took it.

Afterwards, when he'd let go of my hand—which I placed back in my lap—he continued with the piano piece as though nothing had happened. I turned the pages diligently, not wanting to experience any more of his punishments.

"Very good," he said at last, without turning his head in my direction and without any joy or lightness in his voice. My head was bowed, and I couldn't look at him. Half my body was hot with shame, the other cold from the evening chill in a badly heated house.

After everything that had happened, he played me the Debussy three times in a row, presumably to apologise for the punishment he'd just doled out. But for some reason that brought the warmth of my temper back, until the final note, when he looked at me and smiled. He lifted one hand from the piano and brushed a lock of hair away from my face. It cooled my hot temper almost immediately. At the time, I thought of that act as affectionate, showing me that despite the funny little games he liked to play, he did have feelings for me. But in hindsight, I think he was probably neatening my unruly hair.

# CHAPTER TWENTY

A fter the music room, I needed fresh air. It was after ten p.m., and I was exhausted by hours of concentration. When Alex had asked me to turn the pages for him, I hadn't expected how much work it entailed. But I loved the new existence of music in my mind. I loved the way certain musical patterns stayed with me long after he played them and made my step a little lighter. In the music room, I stopped thinking about the dioramas and the past, nothing existed except me, Alex, and the piano in front of us.

Outside the music room, everything came flooding back.

Wood-panelled hallways sprawled through the mansion like veins. Constricted and dark in the evening. They closed in on me, drawing closer and closer until the pressure built around my ribs, a relentless vice with me in its grip. I hadn't bothered to use the servants' corridor because it was late and I knew the door from the entrance hall was quicker to reach. I hurried my way through the house, concerned that I might bump into Lord Bertie and be forced to explain myself.

A high wind raged outside. It caught the baby hairs around my face. The long-sleeved tunic was breathable and ideal for cleaning draughty rooms, but it offered little protection against the cool evening air. I wrapped my arms around my body and crunched down the gravel path until I reached the gardens. Hoping I stayed in the shadows—I didn't want to deal with Mrs Huxley's curiosity—I made my way to the roses at the bottom of the lawn. Bone-white petals shone brightly in the moonlight, like a beacon in the dark. With each step my chest released. The vice slowly opened as though someone else rotated the winch.

At the bottom of the garden, I turned to face the house, its edges jagged and rough in the dark. The climbing plants were in silhouette, little more than blobs of black against the inky sky. My gaze pulled towards the light inside, and I felt like a voyeur, looking in. Just like Alex in the secret cupboard.

A yellow glow emanated from Lottie's bedroom, and every now and then, I saw her move towards the window in a slinky black dress. She was getting ready to go out with her friends. It was late, but also a Friday night, and soon a fancy sports car would arrive to take her out to York, Leeds or even London. I'd heard tales of her weekend partying that stretched across two or three days at least.

Beneath her window, I saw the light on inside the morning room, but it was empty. I wondered whether Lord Bertie was in his office at the back of the house. Then I noticed movement and saw Margot walking the length of the downstairs hallway, her grey hair piled up into a bun on top of her head. She was little more than a silhouette, but I'd recognise her thin frame and the slight hunch to her shoulders anywhere. She walked like a French actress from the sixties. Brigitte Bardot at her sexiest, all hips and cool slouch.

I stood there for a while, thinking about Lottie's diorama. I hadn't spoken to her since helping her with her closet a few days ago. Time ticked on, and I was aware that I needed to do *something*. The conversation I'd overheard between Lord Bertie and Mrs Huxley had made one thing clear—I was no priority to him. He hadn't asked me any questions or talked to me about the diorama. Perhaps I needed to approach him, although doing so could be tricky. Any wrong move or false step could end in me being fired and on my way back to someone's sofa or even the streets. Then I wouldn't uncover any secrets at all.

"What do you think you're doing?"

I yelped like a wounded puppy and spun towards the roses to find Ade raising his hand to his mouth, suppressing a laugh.

"I'm so sorry," he said, grinning from ear to ear. "Oh, that was a fantastic sound you made though. Are you all right? I was just kidding around. I thought I'd make you think you were in trouble, but I guess I didn't think about it being late and dark. I'm such an idiot."

"No, it's fine. I'm just a bit jumpy." A juddering, nervous laugh filled the air between us. He kept three paces away from me as though I were a startled animal he had to approach with caution. "What are you doing here this late anyway? Bit dark for gardening isn't it?"

Before he answered, I noticed the first few drops of drizzle land on my forehead. We both lifted our faces to the sky at the same time.

"Maybe we should go inside," he said. "Were you heading back to the house, or were you running away somewhere?"

"Actually, I was about to dance naked in the woods," I said. "Cavorting with the devil is more my thing."

He glanced at me sideways and let out a small laugh. Perhaps it was the mention of nudity that made him clear his throat as though he was embarrassed.

"I could see Huxley doing that," he said. "I mean, not *see* her, because, you know, it's Mrs Huxley, but I could definitely imagine some witchy behaviour there. She has the look."

"She *definitely* has the look. So, what were you doing out here at night?"

"I stayed late," he said. "I wanted to finish bedding some delphiniums next to the path. I'd spent all day with the privets. Pawel made me a risotto in the kitchen, seeing as I stayed late, and we opened a bottle of his vodka. I was on the way out when I saw you down here." He pointed to the fountain at the top of the drive. "I guess you didn't see me coming from the hedgerows."

"I guess not." We reached the gravel path, and Ade hesitated next to me. For some reason, it almost felt like we were two people at the end of a date. What a strange date this would have been.

"Pawel fed me too much vodka, so I need to walk home now," he said with a laugh. "Don't tell Huxley that I've left my truck in the back driveway. She'll have my head on a platter."

"Don't worry. I won't."

"Has anyone around here told you about Saturday nights?" he asked.

"No, what about them?"

"Sometimes we go down to the Crossed Scythes in Paxby for a few pints. Me, the kitchen guys and Roisin. You should come tomorrow night. If you're not out being witchy in the woods."

I raised a finger as though considering it. "No, it's Mrs Huxley's turn tomorrow. She's going to sacrifice some kittens to Lucifer."

He laughed and pulled up his hood before making his way down the drive. He was easy to make laugh and easy to talk to, and those big brown eyes were a lot warmer than Alex's cold sea tones. I went in through the servants' door, barely noticing how damp my hair was from the drizzle outside. I wiped a spattering of mud from my shoes and walked back to the bedroom. I felt lighter. There was no game to play with Ade, just pleasant conversation. I didn't worry about potential stalkers or sacked maids with grudges or whether I'd need to squeeze myself into an enclosed space in order to entertain him.

Ade was easy. Alex was not.

ROISIN GRABBED me by the arm and gasped when I mentioned the pub that next morning. "Finally! I've put up with *way* too many conversations about football with the lads here. But now I can talk to *you*." She let out a little squeal of joy. "We'll get dressed up. We're booking a taxi so we can wear heels and everything."

When I told her that I couldn't go, she pouted at me for a full hour.

I'd agonised over the decision for much of the night, but the truth was, I couldn't afford it. I hadn't been paid yet, and I had enough money for maybe a few Cokes. I definitely couldn't afford to share a taxi with Roisin *and* buy drinks. Then, what if they wanted to do rounds? How would I tell them that I couldn't afford to buy a pint?

But Roisin was so disappointed that she just couldn't let it go. To her credit, she got the truth out of me before the end of the day. I'd fobbed her off with lame excuses about needing an early night and not wanting to annoy Mrs Huxley during my first month. But she didn't believe a word. She cornered me in the library, blocking my path by holding a long feather duster like a staff.

"What's going on? Is this about Alex?"

Even the sound of his name made me bristle. I found myself growing more and more defensive without fully understanding why.

Though if I admitted it to myself, I'd know it was because I didn't want to keep being warned away from him when I knew full well it was wrong. I knew and yet, I didn't care.

"It's not about Alex."

"Ade? I think he likes you."

"Not him either."

"Then what is it? Oh, is it because you're in the programme?"

I shook my head.

"Tell me. I'm not letting you clean until you tell me."

Through gritted teeth, I explained about how I was waiting to be paid before I had any disposable income. And that wasn't fair to her, but it was how I felt, about being poor, about failing one of the basic necessities for a human being—to be able to pay for shit I needed. But after a few moments, I slowly began to relax, realising that she wasn't going to judge me. Roisin listened attentively, nodding her head, lifting her strawberry blonde eyebrows and expressing sympathy.

"I'll pay for your drinks," she said.

"No, I don't like doing that—"

"Don't you know what friendship is?"

Her question caught me off guard. I had no answer. Maybe I didn't.

"We're friends now. Let me pay this time, and once your first wage comes through, you can buy me a Coke. Deal?"

I smiled. "Deal." And then she grabbed my hand and held it aloft, like two old buddies on an American cop show.

Later that day, once dinner had been served and the Howards filtered back to their rooms, Roisin caught my wrist and dragged me to the bedroom. She forced me into one of her strappy dresses and a pair of wedge heels, and I added a cardigan because it was cold outside at night.

"The clothes shopping around here is dire. There are a few independent stores if you get a bus into town, but the village has nothing. We'll go shopping once you've been paid and get you some nicer things."

She straightened my hair and gave me a lipstick. None of it was quite me. I'd always been a tomboy at school. Flat-chested and dressed in baggy clothes from charity shops, no one flirted with me. Boys talked to me because I liked same music they liked and I wanted to go to the same clubs they did. But rather than kiss me under the strobe lights, they passed me their spliffs or handed me a tab. They introduced me to their girlfriends and said, "She's cool."

Roisin was my first best friend. My first sister. She was an anchor to me at Highwood Hall, someone with a grounding effect on the kind of person who tends to fly too close to the sun. She was too good for that place. I wanted better things for her. I still do.

# CHAPTER TWENTY-ONE

I'd never seen Paxby at night before. There were fewer streetlights compared to the suburb of York where I grew up. Cars crawled infrequently along the narrow roads. The word sleepy came to mind, and with the woods encroaching on the residential space—those thin branches scraping the windows of our taxi—it didn't feel like it truly belonged to the people living there.

Paxby lost its quaint prettiness at night, and instead you saw the flaws that the ivy-covered cottages hid. Young people were scarce because none of them could afford to buy a house in the village. We were the youngest pub patrons by a long margin and certainly the most dressed up. None of that seemed to faze Roisin, however, who beamed at the locals as she ordered me a Diet Coke and herself an Aperol spritz. Hers was bright orange like Irn-Bru in a gin glass. The men at the bar sat straighter on their stools when she approached, and their eyes followed her path as she walked away.

When we'd found a table, Roisin pointedly made sure I sat next to Ade. I pulled the cardigan around me, my self-consciousness no doubt evident to everyone in the room.

"So," Ade said. "You didn't fancy joining Mrs Huxley in the woods for anything witchy?"

We'd kept the joke running, and it was becoming a lifeboat for us to cling to whenever we didn't know what else to talk about. I decided to help us move on.

"Not tonight. I thought I'd give Satan a break. How's your foot?"

"Oh, you know. Lost the toe—and the foot, actually—and I'll never walk again." He maintained his deadpan expression until I began to laugh. "What? It's true."

"How is it really?"

"Fine." He lifted his booted foot to prove it to me, eyes twinkling. Lips twitching. Our gazes met and held. Warmth spread through my body, and I cleared my throat to break the spell.

"I owe you a drink." My eyes dropped to the table, still taken aback by the moment we'd shared.

He held out his full pint. "Maybe later."

I thought of the twenty Roisin had given to me before we left. It was just enough to get a round in case the group wanted to go that route. "All right, you're on."

He placed the pint glass back down on the table. Across from me, Roisin was halfway down her Aperol spritz and leaning close to Pawel, occasionally patting him on the forearm flirtatiously. I couldn't tell if they were in a relationship or still at the courting stages. The giggles, smiles and innuendo stage.

"So," Ade said. "How are you settling into Highwood? Obviously, Mrs Huxley is about as friendly as a trained Doberman, but aside from that."

"You mean apart from someone sending me a threat on my first day? Yeah, it's been great."

"A threat?" He frowned. "What happened?"

I told Ade all about the diorama, from the doll at the bottom of the spiral staircase to the perfectly imitated walls and floors. Then I told him about Lottie's version, of her as a child in the library. As I went on, his eyes widened and his eyebrows lifted until his face could be mistaken for an emoji.

"Why me, and why Lottie? Why would the same person want to torture us both? I'm just a maid. A new maid. I've been here two weeks!"

"Maybe you two are connected in some way," he said.

"She's rich and I'm poor." I shrugged. "I can't see it."

"You have the hall in common. You both live there, sort of. Or maybe it's to do with your past. What about your parents? Could they know the Howards in some way?"

I shifted in my seat, wondering how much to tell him. Part of me assumed he'd think less of me if I told him everything about my life, the mistakes, the misfortunes. And then, of course, my hidden connection to the hall. To give me some time and try to hide the inner conflict, I drank down the last dregs of my Coke.

"I guess you could say I'm estranged from my father in that I've only met him once. My mum..." I hesitated. Should I tell him? I hardly knew him. "No. I don't think so." And it was the truth. Lottie's age meant that my mother had left the hall before she'd been born. I'd never once considered that the dioramas were connected to my mother. There wasn't a strong enough thread between them.

He was quiet for a moment, and then he went to the bar to get us some more drinks. I found myself lost in my thoughts, completely forgetting my promise to buy him a pint. When he came back, we ended up embroiled in a conversation led by Pawel about Mrs Huxley's mysterious persona.

"Does she even have a husband?" Roisin said. "She lives *alone* in her offices at Highwood."

"She used to," Pawel said, "but then she killed him and baked him into a pie."

"Oh, come on, she's not that bad," Roisin said. "Let's not be mean."

"She's not that *bad*, but she is that *weird*. It's like she has nothing better to do than live for the Howards. What does she even do outside work? She doesn't drink. She doesn't socialise with us. Once the Howards are in bed, what does she do?" Pawel lifted his shoulders in an exaggerated shrug.

"She goes somewhere every Sunday," Roisin said. "Every afternoon she leaves for several hours and comes back not herself."

"What do you mean not herself?" I asked.

"I don't know. Sad, I suppose."

"Do you think she has a lover?" Ade suggested.

"Nah. She's too busy servicing *Little* Lord Bertie, if you know what I mean." Pawel snorted and Roisin smacked him on the arm.

"Don't be so gross," she snapped.

Pawel's crude joke killed the conversation, and we went back to other chatter. I bought Ade that drink, and we talked about him for a while. He'd moved to York to study for a diploma in horticulture six years ago. Once he graduated, he applied for a job at Highwood. The Howards were his first steady employers.

"To be honest, I came up north because I needed to get out of London. I love my parents and my little sis, but I've always hated the city."

I found that surprising. "How come?"

"It's just not for me. I like the quiet. I like air that isn't tainted by pollution. You can hear the plants here."

I almost choked on my coke. "I'm sorry, what?"

He laughed. "It's true. Listen to them next time. They sing."

Eventually we started talking about the dioramas again, which I appreciated because it helped me process what was happening. I wanted to hear Ade's ideas because I was fresh out of them.

"There is one part of it that connects," he said. "Lottie ended up getting the maid fired and you're a maid. That's the thread that links everything together. I don't get why now though. The Lottie thing happened over a decade ago."

I sipped my Coke. "Ro told me about Chloe, the maid before me, and I wondered if she was, I don't know, trying to warn me off. Then I thought it was Huxley, who's been there years and must have seen everything. But why would she care about a maid who got sacked all those years ago? The people involved in Lottie's story must have moved on. Don't you think?"

"You know, I've worked here for four years now and noticed that there's a crazy high turnover of maids at Highwood," Ade said. "I always thought it was Margot. She can be pretty demanding. But I guess it's also because Lord Bertie hires so many from the Providence programme and it doesn't always work out."

I stared hard at the glass in front of me, again not wanting to admit to more of my shady past.

"There could be other disgruntled ex-employees out there," Ade said. "But a diorama is a fucking weird thing to send."

# CHAPTER TWENTY-TWO

We staggered out of the pub at midnight. I hooked an arm under Roisin's shoulder to help her wobble her way out onto the pavement. She smiled at me, exhaling acidic alcohol breath in my face. It was impossible to be mad at her though, because she remained just as sweet when drunk, stroking my face and calling me pretty.

"Alex Howard is a dick," she said. "You need to stay away from him. He won't treat you right."

Ade, on the other side of Roisin, cast a quick glance at me and then pointedly away. My cheeks flushed.

"He didn't treat Chloe right," she continued to babble on. "She cried *all the time*. Every night. It made me so sad, but she wouldn't tell me what was wrong. She just cried and cried." She stopped dead on the street and extricated herself from my and Ade's grip. Then she cupped my face in her hand. "I don't want you to cry."

"I'm not, Ro," I told her. "I'm fine. Everything's fine."

"It is?"

"Yeah. Come on. Let's get you in a taxi."

"Oh, you won't find any taxis out here after eleven," Ade said. "We'll have to walk."

"You live in the village though, don't you? You don't have to come with us," I said.

"You can't get her up the hill on your own. Unless you want to stay at mine. I live right around the corner."

"What do you reckon?" I asked Roisin, not that she was in a position to give a sensible answer.

"It's our day off tomorrow," Roisin said. Even in her drunkenness, she seemed to weigh up the pros and cons in her mind. The charming little furrow that appeared between her eyebrows made Ade and I share an amused smile. "Mrs Huxley won't like it. She'd want us at the hall."

"We could walk up first thing in the morning." Still annoyed at Mrs Huxley's iron fist on Highwood Hall, I added, "It's our day off, and we can do whatever we want. Screw Mrs Huxley."

"Screw Mrs Huxley," Roisin said with a grin.

Ade steered us away from the road leading to the hall and back into the heart of the village. Unsteadily, with Roisin propped up between us, we passed the post office and the old-fashioned gift shop. We turned onto a cobbled street that almost upended Roisin in her stilettos, finally coming to a small semi-detached cottage at the end of the road.

"I only have two bedrooms," he warned. "And most of the spare bedroom is taken over by plants. Actually, most of the house is."

Even in the dark, I noticed the greenery outside the house. Long vines reached up trellises, plump flowers hanging from them, and a tall sunflower propped up by garden canes, its wide head looming over mine. Roisin smiled up at it, trying to touch the seeds in the centre. Ade just laughed as he unlocked the front door and let us in.

Roisin was compliant enough to drink some water before we tucked her into blankets on the sofa. Ade placed a large bowl on the floor next to her. Pale-red hair spilled over the armrest. I turned around to apologise to Ade for the intrusion, but he'd already wandered into the kitchen.

"Do you want a cup of tea?"

Caffeine was a bad idea, given the time, but I couldn't stop fidgeting. At least holding a mug would give me something to do with my hands. I nodded my head and sat down at the small round table in the centre of the kitchen. A lush green spider plant sat in the centre, and I idly fingered the leaves. My eyes roamed around the room, finding all the other plants around the kitchen. An orchid on the windowsill, succulents lined up on top of a butcher's block. Tall palms with leaning fronds in the corner of the room. Ade's house was small and busy, but it didn't have that untidy, cluttered feel of most compact homes; it was just cosy.

Aunt Josephine always said that a house told you more about a person than they ever would. A bare, soulless house belonged to an empty human being. But Ade's house had been crammed full of life that he nurtured.

"Sugar?"

"No, thanks." I smiled as he poured the kettle. "You need a pet."

An eyebrow lifted as he looked at me over his shoulder. "What makes you say that?"

"Well, you like caring for living things. So why not get a pet?"

"I do like cats." He placed the mug down on a coaster in front of me with a sigh. "I swear Saturday night drinks don't usually end like this. I'm not sure what got into Roisin tonight."

"I think she needed to blow off some steam. She's had to babysit me for nearly two weeks."

"I can't imagine that's much of a hardship." The twinkle in his eye told me he was being playful, but the curve to his mouth made sensual suggestions.

My fingers gripped hold of the mug, and I dropped my eyes to the table. Things were complicated enough already without adding Ade to the mix. Another sense of claustrophobia washed over me. Those bent fronds seemed impossibly oppressive in the small room.

"Are you all right?" he asked.

"It's been a weird few weeks," I replied. "I'm feeling it. My mood..." I wafted a hand. "I'm all over the place right now. Do you ever feel like you can't trust yourself? Like your heart is going to betray you?"

He tilted his head to one side as though considering the question, then he let out a quiet, humourless laugh. "Honestly, I don't know. Maybe. I... just don't know."

I nodded. "That's okay. You're too sensible for that. You're too together."

"Oh, I don't know. We all have our moments. Hey, try not to let this stuff get to you. That's exactly what the weirdo who sent you that shit wants. Lord Bertie won't tolerate any threat to his family. I bet you this is all resolved within a few weeks."

I tapped my finger against the ceramic mug, recalling Lord Bertie's callous words: *I don't have time to investigate gifts.* Everything he'd said had left a bitter taste in my mouth. Perhaps it was because we were sitting there in the early hours of the morning, a pitch-black sky beyond the kitchen windows, but my insides felt pulled tight, like drum skin.

"Do you think there's something strange about Highwood Hall?" I asked.

Ade blew through his lips as though I'd asked him an impossible question. "There are many strange things about Highwood Hall. There've been rumours for years about it being haunted, which is bullshit."

"It is?"

"Ghosts don't exist." He shrugged. "It's just an old house. You don't believe in that stuff, do you?"

"No." I sipped my tea.

His eyes narrowed slightly, and I could tell he wasn't buying it, but he continued. "Lord Bertie is a strange dude. And... dodgy. His son too."

"What do you mean by dodgy?"

"I've heard things about his fingers and what pies they're in. The people he does business with aren't the nicest. I'm just a fucking gardener, you know? I'm no expert on how you make money in the financial sector. But one of his best mates did go to prison for fraud a few years ago."

"Wow. That's big."

"Yeah." Ade shifted in his seat. "And Alex..."

I leaned forward; my interest piqued. "What about him?"

"I do not like that guy."

"Why not?"

Ade lifted two fingers and waggled them in front of his face. "Nothing behind the eyes. Whenever he smiles at you, it goes nowhere. He creeps me out."

I wrapped both hands around my mug of tea, craving the warmth.

# CHAPTER TWENTY-THREE

While tossing and turning in Ade's spare room, I dreamed that a faceless entity shrank Highwood Hall down to the size of a doll's house and I was smaller than a Barbie as I went about my cleaning. Everything was in proportion, and yet it all seemed uncannily wrong. The wood panelling was just plastic attached to a cardboard wall, and when I looked down at my hands, they were malformed and stiff, the fingers too long, the joints solid. I still had a heart that pounded in my chest cavity, and I walked the corridors just fine, but everything else was frozen. A solid Mrs Huxley stood in the shadowy corner of the library, Lord Bertie reclined on a chaise longue, a newspaper on his lap, his eyes glazed over. Roisin was on her knees, scrubbing the corridor floor, a rag not moving in her hand. Every figure I passed made my throat tighten with fear. My arms and scalp prickled as goosebumps spread across my body.

And then I heard the sound of a piano coming from the music room. It was a romantic melody, one that swelled into a crescendo before returning to a soft caress. Chopin maybe. As I followed the sound, I was aware of a bundle of papers falling from my pocket. Letters, perhaps. I ignored them and carried on, trying to reach the music room. But I was lost. Every time I searched for the music room, I ended up back at the dining room with Alex's mother staring at me from the painted walls. Then I tried to find the servants' door so that I could at least go back to the kitchen, but instead I discovered the portrait of myself painted there. Dark hair, olive skin. A pained, worried expression on my face. The lips began to move. The painted version of me wanted to speak, but I didn't want to hear her. I ran backwards on my plastic legs until I tripped.

A hand touched my shoulder, wrenching me from my dream. And when I woke, Ade's dark brown eyes gazed down at me, a horrified expression on his face.

"I'm so sorry," he said. "I had to come and wake you because we need to get back to Highwood. It's seven. I made you a cup of tea."

As I slowly came round, I became aware of the sweat on my forehead and upper lip. I ran my hand over my face and then into my hair. Ade's eyes remained locked on my face, and I checked that the duvet covered my body. I'd slept in my underwear, not wanting to wear Roisin's dress underneath the bedding. Thankfully, I was covered.

"Are you all right?" he asked.

"Bad dream. Thank you for the tea. How's Roisin?"

"Chugging water," he said with a smile. "She'll be fine in a few hours."

"At least we don't have to clean toilets today."

He nodded. "Anyway, I'll let you get dressed. You're welcome to have a shower."

"That's okay," I said. "I'll shower at the hall. But thank you."

He backed out of the room, and I almost laughed. Ade was the complete opposite of Alex in almost every way. Where Alex was entitled and arrogant, Ade was unsure of himself and a little shy. Alex wouldn't have felt embarrassed waking me. He would've pulled open the curtains and ordered me out of bed. *Who's your boss?* I shivered.

♪

ONE TAXI JOURNEY LATER—ADE's truck was still at the hall—and Mrs Huxley's crow eyes followed us as we tiptoed through the corridor to our rooms. Roisin's hand was in mine, her eyes firmly focused on her feet. I opened my mouth once or twice to speak, but I couldn't muster the courage to do it. It was our day off. We didn't need to explain anything to her, and yet I felt like a child about to receive a thorough telling off by their parent.

Back in our shared room, I peeled away the borrowed dress.

"I want to sleep, but I don't think I can," Roisin said as she climbed into her bed.

I walked over to her, concerned. I'd heard an edge to her voice, almost like an ache or perhaps a croak that suggested she might break down.

"What's wrong, Ro?" Slowly, with my body a little delicate following the late night in high heels, I bent down so that we were face to face.

"I just... I feel like I've made so many mistakes. You know?"

"What sort of mistakes?"

She wiped away a few tears. "Oh God. Sorry. It's the hangover."

But I didn't believe her. Roisin's face was smudged with mascara and drawn tight around her eyes and mouth. I knew she was holding something back. I just didn't know what.

"Come in, sis," she said, lifting the duvet.

Like two sisters in an Austen novel, we lay down together and held hands. Less than five minutes later, she began to snore softly, and I gently eased myself out of her grip. I had a shower, got changed, and went for a walk in the gardens to clear my head. A low-lying mist meandered down to the woods, and a drizzle hung in the air. But the damp was pleasant on my skin after a night of restless sleep. I strolled around the grounds for about thirty minutes, and by the time I got back to the hall, Mrs Huxley was no longer in the kitchen. When I asked Pawel where she was, he said she'd disappeared for her weekly outing.

I went back to my shared room with Roisin, anxiously curling a lock of hair between my fingers. It wasn't any of my business where Mrs Huxley went on her day off, but my suspicions nagged the back of my mind.

Rather than go into my room, I carried on until I reached Mrs Huxley's quarters. She'd have records in there. My mother's name could be in those records. What if my mother had left a forwarding address? What if I could find her?

Pipe dreams. Aunt Josephine would've found her by now if she wanted to be found. I calmed myself and placed a palm on the wood, remembering our jokes about Huxley from the night before. Her situation was strange when you thought about it. Most maids tended to be young people just starting out in life without any attachments. Being a maid at Highwood was more like an extension of school or university. It was like putting your life on hold for a short time while you got your shit together and made some money. Whereas Mrs Huxley living in her "quarters" within the house was odd and old-fashioned. She apparently had no family or connections outside the hall, and long-term staff members like Pawel knew nothing about her private life.

My hand slipped down the wood until it gripped the door handle. It would be locked—I knew it would—and yet I desperately wanted to go in. I wanted to see how she lived, what kind of photographs she put on the walls, whether she was immaculately tidy or a secret slob. I wanted to know what she did in her spare time. Was she in the process of making intricate still life dioramas of Lord Bertie in his office or Margot reclining by the pool with her turban on and a cigarette in hand? Would I find a doll that looked just like me?

Gently, as though I feared someone might hear me snooping, I pressed the handle down. Of course, it was locked. In a stupor, I went back to my room and sat down on my bed. Roisin opened one eye and then the other. She groaned, rubbed mascara further down her face, and turned on her side.

"Do you think Pawel might make me a fry-up if I offer him a favour in return?"

I raised my eyebrows. "What kind of favour?"

"I don't even care at this point. I just need grease." She hesitated, sitting up in bed. "What's the matter?"

"I tried to get into Mrs Huxley's office."

"Why?" She screwed up her face at the ridiculousness of it, and a weariness in her eyes told me loud and clear she was way too hungover for this.

"I think it's her," I said. "It has to be. Who else could it be?"

"What?"

"The dioramas."

"Oh." She sounded tired, like she had better things to do. I didn't resent her for moving on and forgetting about my woes. But I was perturbed that no one else saw them as threatening. "Now why would she? She's strange, I know that, and we had a laugh talking about her in the pub and that. But she doesn't know you, does she? I guess I can see her resenting the Howards, but she's up their arses all day and night. I genuinely think she loves them. Maybe too much."

"I guess so." I didn't have it in me to argue otherwise. "I'll ask Pawel about that fry-up."

"I love you." She grinned at me.

"That's the alcohol talking," I replied, feeling a smile spreading across my face as I went to the kitchen to beg for breakfast.

On the way down the corridor, I heard footsteps behind me. When I turned around, Mrs Huxley was coming out of her quarters.

"But you—" I blurted out.

She straightened her spine and faced me, wearing the same burgundy dress as the day I came for my interview. "But I?"

"I thought you were out."

"Well, clearly I'm back now," she said, and I could have sworn I saw amusement dancing across her face, tugging at the corner of her mouth. "What are you gawping at?"

"Nothing—"

"Where did you go last night?"

"The Crossed Scythes."

She raised an eyebrow. "Is that wise? Considering your background."

"Not that it's any of your business," I said, "but rest assured I spent the night drinking Coke. We left late and stayed at Ade's house in the village." It annoyed me that I justified myself to her, but I couldn't help it.

"Ah, young girls and their desires. I had hoped you might be more disciplined, but the maids from the programme never are."

"Excuse me?"

"I do hope you're enjoying your day off. It's back to work tomorrow, and you have the toilets to scrub." She walked away from me, gliding in that way she did. I hated her then, for judging me, making me feel less-than.

As soon as she was around the corner, I ran down to her office door and tried the handle, but it was still locked. It confused me how she managed to walk past my and Roisin's room without us hearing her. Mrs Huxley glided like a swan on water, but surely we would have heard her movements. The swish of her dress, the hint of a tread on the hard floor. Pawel said she was out before I went back to my room with Roisin. That was, what? An hour ago? Where did she come from? Was there an outside door leading into her office? I needed to know.

After getting Pawel to agree to fry up some bacon and eggs and deliver them to Roisin, I slipped out of the house and walked around the perimeter. There were many doors on the outside of the house, and some of them I had no idea where they led or even if they were in use. I walked around the east side, between the hall and the stable block, to the location of Mrs Huxley's office, but I couldn't find a door, only a window. Peeking through the glass revealed little of note: a tidy desk, a chair and some shelves filled with files.

"Are you planning to rob us?"

I shrieked as I spun around, and an amused smile unfurled across Alex's lips. It was easy to see what kind of mood he was in from nothing but that smile. He was in his charming and handsome mode. The affable Alex.

"Yes," I said, my heart pounding. "And I thought I'd start with the housekeeper's office. That's where all the jewels are, right?"

Alex gazed over my head into Mrs Huxley's room. "Why, I do believe you are snooping. What a little sneak you are. What's she done?"

I shook my head. "Well, aside from biting my head off...? Nothing, I guess. Except every now and then she pops up when I least expect her."

"You mean like now?" He turned around as though about to reveal Huxley behind him. But there was no one there and he started to laugh.

"Very funny." I rolled my eyes. He was easy to like when he was in this mood.

"Come on, I want to show you something." He grabbed my hand. I was powerless to him, again.

# Chapter Twenty-Four

E very nerve in my hand was aware of his touch, the feel of his smooth skin. Hands that had not worked. Hands that had been cared for. My aunt would have ridiculed them. But she ridiculed everyone except for her late husband, a builder who killed himself before I was born. Someone who understood hard work, just like I should. My hands were red, the skin peeling between my fingers. With my hand inside Alex's, I should've been embarrassed of my rough skin, but I wasn't. I suspected he enjoyed the callouses and sores on my hands. There were plenty of smooth-skinned women in his social circles. Alex wanted a different flavour.

We almost ran around the perimeter of the hall, and I became self-conscious, wondering if Lord Bertie or Mrs Huxley were watching from one of the windows above. Alex's brogues kicked up the tiny stones on the path. Every now and then, one of the rambling roses caught me on the arm. By the time we stopped, I had a thorn sticking out of the sleeve of my tunic.

"Here we are," he said. "The north wing."

He stood before a red door. It was far more simplistic than the main entrance, with a regular stone arch that peaked sharply at the top and a large brass knob in the centre. Instead of a door knocker, this door had what appeared to be a modern doorbell fitted. To my surprise, Alex reached into his pocket, removed his wallet, and took out a card. Then he pressed the card to what I'd thought was the doorbell, and it opened with a click.

Alex pushed the door wide open and walked in. His face, half in shadow, half in a dim grey light, was skull-like. For a heartbeat, he reminded me of Mrs Huxley with high, sharp cheekbones and an angular jaw. I followed him through to the darkness, my heart beating fast.

The door closed, plunging us into a penetrating blackness. His voice echoed around me, close and far away at the same time.

"Do you trust me?"

"No."

A light touch on my cheek. Even without sight, I knew he'd caressed me with one of his pale fingers. My heart pounded harder. Every muscle in my body tensed. I heard him breathing close to me, laboured, excited. And then a light came on overhead, and his face emerged from the darkness just a few inches away. The shock sent a ripple through my taut muscles. He had one hand on the wall behind me, his finger still on the light switch, and his other hand was balled into a fist by his hip. His eyes bored into mine. We stayed there for ten seconds, both still, both rigid, until he leaned away from me and strolled away.

A thin, shaky breath expelled from my lungs as my body trembled in either relief or disappointment, or both. But without him close to me, I could relax slightly and take in the surroundings. Dust sheets covered the windows, and a naked bulb hung above our heads, casting a golden light on the rubble strewn across the corridor floor. Part of the plaster had been chipped away from the walls, and the ground beneath my feet was uneven with chunks of it scattered around. Dust infiltrated my nostrils, and I fought the urge to sneeze, not wanting to break the silence. I rubbed my nose and held it in, pondering that this wasn't the dust found in dirty houses; it was the cleaner, sweeter dust of broken mortar.

"How come Lord Bertie hasn't finished renovating this wing yet?" I asked, forgetting my place and making conversation with him as though we were equals.

He didn't turn around to answer the question. He pushed open the door leading into the next section of the wing. He was part way through as he started talking, so his voice felt far away. "Daddy doesn't care about the north wing. He knows it isn't his." He turned to me. "Hurry up."

I quickened my step as I followed him through to the next room, expecting more concrete and broken plaster. Instead, I stepped into a stunning room with painted walls and an embellished ceiling. The mural depicted nature and mythical creatures, with cherubs dancing and butterflies fluttering. I spotted a hummingbird, its delicate wings translucent against the burnt-orange background. I allowed my fingers to reach out towards its beak. Alex slapped my hand away.

"No touching," he said. "Not until I say you can."

I stood still, waiting, playing his game.

"Go on then."

I wanted to please him, so I went along with it and allowed my fingertips to gingerly meet the cold wall. It was like touching Alex. He was made of the coldest stone. His smile never did meet his eyes. Ade had been right.

"Do you like it here?" he asked.

"I do."

"This will be the morning room." He pulled down one of the dust sheets to reveal a beautiful stained-glass window twice as tall as I was. The room immediately filled with a warm glow, highlighting the orange paint. "And this will be where I host parties," he said, gesturing to what might have been some sort of small ballroom or a large dining room. He leant over an old upright piano and played a few bars of Rachmaninoff. It was out of tune and clunky, a honky-tonk version.

"Why are you showing me this?" The question fell from my lips without much thought. Perhaps I should've been warier of him, but he didn't frighten me. I had so little to lose.

He moved away from the piano and sauntered towards me, his hands pushed into his pockets. "When I'm married, I'm going to live here with my wife and children. When we have guests, I'll play the piano for them. Perhaps I'll play the sonata you've been helping me learn. Or some Chopin to keep it romantic. There'll be a nursery. Mrs Huxley can add more staff to the household to help cover the wing. Lottie can fuck off to live with whatever snub-nosed prig she can find with enough money to feed her coke habit. Margot can go on decomposing in the upstairs room, and Daddy can stay in his office, counting his money. I think I'll take the north wing, the forgotten north wing." He came so close to me, I backed away. But Alex wasn't having it, he placed his hands on my shoulders and squeezed and squeezed. I didn't make a sound. Not even when his fingernails dug into my flesh through the fabric of my uniform. "Is this the kind of place you'd like to live?"

"Yes."

"Where did you live before you came here?" He released me, and I ached where his fingers had been.

"I didn't live anywhere. I was sofa surfing."

He gave me a small smile. A knowing one. His finger grazed my cheek again, and he leaned towards me. "Do you trust me yet?"

"No."

He wrapped his arms around my waist. His body was so close to mine, I felt his heart beating. But rather than kiss me, he pressed his cheek against mine.

"What are you doing?" I whispered.

"I want you to trust me," he said, not answering my question.

"Is that what you said to Chloe too?"

At the mention of her name, he stepped away from me and turned around. Her name touched a nerve, but I didn't care. I didn't know what he wanted from me.

"Did you bring her here?" I asked.

"No," he said, still not facing me. It made no difference, I thought.

"I don't believe you."

"Believe what you want. Come on. It's time to go."

Not wanting to end up locked in the north wing, I followed him back the way we came, pausing in the orange room to touch the beak of the hummingbird. Why did he bring me here? Perhaps he wanted to taunt me with a life I'd never have. The touches, the hot and the cold, the soft and the rough, the glimpse into a future that did not belong to me. It was all part of the game.

Alex held the door open for me, and we came out into the fresh air. For the first time since I'd mentioned Chloe's name, he looked at me.

"Listen, I do want you to trust me. I'm sorry if I'm... cold. You have no idea what it's like to live in this family, to be the heir to *this*."

"Yeah, must be a real hardship," I replied.

His eyes narrowed slightly. Around him, the breeze moved through the vines of ivy creeping up the stone walls. While the ivy moved and breathed, Alex stayed as still as a statue. I had felt his heartbeat, seen the twinkle in his eyes once. For the first time, I was frightened by how quickly he changed. "I know I'm privileged. Do you think I don't know?"

I shrugged. "I hardly know you at all."

"Well, I know, all right. But that doesn't change the fact that I have the weight of generations on my shoulders, and I have to carry traditions I'd much rather not."

"You can't use me as escapism," I said. "That's not who I am. I'm worth more than that."

"I know. But you're enjoying it too, don't deny it."

I said nothing.

"I have to go." He took a step back. "We'll talk soon. In the music room, perhaps. I like spending time with you."

"Okay." I leaned back against the red door, waiting for him to leave.

He shoved his hands into his pockets, almost angrily. "Don't spend so much time with the gardener."

My lips twitched with an emerging smile, but I smothered it. "Is that an order?"

He turned around and strode away, his answer coming back to me on the breeze. "Yes."

# CHAPTER TWENTY-FIVE

Monday came and went in a blur. I scrubbed the bathroom floor, but Mrs Huxley found dark spots underneath the sink, so I did it again, and then she decided the toilet wasn't clean enough. I scrubbed the tiles in every bathroom in Highwood Hall that day. My knees were raw and bruised by dinner.

She punished me for staying out on Saturday night. Roisin didn't get quite as much punishment, but she did have to polish the silverware alone while I cleaned the bathrooms, and we didn't serve at lunch either. Mrs Huxley had help from some of the kitchen staff instead. We'd been demoted to the worst jobs, with her always hovering in the background, a harsh word ready and waiting. *Not good enough. Do it again. Concentrate.*

The whole day saw my mind in a state of flux. I'd begun to stagnate in this house, doing nothing but the cleaning I was hired to do. But the diorama of me remained in Lord Bertie's office and I still didn't know who had sent it. I still hadn't figured out a way to get information out of Mrs Huxley without her knowing about my mother.

At the end of the day, Roisin and I collapsed into our beds and slept deeply. There were no late-night chats, and there were no nightmares either. I'd never been so exhausted.

Tuesday was much of the same, with Mrs Huxley again splitting me and Roisin into different parts of the hall. I dragged a heavy vacuum cleaner up and down the stairs, dusted the far corners of the ceilings.

Then she sent me to mop the kitchen floor. I didn't see Alex or Ade for either of the days. Later I learned Alex had gone to work in London for a few days, which meant my constant anxiety about bumping into him had been completely unwarranted.

Mrs Huxley became the bane of my existence, and I wanted nothing more than to snap back. Forcing me to do the same job several times was nothing but torture. And yet every time I thought I was at the end of my rope, I carried on. If I didn't have this job, what did I have? All I could do was grit my teeth and get on with it.

On Wednesday morning, I decided enough was enough. I asked Mrs Huxley for a break so I could speak to Lord Bertie about his investigation into the dioramas.

The two black marbles in her head glared at me. She put her hands on her hips. "He'll tell you if he has any important information. The banisters need polishing." When she turned around, I considered doing nothing, but then I changed my mind.

"Mrs Huxley," I said. "Ten minutes. Please. I have a right to know what's going on."

She stopped, just for a moment, and then she continued walking, the burgundy skirt disappearing around the next corner. I sighed, picked up my caddy of cleaning materials and made my way to the main staircase. But once I was there, I left my caddy on the fifth step and found myself walking up to the next floor. In fact, I carried on until I reached Lord Bertie's office. Then I paused and knocked.

"Come in."

I hesitated before opening the door, trying not to think about the conversation I'd overheard between him and Mrs Huxley. The one that had confirmed he didn't care about my circumstances at all.

"Sorry to bother you," I said tentatively, worried I should say "sir" or "Lord."

"That's quite all right." He smiled and gestured for me to sit on the chair opposite his desk. The Labrador—Leo—sniffed my shoes before settling next to Bertie's chair. It took me a moment to notice the dioramas positioned on the desk between us, the boxes closed. Had he been looking at them? He watched me as I eyeballed them, and then he reached over and opened one of them so that I could see the scene one more time. I'd forgotten the bright red of the blood.

"Did you come about this?" he asked.

I nodded my head.

"I was going to call for you today anyway. I had a private investigator check things over when the police proved to be useless. You've got nothing to be worried about." He leaned back in his chair, placed his arms behind his head. "It's a bad prank, that's all. My friend is an excellent investigator, so you can trust him. I found out this morning that the sender was an ex-employee of ours."

"An ex-employee? Was it Chloe?"

Lord Bertie didn't react for a moment, and then he bunched his eyebrows together as though trying to remember. "No, he didn't say her name was Chloe. Who is that? The girl you replaced?"

I nodded.

"I don't remember much about her. Chloe wasn't here for long. Some maids aren't." He shrugged nonchalantly. "Anyhoo, the police have had a word with the culprit, and she won't be bothering us again."

How do you know that? I thought. But I didn't say it, because I didn't want to challenge him. "Do you know why she's doing it?"

"She stole some money from us," Bertie said. "Not a large amount. It was the petty cash Mrs Huxley kept in her office. Poor girl was suffering from addiction. But she did have an artistic talent, and I suppose this is her way of lashing out. Such a shame." He spun the diorama around. "She's talented."

"What was her name?" I asked. I wondered if it was the same maid Lottie had fired about a decade ago. The way Lord Bertie talked made me think she was young, but I could be mistaken.

"I'd rather not say," he replied, leaning forward again, placing his arms on the desk.

I opened my mouth to ask why, but again found my resolve softened. I had a right to know who had sent me a nasty message through the post, but Lord Bertie was the one person standing between me and sleeping in a cardboard box.

"Look," he said, reading my hesitant expression, "I know she's done a terrible thing, but I want to keep her anonymity. The girl's troubled, but she's not dangerous. She wanted to scare you off, that's all. If I tell you her name, it'll spread around the staff and probably through the village too."

"I wouldn't say anything."

He raised his eyebrows. I'm sure he thought that all women talk. The womenfolk can't help but gossip; it's in their blood.

"How long ago did she work here?" I asked.

"Oh, a few years ago."

"Are you sure she's harmless? The scene sent to me is quite violent."

He laced his fingers together and lowered his chin. "It's certainly unpleasant, and I am sorry you had to deal with that on your first day. Have you talked to anyone about it?"

"Some of the staff here. Roisin, Ade, and Pawel mostly."

"What about outside the hall?"

"No."

He cocked his head to one side. "Not even family? Friends?"

I cleared my throat. "To be honest, I don't talk to my family much and I... Well, I don't have many friends."

He nodded thoughtfully. "Aside from the rather odd first couple of weeks, have you settled in well enough?"

"Yes, thank you."

"And you're getting along with everyone?"

"Yes."

"That's excellent. Huxley told me that you and Roisin went to the pub in the village on Saturday night."

"Yes," I said. "It was just a little staff get-together."

"Oh, of course," he replied. "Nothing wrong with that. But I thought I'd check in and make sure your sobriety was still on track."

"It is."

"Good." He smiled. "Well, I have no complaints. Things seem to be going... quite well. I hope you stay at Highwood for many years to come." He clapped his hands together. "Now. I think it's time for coffee. Could you ask Mrs Huxley to bring me a pot?"

I made my way out of his office, glad to be away from the dioramas. Relieved to not have to smile and nod and seem appreciative. In the corridor outside Bertie's office, I stopped and took a breath. Now I had to tell Mrs Huxley I'd been to see him. If I didn't ask Huxley for the coffee, Lord Bertie would be annoyed I didn't pass on the message, and if I *did* tell her, Huxley would know I defied her orders.

On the way down to the kitchen, I pondered over the conversation

I'd just had with the Lord. He'd protected the identity of the ex-employee sending the parcels. Why? He'd said that the police went to talk to her, but he hadn't told me the consequences of that. I didn't know what counted as an arrestable offence, but he hadn't even mentioned if she'd been cautioned. I thought back to his smiling face and decided that he was holding something back, and I was sure it was important.

# CHAPTER TWENTY-SIX

L ater, after an afternoon of polishing banisters, Roisin and I
unpacked the conversation I'd had with Lord Bertie.

"It wasn't Chloe?" she asked.

"He didn't even remember Chloe," I said. "Unless he acted that way
on purpose to throw me off."

"Well, at least you know it's going to end now." She climbed into
bed, her baggy Smiths T-shirt riding up her thighs, and flopped down
on her pillow. Then she rolled over to face me and waggled her eyebrows
like she had some juicy information to reveal. "Alex comes back
tomorrow."

"Oh cool."

Roisin burst into laughter. "You can pretend like you don't care all
you like, but I know better."

She was still grinning at me as I turned out the light, and once we
were plunged into darkness, she made kissing noises and then giggled.

"Whatever, lassie," I said. "I know that's not your T-shirt. Whose is
it? Pawel's?"

She laughed. "Maybe."

It took us another thirty minutes to settle down and go to sleep, and
during that time, I kept imagining Mrs Huxley standing outside our
room, waiting for an opportunity to scold us for staying up past our
bedtime, not that we had a bedtime.

The next morning, we served breakfast as normal, for once everything went smoothly. Even Margot was fine with her eggs and Hollandaise sauce. Then we had a quick breakfast in the kitchen before splitting off to do our jobs. I went to the entrance hall to dust the paintings and soon found myself lost in my thoughts. Behind me, I heard a chiming sound and realised someone was at the front gates. I waited a moment for Mrs Huxley to come out from the kitchen, but no one emerged. When the bell sounded out the second time, I hesitantly approached and asked who it was through the speaker.

"Got a delivery for you."

I opened the gates and waited by the door, wondering where Mrs Huxley was. She usually stayed on the ground floor in the morning, taking Lord Bertie pots of tea and coffee whenever he requested it, organising the lunches, writing out menus and making phone calls to suppliers. She was the one who opened the gates and took produce from the drivers. Then I realised that I was waiting at the wrong door. The postman always came to the servants' door. I hurried around the side of the house to meet him, pulling open the door just as he was about to knock.

"Just the one parcel today." The postie thrust the box into my hands, and I gripped it tightly, fearful that if I didn't, I'd drop it. He then handed me some envelopes and made his way back to his van. I walked over to the security box system for the gate and watched the black-and-white screen until his van disappeared down the road, and then I shut the gate behind him with a flick of a switch. My heart pounded against my ribs. I looked down at the cardboard box in my arms addressed to Margot. Its size unnerved me. I stared at it for so long that I hardly heard the clicking of Mrs Huxley's heels on the tiles.

"What have you got?" She held out her hand expectedly. I passed her the box, my hands shaking, and Mrs Huxley stared down at it with a frown. "We don't know it's one of them."

"I... It's for Margot. The postman..." I cleared my throat in an attempt to pull myself together. Why were these dioramas unsettling me so much? "Lord Bertie said he'd sorted it out. He said it was some ex-employee. Why are they still coming?"

"We haven't opened it yet." Mrs Huxley frowned and then sighed, sounding more frustrated than disturbed. She turned sharply and strode through the hall. I followed, not sure what else to do but also aware of a strong desire pulling me forwards. I wanted to know what was inside. I wanted to know what this person had sent to Margot and why.

We found her in the morning room, curled up on a sofa with a paperback on her knee, a lit cigarette in an ashtray on the side table, and a half-eaten chocolate eclair balanced precariously on a cushion. Margot jutted out a chin as we approached.

"The help is here," she said, lifting the corner of her mouth. "What could you possibly want, dears? Are we not paying you enough? Has one of you broken some ugly figurine Bertie's ancestors stole from Africa or Taiwan or somewhere? Oh, I have a parcel. Open it, Huxley."

"Yes, madam," Huxley said, placing the box on the coffee table in the centre of the room. She ripped the Sellotape from the outside, opened the top flaps and then paused. I took a step forward, eager to know and yet dreading the answer. After her moment of hesitation, Huxley removed the white box wrapped with a red bow.

"Aha," Margot said. "So it seems my son-in-law is not the great detective he thinks he is. It's my turn, is it? Come on then, let's get it over with."

Mrs Huxley placed the box down on a footstool and pulled open the bow. Quietly, I moved so that I stood behind the sofa and therefore behind Margot. I wanted to see the scene for myself so that I could use that image to compare it with the others. The cardboard front dropped down to reveal the painted miniatures and the backdrop to the scene. This one made me gasp, and my hand flew up to my mouth. Margot froze. I heard a sound escape from her that I never imagined her to make. A whimper. She whispered to herself, and then she scrunched her eyes closed.

This miniature depicted the dining room in its usual exquisite detail. Even down to the cherubs and angels painted across the wood panels. Above the dining table was a tiny doll, a lot like the one illustrating my fall down the stairs. It hung from a well-sculpted version of the chandelier made out of miniscule plastic beads. The doll swung slightly, still unbalanced from its journey into the morning room. I didn't recognise the doll, but it was dressed in what appeared to be regular, modern clothing. She had on jeans, socks, a white shirt. The hair was long and hung down to the doll's waist. It was beautifully created, with pockets and buttons stitched into the fabric. But my gaze was drawn to not the doll's clothes or the delicately painted make-up on her face or the pretty portraits around the room, but to the rope around the doll's neck. She swung, along with the chandelier, from side to side on a simple hessian string shaped into a noose. The doll's legs were slightly pulled apart and purple bruising painted carefully around the face and neck.

Margot opened her eyes and shook her head in disgust. "Close it then. Close the damn thing before I have you fired."

Mrs Huxley did what she was told, tying the bow around the top. "I'll take it to Lord Bertie."

"Go on then. Get it out of here."

I forgot to move when Mrs Huxley walked out of the room with the box in her hands. I remained there, watching the normally steely Margot crumple into a ball. Instinctively I grabbed some tissues from a dispenser in the dresser and sat down next to her.

"Are you all right?" I asked.

She blew her nose loudly and shook her head. "This person has a sick sense of humour. Sick."

"I know," I said. "I'm so sorry."

"They should be strung up themselves," she said fiercely.

I handed her another tissue. "Can I ask who it was? The doll?"

She dabbed her eyes once more and then let out one long sigh as though expelling the pain. "My daughter."

# CHAPTER TWENTY-SEVEN

I waited for a moment, confused by her answer. I'd thought Margot's daughter—Lord Bertie's late wife—had died falling down the stairs. It wasn't a story I would easily forget, not when I'd heard that Alex had possibly seen the fall himself, hiding in the secret nook behind the painting.

"It happened a year before she died," Margot said, continuing her explanation. "She wasn't well, you know. I suppose it was depression or whatever it is you young people call it, but I hadn't grown up with those labels. I'm an old dinosaur, and I didn't know how to help her."

"I'm sure you did the best you could," I replied.

Margot placed her hands on her knees. Frail hands with long red nails, blue veins and mottled skin. "Bertie cut her down before she could do any real damage, but she was never the same afterwards." Her hands gripped her knees tightly. "She was so sad. So very sad, and there was nothing I could do."

Tentatively, I placed a hand on her shoulder. I wasn't sure what else to do. It felt like crossing a line between two people who shouldn't touch. She'd seemed untouchable to me until she broke down. Now she sniffed and trembled as she cried, just like anyone else would.

"Do me a favour, would you, dear? Go to the cupboard by the television. There are some leather-bound photograph albums. I'd like to look at them."

I found the albums stacked up on a shelf and brought the lot over to her on the sofa, balancing them under my chin. When I'd spread them out on the footstool and the sofa, she picked one of them up and thumbed through them.

"Most of these are Bertie's," she said, flicking the pages. "Look." She held the book out, and it wobbled unsteadily as she clasped it with her thin hands. I saw two distinguished Victorians sitting tight-lipped. A bearded man in uniform and a corseted moon-faced woman with beautiful curly hair. "Some duke in the family, I suppose. Most of them lived here at Highwood. It's been in his family since the Tudor times. Anne Boleyn stayed here on more than one occasion." She closed the album and handed it to me.

"It's a beautiful home. It's a shame no one else gets to see it," I blurted out, regarding her cautiously. Would she chastise me for my opinions?

"It is," she said. "It's selfish to keep this place locked away, but that's Bertie. He does what he wants, not what's right. Ah, now this one is mine." She opened the album and spread it out on her knee. "I used to be an actress, you know."

"Really?"

"Oh, yes. I met all kinds of people. Here's me with Marilyn."

"Monroe?"

"Look at the picture, dear." She rolled her eyes.

The photograph was clearly Marilyn Monroe next to a brunette woman who competed, if not eclipsed, Marilyn's beauty. "Is that you?"

"Well, it isn't Liberace is it? Yes, it's me."

"You're more beautiful than Marilyn there."

She smiled. "I was younger." Then she flipped more of the pages, and I saw her black-and-white frame standing next to the people I'd seen in old movies when I was off school with a cold, laid out on the sofa watching Audrey Hepburn and Grace Kelly. Part way through, Margot appeared in white lace, beaming next to a tall, attractive man, and a few pages later she had a baby in her arms. "Ah, there's my Laura. She was a beautiful baby and so calm. All the other women complained about their children all the time, but I didn't have to."

"She's lovely."

"Yes, she is." Margot touched the picture with two fingertips. Her voice was shaky after she withdrew them and turned the page. "Robert and I tried for more children. We lost two in the first few months, and then…" She lifted her empty hands. "Then nothing. Laura was all I had, and I never… I never expected to outlive her." She brushed away a few tears. "I'm glad Robert didn't get to see her like that."

I looked down at the photo album on Margot's lap. Laura was a toddler now, dressed in a bonnet and booties. A few pages later she was in a cute dress, her hair in pigtails. There were pictures of Margot with her husband on the beach, Laura by their side, building a sandcastle. Before my eyes, I saw this woman's life unfold. It was glossy and privileged, dressed up in clothes as beautiful as their faces, but it was life. It was real, and I saw Margot's pain as she relived it.

"This was the beginning of the end," Margot said, stopping as we reached Laura's wedding to Bertie, now in the early nineties, complete with hazy, colour photography, large puffy gowns and even larger hair. Margot was greying, a Chanel twinset draping fashionably from her slim frame, still as fabulous as ever with a cigarette dangling from the corner of her lips.

"What was?" I asked, pulling my eyes away from the wedding photo.

"Her marriage to Bertie. He made her crazy."

"What happened between them?"

She slammed the photo album shut, and the echoing slap made me cower back. "Put these away, will you? I don't know why you got them for me. What am I going to do? Sit here crying all day? Preposterous! Take them away. Now!"

Hastily, I piled the albums up under my chin and hurried, stooped over, to the cupboard by the TV. My breathing came out slightly panicked, alarmed by the sudden change in tone. Margot had been pleasant up until that moment, willing to tell me all about her life. After slamming the cupboard door closed, I turned around, debating whether to ask if she was all right, but Margot stared firmly away from me, the cigarette back between her fingers. She'd closed down.

I ducked my head and walked out of the room. The Howards rarely directed their spotlight in my direction. The problem was, when they did, it was intoxicating, and when they took it away and you became the ghost again, it left you with a burgeoning, freezing cold in your veins. I disappeared into the servants' corridor, wrapping my arms around my body. The chill seeped down to my bones.

No one mentioned the diorama Margot had received. Lord Bertie never pulled me into his office to update me on what was going to happen next. Margot's diorama hadn't been a threat, but it had been distasteful and nasty. Surely Bertie would want to get the police involved and maybe take out a restraining order against the disgruntled ex-employee. Mrs Huxley never mentioned it either and we went through the motions at dinner, laying out the plates, serving the food. Mrs Huxley took a plate to Margot in her room because she wasn't feeling well.

Bertie, Lottie and Alex started their meal in silence. They continued in silence without a word spoken until Mrs Huxley dismissed us from the room. On our way back to the kitchen, I told Roisin about Margot's parcel and what I'd seen inside.

"I never knew Lady Laura tried to hang herself," Roisin said. "How awful."

And that was all we said.

Later, in my room, I tried searching Facebook for Highwood Hall, wondering if any ex staff members had set up a Facebook group, something like that. Then I tried searching for Susan Cole, Lottie's ex-nanny, but there were many results, most of whom had private accounts. Without knowing what she looked like, I had no way of knowing which woman could be the Susan Cole I was searching for. I soon gave up, and instead, I read my mother's letters, using the light of my phone underneath the duvet. *This place can make you feel so alone at times. It isn't a happy place here. I wouldn't live here even if I was as rich as this family because it isn't happy here at all. In some ways, I pity the Howards.*

I pictured a young Lord Bertie with his young wife. My mother started working here when I was a baby, so twenty years ago. Bertie and Laura would have been married five or six years, making Alex about five. And then my thoughts drifted to Lady Laura as I fell asleep that night. I pictured her smiling face on her wedding day, dwarfed by the size of her puffed sleeves, like the tiny Lady Diana in her gargantuan frock. When I closed my eyes, I saw the flowers in her hair, the long, trailing bouquet of lilies. *This was the beginning of the end.* The way Margot had said those words steeped in vinegar. She still lived in Bertie's house, and yet she blamed him for Laura's death. I could feel it: the pain, the animosity.

Margot must believe that Bertie behaved egregiously towards her daughter. But what did he do?

Poor Lady Laura. She was a small paragraph on Lord Bertie's Wikipedia page. Her troubles with mental illness had been ignored. She must have led a complex life in this place with her husband, children and mother. And now she had been immortalised on the wall of the room where she once tried to kill herself. Anger bubbled up inside me, for her and all the other women pushed to the sidelines in their own stories.

# THE MUSIC ROOM

He played Liszt for the first time. It wouldn't be the last. I sat there in awe as his fingers moved impossibly fast up and down the keys. I listened to the way the notes clashed at times and loved the challenge of it. Debussy was calming and romantic. Liszt was a showpiece designed for the performance. I stood a few paces away from the piano stool, and when he was finished, I clapped and he gave a little bow.

"When are you going to perform for other people?" I asked, taking my place next to him on the stool.

He shrugged. "I haven't decided. The next time we have a function at the hall, I suppose. Or maybe I'll arrange an informal gathering."

"Did you ever want to be a professional pianist?"

He raised his eyebrows. "Oh, only every day. But Father would prefer I work in the business. Here I am, I suppose, not letting go."

"I don't think you should give up."

My words clearly irked him. A ripple of tension worked its way up his jaw, and he scrunched up his eyes before breathing slowly out. "Don't pretend to know what's best for me or who I am. You have no idea."

I inched away from him, afraid of the way his body tensed, wound up tight like a mechanical toy. He didn't say another word, simply launched into his sonata, and I turned my attention to the notes, both on the paper and the fingers moving up and down the keys. I was learning, slowly. Most of the time the music washed away like a tide, moving too quickly for me to read it, but in other moments I understood. Sometimes I found myself gazing at his face, distracted by the intensity in his eyes, before I forced myself to concentrate again. By the time he finished, he was sweating across his brow. He sighed, stood up and paced the room.

"That middle section. It's all wrong."

"It sounded beautiful," I said.

"Well, it would to you," he replied.

His mood had turned, sharply. For the first hour, he'd been cheerful, playing me several of his favourite pieces, most of them from memory. A storm cloud travelled across his eyes. They were lovely when he was happy and animated, but now they were dark and unreadable. When he reached out to me, it took all my willpower not to flinch. All he did was tuck a lock of my hair behind my ear.

"Huxley wouldn't like you with your hair loose." He smiled. I wished it reached his eyes.

"She hates me coming here. She's never said anything, but I can tell. She sits in the kitchen and watches me walk past when I go back to my room."

"She's a ghoul," he said and laughed. "Come on, let's do that middle section one more time. When I play this in front of Father, I want it to be perfect."

I saw the little boy in him then, the one who craved his father's admiration. Despite everything, I pitied him. He fascinated me in the strangest of ways. He was wrong about me. I saw who he was. I saw the darkness in him. I knew he was a controlling man, and I suspected he liked maids because they were easier to dominate. Sometimes I thought he led me on because he saw me as disposable, a woman with whom he had no future. The stakes were low, practically non-existent. Other times I felt deeply connected to him because he revealed vulnerable sides to his personality that I suspected—or hoped—he didn't show anyone else.

This time, even I knew he played the piece perfectly. The world shrank to just us. I stopped watching his hands and instead watched him. When I turned the page, it was instinctual, because I knew the music now and I knew the note and where it fell. Towards the end of his run through, he stopped looking at the sheet music and instead turned his face to me. On the final note, he kissed me.

He tasted faintly of brandy and the aftershave on his skin. He held my arms by my side as we kissed, and I allowed myself to surrender to that vice-like grip. It excited me in the right way. Frightened me in the right way. It hurt in the right way too when our teeth collided for a split second. Eventually he softened, and his arms circled me. He pulled us close together on the piano stool, his elbow catching the keys, the clashing notes like our teeth. I melted away, a crescendo in my mind.

# CHAPTER TWENTY-EIGHT

We didn't go to the Crossed Scythes that Saturday. Instead, Pawel made us dinner with spare food from the kitchen that needed using up, and the others drank homemade elderflower cider that Ade brought from his home brewery. Mrs Huxley stayed in her room as we took over the kitchen. We were glad for it, obviously. We didn't want her judgemental gaze on us.

Ade showed me his gardening explanation YouTube channel, and the others had a giggle about the delivery of his script as he went through his top tips for growing tomatoes.

"Ha ha, dickheads. I'd like to see you try it," he said, somewhat huffily.

The food was delicious. Tapenades and an aubergine casserole with fresh bread and pavlova for dessert. I gazed longingly at the cider, sure that I could have a glass or two but decided not to give Huxley the opportunity to sack me for not staying sober.

"Oh, let's go outside," Roisin said. "It's a beautiful night." She skipped across the kitchen to the large window above the sink. "You can see all the stars."

"You mean it's not raining for once?" Pawel said. "Makes a fucking change."

"Come on," she said, grabbing my arm. "Let's get our coats."

A few minutes later, we walked down the lawns towards the rose garden. The floral aroma of Ade's flowers floated along on a warm zephyr. But I couldn't quite relax. I cast a couple of guilty looks up at the hall, concerned that Lord Bertie would see us gallivanting around his grounds and discipline us tomorrow. Ade noticed and smiled.

"He went to London for the night. Alex too."

"Oh." I tried to keep my voice disinterested.

"What's going on between you and Alex?" Ade asked. His forth-right tone caught me off guard, and I struggled to find a way to answer his question.

"N-nothing."

He gave me a wry smile, clearly not believing it for a moment. I cursed his intuition.

"I don't know," I admitted. "It's complicated. He's complicated."

"He's dangerous," Ade said.

I didn't say anything. I didn't get a chance. Roisin had hopped onto the retaining wall at the bottom of the garden and walked along it like a gymnast, pointing her toes. Then she did the funky chicken and we all laughed.

"Sing us a song," Pawel said, lifting a bottle of beer into the air. He turned back to me. "Have you heard her sing yet?"

I shook my head.

"It's for the best. She's terrible." He gave me an exaggerated grimace to signal the joke, and Roisin kicked out her foot in his direction.

I laughed, watching them muck about. Behind them, the night sky bled into the cluster of dark forest leading down to Paxby. As Pawel pretended to grab Roisin's ankles and she hopped and skipped along the wall, I thought of my walk up the hill to Highwood for my initial inter-view. I pictured the bent boughs in the woods, the moss-covered trunks, and the thorny vines spread out across the forest floor. For some reason I imagined them moving towards us, like a tidal wave of shifting branches here to sweep us away. I trembled.

"Are you cold?" Ade said. He fingered the edge of his jacket as though considering whether to lend it to me.

"No, I'm fine."

Before he asked me again, Roisin began to sing, and suddenly the messing around stopped. I don't know what she sang. A folk song, I think. Her lilting voice rang purely. Lifting and falling as she walked back and forth along the wall. The moonlight fell on her face and her coppery hair, throwing her into a pale blue light. She was beautiful, of course she was, and I saw Pawel's usually sarcastic smile fade from his lips. Even in the late-evening gloom I saw how his eyes shone with emotion, and I saw the way Roisin returned the gaze. Ade shuffled closer to me, and I became aware of the arm of his jacket close to mine. Part of me longed to lean in, to allow him to put an arm around my shoulder like I thought he wanted. It felt childlike but sweet, the opposite of Alex Howard.

And then she stopped. Roisin dropped down from the wall, her face flushed and crumpled. There were tear tracks running down her cheeks.

"What is it?" Pawel stepped forward first. He tried to put a hand on her shoulder, but she ducked away and started running.

"Ro?" I called after her. But she ignored me and carried on. I turned to Ade. "I need to go after her. I don't know what's wrong."

"Make sure she's okay," Pawel said.

I FOUND her curled up in a ball on her bed, her body rising and falling. My heart tugged when I approached and placed a hand on her shoulder.

"Can you talk about it?" I asked.

She didn't respond. For a moment I wasn't sure if she knew I was there.

"Do you miss home?" I thought that perhaps the song had brought back happy or sad memories.

"It isn't that," she said quietly.

"What is it?"

The sobbing finally subsided, and she lifted herself up to a sitting position. I'd spent too much time comforting others that week, from Margot reminiscing about her life to Roisin's abrupt turn. But even though a wave of exhaustion washed over me, I realised on some level that I enjoyed comforting others. She wiped away her tears and exhaled.

"I want to love him, but I can't."

"Who?" I asked. "Pawel?"

She nodded.

"Does he love you?"

She nodded again.

"Have you told him how you feel?"

She shook her head. We were silent for a moment, and then she began to speak. "We've been together off and on. It's never been serious, but recently he's started to tell me how he feels. He even bought me a present." She leaned across the bed and opened a drawer from the side table. It was a slim, pocket-sized book. "It's poetry. Love poems."

"Oh."

"Yeah. He wrote a message inside about how the poems in this book remind him of me, and then he told me he loved me and that he wanted us to be exclusive."

"You're not exclusive?" I asked.

"No. And at first it was fine because it was casual, and I knew he hooked up with people when he went out in York. But now..."

"Now he wants more but you're hooking up with other people?"

She nodded. "One person."

"Oh," I said, beginning to understand. "Someone from the village."

Her gaze dropped down to the book in her hands. She turned it over and then placed it on top of the table. "Not the village, no. Not quite."

"It's someone at Highwood Hall. It's Alex, isn't it?"

She reached out and clutched my arm. "No, it's not him. I promise. He's all yours."

"Ade?"

She shook her head and her chin wobbled. "It's bad. It's so bad."

"Please tell me it's either Mrs Huxley or Lottie."

She bit her lip. "No."

I stood up then and placed my hands over my eyes. It was... wrong. Revulsion rippled across my flesh just thinking about it. "You're with Lord Bertie."

"Jesus, I didn't think you'd judge me," Roisin snapped.

I dropped my hands. "Hey, I wasn't. I didn't mean it like that."

"You're just as bad. You're with Alex."

"I'm not *with* Alex," I replied.

She rolled her eyes.

"I'm sorry," I said, sitting back down. "I didn't mean to judge. It's just that he's so much older than you. I had a bit of trouble picturing you with Pawel at first, but Lord Bertie is an even bigger step. Sorry."

"He's kind to me," she said.

"Okay."

"You're still judging me."

"I'm not," I replied. "I'm judging him actually. Look, I'm sure you know this already, but he could be taking advantage of you. You're so much younger, and he's your boss."

"I know," she said. "I just don't care." Her expression had hardened. She gazed up at me with red-rimmed eyes that narrowed with stubbornness.

I lifted my hands as though in surrender. "Okay. If you're happy, then that's... your business. How did it start? How have you managed to keep this a secret from Mrs Huxley?"

"I think she knows," Roisin said. "She saw us talking in the servants' corridor once. He'd followed me in for a kiss. He doesn't want Margot to know, you see. Not after the way Lady Laura died."

Hearing her name sent another shudder through my body. I wondered how many pretty maids Bertie had screwed while they were together. *Like father, like son.* I pressed my eyes closed briefly, trying to stop my thoughts from going down that dark path. And then I thought about her, a young mother, naive probably, eager to start a new life with her baby. My father had been a drug addict at the time. She'd had no one. She'd talked about Lord Bertie in her letters...

"It started how anything else starts," Roisin said, interrupting my thoughts. "By talking. He needed me to clean up a wine spill in his room, and he happened to be in there reading. We started talking and hit it off. He's so smart and witty."

Of course he seemed that way to her, I thought. He was over twice her age, had attended the best schools in the country, and had an entire lifetime of experience, whereas she'd had precious little.

"Then he started telling me about different kinds of wine. We'd go down to the wine cellar together, and he'd uncork a bottle and tell me all about the grape and the flavours of each one." She blushed. "That was how it started, over wine."

I wanted to tell her that he'd asked her to be in vulnerable situations with him, plied her with alcohol and then used his superficial charm to get his way. What would've happened if she'd turned down his advances? She was so pure that I hated the thought of it. I was already sullied. I knew how to play Alex's games. But Roisin? No. It made my blood boil just thinking about it.

"Please don't tell anyone. Don't tell Pawel."

"I won't. I promise. But you're going to have to break it off with him. Or with Bertie."

She nodded. "I know."

# CHAPTER TWENTY-NINE

Roisin and I spent our Sunday apart from each other. She had breakfast with Pawel in the kitchen, whereas I took a croissant out to the garden and sat on the retaining wall to look out at the woods. I had a lot to think about, from the dioramas to Alex Howard to Lord Bertie and the confirmation that he'd slept with at least one maid. There were decisions I needed to make and information to uncover. Part of me longed to talk to Roisin about my suspicions; things were awkward between us since she'd revealed her secret. I picked at a rose petal and tried to get the thought of them together out of my head.

I spent the morning waiting and wishing I could tell Roisin everything I planned to do, even though she'd probably try to talk me out of it. But I had a hunch, and I wanted to follow through on that hunch.

When Mrs Huxley left the hall, as she did every Sunday, I did too, but I cut through the forest while she walked down the road. I knew she didn't have a car, so I knew she'd have to walk to Paxby before she went anywhere else. I'd thought about heading there before she left, but I didn't want to miss her if she jumped straight on a bus or took a taxi.

It was my first time in the woods, and I hoped that the path was relatively straight through the trees. If I ended up getting lost, I'd never be able to keep up with her. I'd worn appropriate footwear and clothing for the walk. I had on my trainers and thickest pair of jeans. Even though it was warm, I wore long sleeves to help beat back the branches and vines.

Every step brought with it a sense of unease. These woods were not the kind you walked your Yorkshire terrier through with your husband and your North Face jacket undone at the collar. No, these were woods that weren't particularly welcoming to your average dog walker. I almost fell three times, feet sliding on the mossy stones. The place made you believe that nature was capable of rejection, that it could close up around an outsider and spit them out.

Luckily, I wasn't rejected after all, and I stumbled out across from the village before Mrs Huxley emerged from the road. I quickly smoothed down my hair, brushed off as much mud from my shoes as I could, and picked thorns from my clothes. Then I walked in a semicircle across the road, hurrying so as not to stay out in the open for too long. I hovered in between a newsagent and a dentist, keeping one eye on the bus stop in case the housekeeper left before I had a chance to follow her.

She walked confidently towards the village in her dark burgundy dress, a tan leather bag slung over her shoulder. When she reached the shelter, she took a seat on the bench, crossing one ankle over the other. Concealed in the passageway, I waited, considering my options. There were a couple of taxis waiting in a lay-by. Perhaps I could jump in one and follow the bus. But what happened if Mrs Huxley went far out of the village? Then what? I had some money left over from the night in the pub that Roisin had insisted I keep for emergencies, but I couldn't afford a taxi ride for a long journey.

I decided to wait and see what kind of bus pulled up. If it was a bus to York, I'd have to let her go. If it was a small, local run bus that circled around the villages, I'd hire a taxi and *follow that bus*.

The last diorama had done it for me. I knew then that Lord Bertie was either delusional or lying or both. Margot's diorama had been so personal, so nasty and cruel that I couldn't think of anyone but Mrs Huxley. She was the one constant at Highwood Hall. She must have been a witness to many awful things over the years, from Lottie's bad behaviour to Lady Laura's death and, possibly, Lord Bertie's affairs. Perhaps one of those events had made her snap and now she wanted revenge. What if the first diorama wasn't a threat but an attempt to frighten me away? And now she was taking down each of the Howards one by one.

Whatever her motivations, I needed evidence. I needed the truth.

I'd thought about what to do. It was possible Mrs Huxley made the dioramas herself, painting and painstakingly constructing them in her room. But how and when did she buy supplies? Wouldn't we notice her bringing special cardboard boxes into the hall? Perhaps I could catch her in the act today. On the other hand, it was possible that Huxley was commissioning those pieces, and every Sunday she went to see the artist creating them. I'd decided that even if she wasn't doing anything nefarious, I'd at least gain some insight into her strange little world if I followed her.

A small, local run bus trundled up to the shelter, and I decided that was enough to tell me she wouldn't be going far. I remained tucked away between the buildings until she stepped onto the vehicle, and then I hurried over to the taxi stand and asked the driver to follow it. He gave me an odd expression before shrugging and letting me in.

"Isn't it supposed to be the opposite way around?" he said.

I hardly heard him; I stared at the bus in front of us instead. "What?"

"Aren't you supposed to follow the taxi?"

"On a bus?" I said, confused.

"No," he said, grinning. "In *another taxi*."

He was older, perhaps in his fifties, and I sensed he wanted me to laugh, so I did.

"You might want to hang back a bit. They'll be making stops. I'm waiting for someone to get off, but I don't know which stop it'll be," I told him.

He slowed down, waved a couple of cars past, and then maintained a steady speed so I could watch the bus pull in and out of its countryside stops. My eyes were glued to its back window as adrenaline coursed through me. It wasn't exactly a high-speed car chase, but the thrill of figuring out a mystery ignited a fire within me. I fidgeted around in my seat, tapping my knee, biting a thumbnail. I wondered what my aunt would make of this side of me.

"Stop," I called out. The taxi driver pulled onto the side of the road. Mrs Huxley stepped off the bus at the corner of a deserted shelter near a narrow road. "Is there even anything here?"

"There's a village up the road," the taxi driver replied. "And some sort of care home, I think. The kind for people with... difficulties."

"Oh," I said. "Like a psychiatric facility?"

"I suppose so. That's all I know about it. Why are you following that woman anyway? Or shouldn't I ask?"

"She's... my aunt," I said. "And she lied to me."

The driver shrugged one more time before asking me for £5.50. I handed over the money, waited for change, and then got out. By that time, Mrs Huxley was a minute or two ahead of me, but seeing as there was only one road, I wasn't too concerned.

I walked slowly, keeping an eye on the distance ahead. There were a few bends and a narrow pavement. Every now and then she came into view and I tensed up, expecting her to see me. She never looked back.

We were deep into the countryside now, passing the bobbing heads of cows and sheep as they watched me. I smelled the farm before seeing it and heard a tractor rumbling around a field somewhere. I rolled up my sleeves, feeling the burgeoning of perspiration along my hairline.

Around four or five minutes after getting out of the taxi, I came to the small village of Wicklesworth, which appeared to be structured around a small park. The road signs mentioned York, Bishoptown-on-Ouse and Paxby. I stopped for a moment because for the first time, I couldn't see her ahead of me. And then my heartbeat quickened, expecting her to pop up behind me. One fingernail tapping me on the shoulder and her stern face tilted downwards, demanding what I was doing following her. But all I needed to do was round a corner away from the park, and there I saw her heading towards a facility called Heather Grove.

The psychiatric facility. What was she doing going there? I walked closer but hung back out of sight. I plonked myself on a skinny wooden bench across the road from the home, taking a book out of my bag. It didn't matter which page I opened. I wasn't planning to read it. Across the road, Mrs Huxley disappeared into a white painted building.

She must be visiting someone, but whom? I'd hoped to catch her going into an artist's workshop, but there I was at a care home. Who was Mrs Huxley visiting? Her husband or wife?

I remained on the bench for about fifteen minutes before I saw her leave the building with a person by her side. They walked down the front lawn together, strolling and chatting. They were close but didn't touch. My book was on my lap. My eyes were fixed on them.

The other person was slightly taller than her, male, and younger. He walked with a slight stoop, with his face mostly watching the ground and his hands clasped in front of his body. Every now and then he pointed at flowers in a childlike way, one finger jabbing excitedly. Outside of Highwood, Mrs Huxley walked with a completely different posture. Not quite so upright, her shoulders set at a natural angle instead of pulled back. She took the flowers he picked for her, smiling broadly. If she'd worn a different outfit, I would've thought she was a different woman.

And while I was there, watching, a change washed over me. I felt ashamed for following her. Mrs Huxley was visiting a family member— I'd guessed her son in my mind, the approximate ages seemed to fit— and I watched them, creepily, from my bench. I packed my book away and hurried back along the road towards the bus stop. If I left now, I could catch a bus to Paxby and return to the hall before her. On my way, tears pricked the backs of my eyes, and for the first time in a while, I felt lost.

# CHAPTER THIRTY

I'd brought them with me in my bag. I allowed my fingers to grope inside and touch the edges as I sat at the back of the bus. The letters from my mother to my dad. Pages that I knew off by heart that talked about me and what I'd meant to her and why she did what she did. They were a comfort blanket to me. They were dog-eared and worn thin from my fingers and thumbs as I read and reread them. I'm not sure why I'd slipped them into my bag that day. I was scared of what I might find Mrs Huxley doing or the potential confrontation that could occur, and before I knew it, they were in my bag with me.

*Sometimes I think about running away from it all. From my baby.*

My father, David, had given me the letters when I went to find him for the first time. He lived in a run-down terraced house between Leeds and York. Even though I saw he'd cleaned for my arrival, the place was still grimy. Mould mottled the grouting between the kitchen tiles, and limescale edged the circumference of the taps. The mug he gave me was chipped, and the tea tasted watery.

"You look like her," he'd said, pale, watery eyes bloodshot and difficult to scrutinise. "Just like her. It's remarkable."

And then he'd told me about how young they were when she found out she was pregnant and the difficult conversations they'd had. He hadn't been in a good place, not that he'd ever been in a good place, but it'd been especially bad when I reared my ugly presence into their lives. He'd taken recreational drugs that developed into an all-consuming addiction, not unlike my own story. He'd spent much of his life home-less, never able to keep a job for more than a week or two. By the time I met him, he'd been in prison twice and since then, found God and a decent charity to get him back on his feet. By then, caffeine remained his last addiction.

He worked in the coffee shop at the local church, cooked food at a pub on the weekends, and in between went from washing windows to mowing lawns to cleaning wheelie bins and guttering. His pressure washer was his pride and joy.

I felt the tiniest bit jealous that I'd been replaced by a pressure washer.

He had no other children, which meant I didn't have to worry about half brothers and sisters. From what I gathered, there wasn't a significant other in his life when I met him, though he did talk about an ex. He'd shown me photographs of my mother when she was young, dressed in oversized jeans and T-shirts emblazoned with band names like the Offspring and Blink-182. Her eyes were lined with thick black eyeliner.

"I haven't spoken to her since you were born," he'd said. "Every time I answered the phone, I thought it might be her. It makes no sense because she doesn't know my number or where I live now, but I always thought I'd hear her voice."

"Sometimes I think that too," I'd admitted. "Whenever the doorbell rang, I imagined her on the doorstep ready to pull me into a hug and tell me who she was. But it was always a delivery or someone wanting money."

At least Mrs Huxley stood by her kid. At least she visited him every week. At least she smiled and took the flowers and talked to him, loved him. Now a lot of things about her clicked into place for me. He was the reason she'd stayed at Highwood. I was sure about that. Not only was Highwood Hall close to Heather Grove, but Mrs Huxley, as the head housekeeper, had a stable, well-paying job that helped to pay for her child's care. She needed the money, and where else was she going to get a wage like that around here?

There were many other mysteries about the housekeeper, like why the Mrs, but for now I understood her better. Could she still be the person sending the dioramas? Possibly, but now I knew she had more to lose than I'd thought. It seemed as though I was back to square one, and I'd spent bus fare and taxi fare for no reason. Luckily, it was payday tomorrow, which was a huge relief.

When the bus pulled into the Paxby bus stop, I decided to spend a little time in the village before heading back to Highwood. And yes, it was partly to avoid Roisin, but also to acclimatise to the area I lived in but knew nothing about. Perhaps it was time to get used to its eccentricities and find the best place to buy the flakiest pastries. But as I walked around, browsing the few shops and cafes there, I constantly felt as though people were watching me. It came from a paranoia I'd never been able to shift, that someone would look at me and they'd know I came from nothing. They'd see it written on me—*rejected by her own mother*. They'd know.

With one hand on my bag, thinking about my father and the letters he'd given me as I'd left his house, I slipped into the woods to be alone. It was cold in the dark. I wrapped my arms around my body, waiting for the hall to emerge above the canopy of bent trees. Soon I witnessed its ramparts blocking out the afternoon sun. A cloudy sky surrounded those turrets.

The woods had been suffocating, but I wasn't relieved to be back at the hall. Nerves tickled at my stomach as I made my way through the hallway into the kitchen. I placed my bag next to a chair and sat down for a few moments. Before I knew it, a plate appeared before me. Pawel had made a cheese sandwich. Next to it was a homemade chocolate truffle. I started with the chocolate first.

"Is it nice?" he asked, sitting opposite me with a plate of more tempting truffles.

"Delicious." I reached out for another, but he slapped my hand away.

"One for you, greedy girl. I'm setting up a business. Letterbox chocolates."

"That's a great idea."

He nodded solemnly. "It is. And I can do it outside my hours here. At the beginning anyway. If things go well, I'd have to leave I suppose."

"I'd miss you."

"At least someone would." He frowned, and I understood immediately that he was talking about Roisin.

"We'd all miss you," I added.

He rolled his eyes. "All right. You can have another if you're desperate enough to compliment me."

I grinned and snatched the chocolate before he changed his mind.

"Where is she?" he asked, taking me by surprise.

At first I thought he meant Mrs Huxley and that he'd figured out I followed her. But then I realised he was talking about Roisin. "Isn't she in the hall?"

He shrugged. "I haven't seen her all day. She's avoiding me."

"Don't take it personally," I said. "I think she's avoiding me too."

He propped up his head on one hand and frowned. "Why would she avoid you? You're her best friend."

His eyes were a pale grey searchlight that narrowed on me, making me squirm. I had a secret that he wanted—needed—to know, but I didn't want to be the person to reveal it. I *shouldn't* be the one to tell him; it should come from Roisin. And now I had to lie. Or at least obscure. I fixed my eyes on the plate of chocolate between us. "Oh, no reason."

Pawel pulled the plate away from me. "There is a reason. She didn't cry last night for no reason. She isn't avoiding you or me for no reason. Tell me."

"I can't, Pawel," I said. "She needs to tell you herself."

He paled then. I think he probably always knew, and now I'd given him the proof he needed. He saw it written all over my face. There wasn't anything I could do or say, so I backed out of the kitchen and left him alone. When I went to my and Roisin's room, it was empty. I put my mother's letters away and decided it might be best to try to find her. I could at least give her a heads-up that Pawel had guessed what was going on. But on my way to the front of the house, Lord Bertie pulled up in his Porsche with Alex in the passenger seat. Seeing them changed my mind. I didn't want to be walking through their private quarters on my day off. Instead, I made my way back to the servants' entrance and decided to walk around the grounds at the back of the house. I noticed Ade's truck parked there, which was unusual for a Sunday. Then again, he was dedicated to the plants and would often pop back to the hall to finish up any jobs that needed it on the weekend.

I made my way around the hall, avoiding Alex and Bertie. I didn't feel like dealing with Alex's games. But as I walked closer to the stables, I saw him watching me through a window, and I worried that he'd come to find me. I quickened my pace, coming back out to the front of the house, which was where I found her.

Halfway down the lawn, I saw Roisin and Ade talking by the rose garden. That in itself wasn't odd, or maybe it was, because Roisin and Ade didn't tend to talk much. I thought about walking down there and joining in, but the conversation didn't seem casual—it felt as though it was intense—and I got the sense that I'd be intruding if I interrupted them. Instead, I turned around and headed back to the hall, which was when I saw Mrs Huxley coming up the drive. The surprise of finding myself face to face with her and the fact that I'd followed her earlier made me jolt. I hoped she didn't notice. In an attempt to cover up my reaction, I smiled and waved. She did not return either.

I thought nothing of it and returned my attention to Roisin and Ade. Roisin wasn't there anymore.

# CHAPTER THIRTY-ONE

R oisin didn't come back to the hall that evening, which seemed out of character for her, leaving me with a sour taste in my mouth. I waited up until after midnight, unable to concentrate on the romance novel I was skim reading. Every text I sent to her went unanswered. When I tried Pawel and Ade, they sent back messages saying she wasn't with them. Eventually I fell asleep around one a.m. and woke up again around five, immediately turning on my lamp to check if she'd come back. Her bed was empty. Panicked, I called her phone only to find it vibrating underneath her pillow. A prickling sensation spread across my scalp. That was the point when I flung the door open and ran barefoot down the corridor, still in a T-shirt and shorts, to Mrs Huxley's room. Breathless, I pounded the door until she opened it.

She was in a red dressing gown and slippers with her hair tucked into a silk headwrap. She didn't seem angry—more confused—when she saw me.

"Roisin is missing," I said, the words coming out rapid-fire. "She never came to bed last night. I just woke up, and she's not there. Her phone is underneath her pillow, and Pawel hasn't seen her since earlier. I don't know where she is." My hand reached out, tensed, and returned to my side.

"Okay, I'll help you look," Mrs Huxley said. "You should put warm clothes on and some shoes. Highwood is a big place."

She was right. I ran back to my room, pulled on a pair of jeans and some trainers, then met Mrs Huxley back at the kitchen.

"I'll need to inform Lord Bertie," Huxley said. "While I do that, you can check the servants' corridors. Perhaps she's slipped and fallen somewhere."

I nodded my head and began the search, hurrying into the network of hallways behind the walls. There were bare bulbs above my head as I worked through them, making me feel like a prisoner escaping through a tunnel. I pictured every room I passed—the library, the bedrooms, the dining room—and considered stepping through the tiny hidden doors into those spaces. But we needed to be systematic, and I had to be sure she wasn't passed out or hurt somewhere.

A feeling of claustrophobia swept over me the longer I stayed in the corridors, yet at the same time I was devastated not to have found her. I didn't want to leave. I didn't want to admit that she was gone. I came out on the upper level near the stairs, just about to make my way down —I'd decided to avoid the spiral staircase, having already checked it on the way up—when I heard voices coming from the entrance hall. Instinct told me to hide. Silently I folded myself into the tiny cupboard behind the painting.

I didn't dwell on why I hid, but I did gently move the tiny piece of metal covering the peephole and watched Lord Bertie and Mrs Huxley standing there in their pyjamas. Huxley stayed close to the door with Bertie above her on the last staircase step. I saw from the way Mrs Huxley held herself that she was tense, whereas Bertie seemed more relaxed, one arm resting on the banister.

"When did you last see her?" Huxley asked him.

"Before I left for London," he said. "I'm not sure when it was. Perhaps Thursday evening."

Mrs Huxley's frown led me to believe she knew about Roisin and Lord Bertie. If I hadn't known it, I would've thought nothing of her standard question.

"I'm worried," Huxley said. "We'll have to phone the police."

"Let's not be hasty," Bertie replied. "I'm sure she'll turn up. She's a young girl; she's probably out partying. Where's the other girl?"

"I sent her through the servants' corridors."

"Good," Bertie replied.

"Should I check the north wing?" Huxley said.

Lord Bertie simply shook his head. She nodded, and then she walked away, heading towards the Howards' living quarters. I stayed where I was, frozen in place, as Bertie turned around and started walking back up the stairs. Gently I closed the peephole in case he noticed it was open. And then I remained, very, very still, too afraid to even breathe. Why was he walking up the stairs so slowly, practically pausing before moving each foot? Or was I imagining it? The gentle creak of one step, then the next. The hushed shuffle of slippers on carpet. And then finally... silence.

Or not. I could no longer see what he was doing, but I was sure that he'd paused extremely close to the cupboard. Was he there? Outside the door, leaning close? Listening? Was that the sound of him breathing, the tiniest hint of a whistle through the nose?

Hot, viscous air swamped me, infiltrating my lungs. Everything smelled like old wood, dust and oil paint. Every part of me wanted to fling the door open and escape that tiny space, but I couldn't. I pressed a hand over my mouth, and I listened, waiting for a sign that he'd walked away. What if he was gone and I was waiting needlessly? A man in slippers and a dressing gown would be quiet, but surely I'd hear movement.

And then, just as I was about to exit the hole, I heard the barest swish of fabric. The hushed shuffle of his slippers continued, growing fainter and fainter as he walked away. Finally, while silence settled in the house, I pressed my forehead against the wooden frame and allowed myself to breathe. As I crept out of the cupboard, I wiped sweat from the back of my neck with shaking hands, making my way down the stairs to see if I could find Mrs Huxley.

I'd been sure at the time that Lord Bertie waited at the top of the stairs, suspicious of being watched. But if that was true, why didn't he just open the cupboard door? This was his house; he could do what he wanted. But perhaps he'd paused to check his phone or catch his breath. Either that or I'd let nerves and paranoia take hold of my senses.

I hurried through the house, checking the morning room, the dining room, the snug and the living room, but there was no sign of Roisin or Huxley. When I reached the window that overlooked the fields out towards Paxby, I double-backed on myself following the long corridor towards the kitchen. It was there I found Mrs Huxley in the dining room, staring at Lady Laura's portrait. Surprised, I entered, wondering where she'd been before. She didn't turn around as I entered, so I cleared my throat to announce my presence. She turned quickly, startled, a rare expression of concern on her face. Again, it surprised me to see her so *human*.

"I didn't find her."

"Okay," she said thoughtfully. "Perhaps we should try the grounds."

"And then call the police?"

She bit her lip. "Yes, and then we call the police." She made her way out of the dining room, crossed the great hallway, and pulled back a heavy drape. "It's still dark out. We should get torches. There's some in the kitchen."

This time I had no problem keeping up with the housekeeper. I ran on adrenaline now. My stomach churned with nerves. Even though I'd known Roisin for little more than a few weeks, I knew she wasn't the kind of girl to run off without her phone and not tell anyone where she was going. I knew she wasn't this flaky. She liked the people at Highwood far too much to put them through needless stress. No, none of that was like her, and when the realisation hit, it made me want to double over and vomit onto the antique carpet. Once we'd reached the kitchen, I experienced a strange sort of reluctance to everything I was faced with past that point. I didn't want to take the battery-powered torch that Mrs Huxley passed to me. I didn't want to leave the building and split up so we could cover more ground. But I did it because every second counted.

I wanted nothing less than to walk down the lawns towards the rose garden, but I did. I even continued past the roses, ignoring their sickly sweet scent because it added to the nausea. I continued down to the retaining wall. The sound of her voice filled the air, and I didn't want to hear it. As I replayed her song in my mind, I heard the pain in the melody. I even saw the ghost of her jump down from the wall and run away. *Ghosts.* That's what we are. What we'll ever be to the men who go back to bed when one of us is missing.

I placed my hands on the wall and gazed out at the dark woods. Nothing. I lifted the torch and waved it up and down the line of trees. Nothing. No. Something. I wafted the torch beam again. Yes, something.

Even though I didn't want to, I climbed over the wall and walked slowly towards the woods. With every step, my body longed to turn around and run back. Every instinct screamed at me. The blurry image before me became clearer the closer I got. The pale length, hanging, swinging gently, grew bigger and bigger until my body told my mind that I had to run. I broke into a wobbly sprint that shook the light so vigorously that it bounced around, turning my vision into an unsteady camera. The pale length came closer until I was right next to it. I flung my arms around her dangling feet, imagining that I was Margot helping her daughter down from the chandelier in the dining room. But what I wrapped my arms around was cold and lifeless.

# CHAPTER THIRTY-TWO

**M**rs Huxley found me on the grass, staring at the torch beam. The torch itself I'd dumped near my feet. I sat there, alone, waiting for the police, staring into the bright light to block out the sight of her swinging legs. The housekeeper silently placed her dressing gown over my shoulders and walked towards Roisin's body. I opened my mouth to tell her not to, but nothing but a raw squeak came out. I pulled my eyes away from the light and saw her place a hand on Roisin's foot, before staggering back.

Roisin deserved more than this. The beautiful girl with the beautiful voice deserved more than to die in the cold below a twisted, malformed branch. And for the briefest of moments, I thought to myself that it should have been me instead. Then there were flashing lights, a wailing noise, and a car that hurried across the gravel drive. Someone helped me to my feet and walked me back to the hall where I saw the Howards lined up outside the entrance in their pyjamas except for Lord Bertie, who had changed into trousers and a shirt. Alex stood with his hands deep in the pockets of his purple silk dressing gown. Lottie chewed her thumbnail, pressing her weight from one leg to the other, shivering in her shorts and strappy top. Margot stepped forward and embraced me. Her scrawny arms wrapped around my neck.

"Oh, you girls," she said. "You shouldn't have come."

I pulled myself away from her, confused and upset. Lord Bertie took her by the arm and moved her away from me while Alex's cold blue eyes observed me.

"What is she saying?" I asked someone. I don't know who. Not Alex.

"Mo-mo gets confused sometimes," Lottie answered. She was crying. I wanted to slap the tears from her cheeks. She had no right to cry.

After that, everything went by in a blur. I was given a hot cup of tea in the living room. It felt strange to be sitting on one of the Howards' sofas. I stroked the fabric in bewilderment, my mind fractured and easily confused. A policewoman sat next to me and asked me questions I mumbled the answers to. Across the room, Lord Bertie leaned against the wall, one hand on his hip. I saw him refuse a drink. He spoke to no one. All he did was watch.

I had never felt as alone as I did, sitting in that room full of people as I answered question after question. Alex and Lottie hovered around in the background while Mrs Huxley spoke to another officer close to the door. Margot was sitting on the sofa opposite, her skinny legs crossed, a cigarette burning through as she stared into space. Her grey hair was loose and frizzy around her face. Once the police officers were done talking to us, they spoke to each other in hushed tones. And then Pawel arrived for work. I watched his features crumple in as the policewoman took him to one side.

After she had informed Pawel of Roisin's death, the policewoman made her way back and took her place on the sofa next to me again. "I found a letter addressed to you in Roisin's bedside table."

I turned sharply. "What sort of letter?"

"A suicide note, I'm afraid," she said.

I couldn't believe it. Not Roisin. No. This wasn't happening. "Can I see it?"

"Of course," she said, passing me an A4 piece of white paper that had already been placed in a plastic bag. It was evidence now, I supposed. There would be an inquest or an investigation. I didn't understand the terminology, but I knew they'd need to make sure Roisin killed herself.

I found it difficult to hold the letter with my cold, shaking fingers. I placed it on my knees and leaned over to read it, but the contents left me cold. The note showed me nothing of the Roisin I knew.

*I'M SO SORRY. Please contact my family and tell them I loved them. This isn't because of them. I just can't go on.*

"TAKE IT AWAY," I said, closing my eyes tightly.

"I need to ask you a question first." I opened my eyes and turned to the officer. She had a round face and a widow's peak, giving her a heart-shaped appearance. The softness must be useful for a police officer, I thought. Constantly being underestimated can be an advantage. "Can you identify Roisin's handwriting for us?"

I shook my head. "I don't think I've ever seen her write. You'll have to ask her family. Or maybe Mrs Huxley."

She nodded. "Okay. Thank you. We will be in touch with Roisin's parents very soon. I'm so sorry for your loss." Gently, she pulled the note from my lap.

"What happens... What happens to her body? Have you cut her down? From the tree?"

"Yes," she replied. "We're taking her to the morgue."

I pulled my knees up beneath my chin, closed my eyes and felt tears wash down my cheeks. The cup of tea cooled on the table beside the sofa as the police slowly filtered out of the room. I couldn't stop thinking about Roisin's song in the gardens. Did I miss her pain? I didn't understand. I was the one who received the threat when I first started here. If anyone was supposed to die, it'd be me falling down that spiral staircase.

This place had a history with dead women. First Lady Laura, now Ro. I lifted my head and watched Lord Bertie, sitting next to Margot, his face turned towards the window. He was the connection between the two dead women. Him. I remembered the photo album, the pictures of Laura and Bertie's wedding with the lace and crinoline, those big smiles and bigger hair. Margot told me he was the catalyst for Laura's downfall, and now he'd done it to Roisin.

# Chapter Thirty-Three

No toilets were cleaned that day. The Howards generously offered to take care of themselves, and the staff were sent home. Mrs Huxley and I had no other home to go to, and I didn't want to go back to my room and stare at Roisin's empty bed, so I walked the grounds of Highwood until my feet hurt. I sat down on the damp grass next to the roses and played back the last few weeks in my mind, trying to find places where I could've done or said anything differently.

I finally dragged myself back to the hall when it started to rain, forcing myself into the bedroom because I needed to shower and change. But of course, I found myself staring at Roisin's unused bed. Then my eyes drifted over to the bedside table. When did she put the note in the table drawer? And when did she hang herself? How did she find the rope? She must have planned all this in order for it to be executed properly, and yet Roisin never struck me as a planner. She was more of an instinctual person. If I had to imagine her killing herself, it would be with a much less complicated method. Jumping from a great height, taking an overdose.

The world had tilted and everything was askew. Roisin no longer alive made everything seem off. My dark thoughts about whether she did or didn't kill herself were so preposterous that I almost laughed. And yet, I had to think those things because I didn't believe it. I didn't think she'd committed suicide.

It was after I'd showered and changed that I remembered seeing Roisin and Ade in the garden together. He just might be the last person who'd spoken to her. I decided then I needed to see him. I pulled on a hooded jacket and left Highwood, not bothering to tell Mrs Huxley where I was headed. To be honest, it hadn't even occurred to me. All my focus was concentrated on Roisin. Even in the fog of my shock and grief, I had enough clarity to know that if she didn't kill herself, that meant someone murdered her.

She hadn't received any threatening dioramas, but Roisin was in the middle of a love triangle with two men. Lord Bertie, who had the power and privilege that made a man think he can do whatever he wanted, and Pawel, a passionate young man with a flair for creativity. And then you had the house itself, a place filled to the ceiling with secrets.

It took me less than half the time it usually takes me to walk to Paxby. I was out of breath and sweating despite the chill and the drizzle in the air. I strode past the Crossed Scythes and retraced my steps to Ade's house by memory. If Roisin had been hurt by someone, did that make Ade a suspect along with Pawel and Lord Bertie? My mind swam with conflicting thoughts. It was far too soon to be speculating about murder, and yet I couldn't help it.

He opened the door on my second knock, his eyes widening in surprise. "Come in."

In the hallway, I tried to unzip my jacket, but the zipper kept getting stuck. He quietly put his hand over mine, easing the zipper down and helping me out of the jacket. It made me feel like a child, but not in a bad way, more in the sense that someone was there to care for me when I needed it. Then he led me through to the kitchen, filled the kettle and sat me down at the table.

"How are you?" he asked. "And don't say fine. I know you're not fine."

"Not fine," I said. "Pretty far from it."

"Mrs Huxley called me," he said. "And she told me you found her."

"Swinging from the tree. All the life had gone out of her. She wasn't singing anymore; she was cold and..." I trailed off, horrified by the words coming out of my mouth, by the memory of finding my best friend in the woods. Ade reached across the table and took my hand while the kettle boiled in the background. He had tears in his eyes.

"I had no idea she was depressed," he said. "Apart from crying the other night, I'd never seen her upset."

"You knew her longer than I did."

"Yeah," he said. "But I didn't know her very well. We didn't talk much."

"You were talking in the rose garden yesterday. What was that about?"

Ade let go of my hand and leaned back in his chair. "God, that feels like a lifetime ago already." He shook his head. "I asked her if she was all right, because she'd got upset. And then I asked if everything was okay between her and Pawel, but she was... avoidant, like she didn't want to talk about it. And that was about it."

"I think she killed herself not long after then," I said. "If she even killed herself at all."

"What are you saying?"

I shrugged. "Weird shit has been going on at Highwood since I started working there. Those dioramas turned up, and now someone's dead. I mean, I know Roisin didn't get one, but it's too strange to be a coincidence, don't you think?"

"I guess," he said. "But why Roisin?"

I paused so I could examine his expression. He had an open face, kind and honest.

A heavy weight settled on my chest and shoulders. A potato sack of grief and fear and regret. I pulled in a deep breath and made a decision.

"Roisin was having an affair with Lord Bertie."

"What?"

"It's true. She told me yesterday. It's the reason she got so upset. She didn't know whether to tell Pawel and break up with him or not. I think she loved Pawel, but Bertie had her in this toxic relationship." I shook my head, a sudden burst of pure rage ran through me. "She was young and naive enough to think it might work with him."

Ade rubbed the back of his head thoughtfully. "This changes everything."

"Do you think it gives Lord Bertie a motive?"

His expression sharpened; his eyes narrowed. "That's a big accusation." He folded his arms and frowned. "Why though? He's single. I know she's a maid, but I think we're past that kind of prejudice, right?"

I shrugged. "Maybe not in his world."

Ade sighed. "I think we should have a cup of tea and, I don't know, just chill a bit. We don't know what happened, and to be honest, neither of us knew Roisin all that well. The police will get to the bottom of anything suspicious."

He got up to pour the tea while I tried to calm the nerves running through my body. Ade was being cool-headed and sensible, but he didn't know the things I knew about the past and about the men at that place. He hadn't read the concerns my mother had as a maid. *I think there's something wrong with Highwood Hall.*

# CHAPTER THIRTY-FOUR

R oisin's parents arrived from Sligo the day after I'd found her body. They were short people with roundish features and pink in their cheeks. Her mother had the same strawberry blonde hair, though hers was curly and cut shorter.

I saw the people they could be, and I saw what they were now: a creased, pale imitation with wet eyes and crumpled clothes. But Roisin's mother hugged me when we met, and I sank into the soft warmth of her. It almost broke me, that hug, but I wanted to hold it together enough to talk them through Roisin's final days. Afterwards, I showed her mum our shared room and all of Roisin's belongings. They then packed them away into boxes, silent tears running down their cheeks. With hands held over those boxes, I told them that she loved them. She'd wanted them to know that.

"We fell out sometimes," Mrs Byrne said. "But she was always our little girl."

I looked into her eyes and couldn't tell her my suspicions about Roisin's death. I couldn't speak at all. Nor could I tell her that her little girl had been involved with a man over twice her age.

"We're staying in the village tonight," she said. "We need to wait a few days for her... body to be released so we can take her back to Ireland. Please keep in touch, won't you?" She scribbled down a number and passed it to me. "I can see that Roisin cared about you and that you were a loyal friend to her. I'd like to let you know when the funeral is arranged."

I took the number and nodded my head. But inside I already knew that I wouldn't be able to afford to travel to Ireland even though I wanted to say goodbye. When they left, taking Roisin's belongings with them, I lay down on my bed and stared at the empty side of the room.

Somehow I'd slipped into a restful sleep—exhaustion will do that—and woke up to find Mrs Huxley standing by the bed.

"Would you like anything to eat?" she asked. "There's no hot food with half the kitchen staff still off, but there's a spread of sandwiches if you're hungry." As she stood before me, I searched her face for some sort of human emotion, thinking of her smiling at Heather Grove. She'd been affected by Roisin's death. There were shadows beneath her eyes, and her hair wasn't quite as neatly pinned as usual. She turned on her heel, leaving me to make the decision for myself.

Reluctantly I forced myself out of bed and stumbled bleary-eyed into the kitchen. Mrs Huxley sat at her usual spot at the head of the table. I nodded to her, taking a plate from a stack next to the sandwiches. The world was about to go on turning, and there was no way to stop it.

After a silent lunch, I put on my uniform and cleaned the library, hoovered the carpets and helped Mrs Huxley with dinner. None of the Howards looked at us as we served them. Bertie had his nose in the newspaper while Alex and Lottie stared at their phones. Margot ate her food in her room, taken to her by Huxley.

For the days that followed, I worked twice as hard, picking up Roisin's jobs as well as my own. I felt as though I had to prove I could cope, and I certainly didn't want Mrs Huxley to hire another maid. The thought of her replacing my kind and gentle friend made my stomach churn.

It was towards the end of the week when the police report ruled cause of death as suicide, and the Byrne's took Roisin's body back to Ireland. I thought of her in a coffin and shuddered. No, I couldn't go to the funeral. I couldn't watch her body lowered into the cold ground. Not with the gnawing, clawing sensation in the pit of my stomach, the one telling me I could've prevented it. I should've seen her hurtling towards disaster. I should've done more to stop it. To help her.

Cleaning became an escape from the grief, and I poured myself into it. I scrubbed and dusted and vacuumed and mopped and polished. I spoke to no one for days. I took no time to myself, and I ate little. When Pawel came back, we found we could barely speak to each other, perhaps each one of us sensing the pain the other was experiencing, or perhaps it was because I hadn't made my mind up about him. Pawel had been wronged by Roisin. What if he'd lost his temper with her? What if he'd hurt her?

No. Stop it. The police report... Again, it gnawed and clawed and nagged. What if the police were wrong?

I kept finding myself in the dining room, staring at the women on the walls, feeling a complete and utter sense of impotence. I wanted to piece together Roisin's final moments, but every time I tried to read the police report, I found my eyes filling with tears. Even if I did uncover some sort of anomaly, who would listen to a maid? Instead, I kept my head down, and I waited until I was ready to pick up the train of thought I'd started. And at night, when I found that I couldn't sleep, I reread the letters my mother had sent to my father. I read about what I looked like as a baby and how much she missed me when she went away to work. I read about her money troubles and her desperation. I read until my eyelids drooped and my mind drifted.

But during the day, I was drawn to the dining room over and over again. As the Howards ate their dinner, I picked out images of the women on the wood-panelled wall and fixated on them. I gave them backstories and invented families for them. I was one of them, forever imprinted on the walls of this house. That one face, the one I'd seen on my first day, with the passing resemblance to me, became an avatar for me. None of the portraits captured Roisin's pretty, elfin features, but I knew she would forever be etched here.

I'd applied for the job at Highwood Hall about six weeks before Roisin died. No one, certainly not me, could have predicted what had happened since I'd joined the staff. I'd expected to grow closer to the one woman I'd always wanted to meet, but never had been able to. And I'd wondered if perhaps after a few weeks I could learn more about her, uncover a few titbits about her past, either through Mrs Huxley or Lord Bertie. But I'd never expected to work through this sense of loss. Never before had I felt like such a failure. And now I had a difficult decision to make. Now I needed to decide whether to pull at the threads I saw around me or leave them and get out. Because it seemed obvious to me now. Highwood Hall had a rotten core.

# The Music Room

I didn't want to be there, and he knew it, but instead of the same old roughness—the orders and the punishments—he was softer that day. He didn't play the sonata at all. Instead, he played different pieces for me and asked me which was my favourite. He told me he was sorry we hadn't talked since last Friday, that he didn't like to see me upset, and then he began to let me in, bit by bit, which helped to take my mind off everything else.

"Daddy never wanted me to be a professional pianist, but he made me learn. All the men in the family learned to play an instrument."

"That's an unusual tradition," I noted.

"Believe me, there are many strange traditions in my family." He smiled. "He's a brilliant violin player, my father. But all this, the music, the practice—it's playtime. The business is what's real. Every man needs a hobby. It's healthy, apparently, to have a creative pursuit outside work. In my world, you get a wife and a hobby outside the business, and you'll be happy with it."

But my mind was elsewhere. He noticed me staring at the other side of the room and brushed some hair away from my ears. Still gentle. I'd never known him like this.

"Are you all right? I know you miss her."

I wiped tears from my eyes, and for once, I leaned into him. He readjusted himself on the piano stool so that I could nestle into his shoulder, and as I made myself comfortable, I inhaled the scent of his juniper aftershave. His hands smoothed over the crown of my head, and then his fingers worked the hair tie, loosening the waves from their knot. His face was close to mine when he ran his fingers through my hair.

"I do," I said. "I miss her so much."

"You'll see her again," he said. "I know you will."

I half listened to him as my hands rested on his chest, balling up his shirt in my fist. This shouldn't be happening—it was unprofessional, dangerous even—but I craved the warmth of him.

"Do you trust me, Emily?" he said.

I nodded my head. His lips met mine while his hands ran through my hair. As I leaned into his kiss, those fingers tightened until they formed a fist, tugging my head back just slightly. He broke away from me and continued to pull, harder now. And as he pulled, he watched me, his eyes dark. And then he let me go.

"Perhaps you shouldn't trust me," he said. He turned away and stared at the piano. "I'm fucked up."

"Everyone is." I wanted his hands in my hair again. I ached for the pressure on my scalp, the slight prickling of pain that blocked out all the bad thoughts. "I don't care what you do to me. I like it. I want more."

When I reached for him, he scooted from the piano stool so quickly that he almost tripped over his feet, stumbling back into a music stand. It clattered to the floor, the sudden cacophonous noise making me jolt. "No. Don't say that. Don't ever say that."

He seemed disgusted with me, and I couldn't stand the expression on his face. I needed to get out of there fast, but when I moved past him to get to the door, he caught me by the elbow and kissed me again. Soft and lazily at first, but soon he was pushing me back against the wall, his weight pressed against me. I was pliable, like clay—or a doll—to be played with. When he was in control, I left my body. It made me numb from head to toe, taking away the sadness locked inside me. But it made me wonder if I felt anything for him at all or whether I used him as some sort of conduit for my own pain. His hands moved up to my throat, a thumbnail pressing into the flesh. Not too hard but not gentle either. I wanted to egg him on, to tell him to go harder. I deserved the pain. I wanted it. But I didn't, and he didn't. He broke off and shook his head as he walked away from me. I watched the ripple of tension work through his back muscles, the flex of his arms as he balled his hands into fists.

"This isn't right," he said. "We should stop."

"Why?"

"Because..."

"I'm a maid?"

"Yes!"

I placed my fingers on my lips, the echo of the kiss still there. "Does it matter?"

"Yes," he said. "No. I don't know." He turned to face me again. "Do you want to live in the north wing with me?"

"Of course I do!" I said. And it was true. But why was it true? Did I love him, or did I want a home?

"They'd think you were a gold digger," he said, half laughing at his own words.

I shrugged. "Let them."

"You're just agreeing to all this because you're upset right now," he said. "You're not thinking clearly."

Perhaps he was right. Yearning made my heart raw, and perhaps I'd allowed desperation to make the decision for me. "Then wait a few weeks and ask me again."

He smiled. "All right then."

# CHAPTER THIRTY-FIVE

I woke up confused on Saturday morning. For some reason I'd expected to be in my bed at Aunt Josephine's. When I didn't hear her calling me for breakfast, I didn't know what was going on. And then I noticed a second bed in the room, and I knew I was at Highwood Hall. That second bed had been stripped bare, the battered old mattress resting on top of the frame. Looking at that lumpy thing brought everything flooding back.

It was the day of Roisin's funeral.

Mrs Huxley had offered to give me time off for the funeral, but I couldn't afford to fly to Ireland anyway, so I told her I'd be working as usual. She'd hired freelance cleaners to help get the hall in shape that weekend, which meant I could have the day off. I'd decided against it. I needed to keep busy.

As I showered and changed, I thought about the music room, about the way the piano music had lifted me, transported me to another time and place. When I was in that room, I didn't trust myself. I didn't trust Alex. Roisin had warned me about him so many times, but did that mean much when she was seeing a man like Lord Bertie? He wasn't going to her funeral. He hadn't cried for her as far as I knew. He acted like she was a person he'd never known. He hadn't shown even the slightest bit of sadness.

Perhaps *he* was the root of it all, a cancer at Highwood Hall that my mother had sensed all those years ago. And then my mind drifted back to the conversation between Lord Bertie and Mrs Huxley the night Roisin died. The way she'd spoken to him, as though she were putting feelers out to decipher whether his guilty deeds needed to be covered up. What did she know? I desperately wanted to find out.

While drying my hair, I put together a short list of questions I wanted answered.

How does Mrs Huxley move around Highwood so quickly? Could there be another secret corridor?

Did Roisin really kill herself?

What happened to my mother when she worked here?

Who sent the dioramas?

But the more I thought about those questions, the more alone I felt. Things hadn't gone the way I'd planned since I came to Highwood Hall, and I began to wonder if I should have come at all. My aunt would call me a quitter if I didn't see this through.

A commotion came from the kitchen. Pawel had decided to travel to Ireland for Roisin's funeral, so we were short-staffed again. I walked into chaos and quickly dived in, taking pastries out of the oven, handing over spoons, wiping icing sugar from the kitchen surfaces. As we worked through it all, the doorbell rang, and Mrs Huxley muttered under her breath as she strode out of the room.

My stomach rumbled with hunger as I arranged croissants. It was the first time I'd felt any kind of appetite since Roisin's death, and I actually felt guilty about it. But Mrs Huxley's return soon put a stop to the hunger pangs. Her skin, usually a deep russet brown, had turned ashen grey. She carried a gift box tied with a ribbon exactly like the one I'd received on my first day. I rushed over to the table as she placed the box down.

"Who is it addressed to?" I asked. My heart was in my mouth. I was sure that this box was for Roisin. I'd already conjured the image of it in my mind. A monstrous miniature portrayal of her cold, blue-tinged legs swinging from side to side among the branches.

"It's addressed to me," she said.

I wrapped my arms around my body to stop my hands from shaking. The appearance of these boxes accelerated my heart rate so rapidly that I doubted I'd be able to look at a present in the same way ever again.

Slowly Mrs Huxley tugged on the red ribbon until it slid from the surface of the box. The front flap fell, and we peered inside.

This time Highwood Hall was depicted from the outside. I saw the bricks and the windows painted on the back wall of the box. There were tiny stones of many different colours glued on to form a path, and next to the path were little flowers, the stems made out of plastic but the petals made from fabric, glued until they were stiff enough to retain their shape. In the centre of all that, a tall woman in a red dress stood outside the house, looking in, her dark hair pulled back into a tight bun. Mrs Huxley.

"What does it mean?" I asked.

She didn't answer right away; she was staring at the diorama. I took a step closer so that I could examine it more myself, and I could've sworn I saw a face in the window of the hall. The face of a young woman. But before I could get a better look, Mrs Huxley slammed the front flap shut and picked up the box in her arms. She turned around and strode out of the room.

I glanced at my phone. It was seven thirty a.m., and we needed to take the food to the dining room. I had no choice. I had to organise it myself. Grabbing a silver tray, I piled some dishes on it and made my way through the bare corridor, ignoring the ache spreading through my taut muscles. The secret door clicked open, and I entered the dining room, keeping my eyes down so as not to look at any of the Howards, especially not Alex or Bertie.

But unfortunately, they noticed me.

"Should you be working, dear?" Margot asked, a kindness in her voice that took me by surprise.

"I'm okay, thank you." I placed bread down on the table and helped the others bring in eggs, bacon and pastries for the stainless steel food warmer along the far wall.

"Where's Huxley?" Bertie asked.

Without looking at him, I said, "She went to her room. She wasn't feeling well."

"I saw her just thirty minutes ago, and she was fine," he replied.

His nonchalance pissed me off. Why were any of us here serving him food? Roisin—his lover—was dead, and here I was putting his spoon next to his fucking plate.

"Actually, she received an unpleasant parcel in the mail. Another diorama." I stood up straight and looked him right in the eye. "It upset her, so she went to her room. It seems this ex-employee is still angry even though you said you'd handled it." I forced my mouth to close before saying anything else. It was already a huge mistake to have blurted out as much as I had. Quietly I backed away from the table, my legs unsteady, and caught Alex staring at me. I saw no trace of a smile on his face, but I got the feeling, from the way his head was cocked slightly, that he sized me up, trying to decide whether what I'd done was brave or stupid.

I thought stupid. Either I'd pissed off a murderer or I'd spoken back to my boss, a powerful man who could fire me at any moment. The air in the dining room cooled. Bertie's eyes focused on mine, but he didn't seem fazed by my outburst.

"Well, that is a shame," he said. "Please tell Mrs Huxley that I'd like to see the threatening gift she received. My investigator is still building a body of evidence. I'm sure the matter will be dealt with soon. Unfortunately, the girl is more unhinged than I'd originally thought." The corners of his mouth twitched up. "Though I do pity her. As I do anyone with a mental illness. Thank you for organising breakfast. I'm sure this is a difficult day for you."

And what a difficult day it is for *you*, I thought, as I nodded my head, leaving through the servants' door. On my way back to the kitchen, a sudden burst of almost uncontrollable rage spread all the way from my head to my toes. I pressed my knuckles into the wall and ground my teeth to try to make it stop. It would not.

WHILE I WAS DUSTING and scrubbing and mopping, working my hands until they were red and flaky, I imagined Roisin's family. I saw them waiting for the hearse, driving to the cemetery, the sound of sniffles over the engine. I saw them walking down the church aisle in procession with the coffin, arms over shoulders, chests heaving up and down as relatives sobbed. I wondered what music they'd chosen for her.

It drove me mad. I'd lived it without even going there and giving myself the closure to my grief. So I cleaned harder until the wooden handle of a scrubbing brush gave me a blister.

At lunchtime, I wandered down to the bottom of the garden and found Ade staring at one red rose, a shovel by his feet. He turned to me as I approached, a sad smile on his face.

"You didn't go," he said.

I shook my head. "I couldn't."

"They didn't give you time off?"

"No, nothing like that. I just... I couldn't."

He was quiet then. He simply nodded and glanced down at his shovel. "I can't seem to concentrate today. You know?"

"Same."

"If you need someone to talk to—"

"Huxley got a diorama this morning," I said, cutting him off. I didn't feel ready to accept his kindness. "I thought it was her. All this time, I was convinced. But now she'd got one herself. And... she seemed super spooked, you know? Pale and freaked out. You can't fake that." I chewed at the inside of my cheek, trying to piece together everything that had happened. None of it fit.

"Did you see it? What was it like?"

"Yeah, I saw it. It was the hall from the outside, and Mrs Huxley was looking in. I think I saw a woman's face in the window."

"Well, that's creepy."

"Yeah." My voice sounded far away as my mind whirred, trying to make sense of it all. "The one person who died didn't get one of them. These things seem to be some sort of bizarre, veiled threat, and yet Roisin never got one."

Ade tapped the soil with the toe of his boot. "It could be a coincidence."

"It could be. Maybe there's more than one strange thing happening at the hall. Maybe they're not connected at all." I searched his eyes. I wanted him to be on my level, to be willing to believe that anything was possible with this family. But I saw caution. I saw disbelief.

"I guess so," he said. "Are you all right? You seem wired."

He knew I wasn't telling him everything. I supposed he knew me well enough for that. I thought about Alex in the music room, his fingers brushing the hair from my face, his lips whispering promises into my ear. I thought about the north wing, the place he told me his wife would live. He'd hinted that it could be me, but it almost made me feel like it was a competition to be won. Play the game and you could have a piece of this fortune. I thought about Lord Bertie at breakfast, his nonchalance, his complete disregard for us. His private conversations with Huxley. Margot with the photo albums pointing at him, blaming him. Lady Laura falling down the stairs and her adult son watching...

"I might need your help soon," I said. "And I might need you to trust me when I come to you and ask for it."

He straightened his back, and a wave of calm seemed to wash over him. Resolve, I thought. I hoped. And I knew then that I could rely on him. Immeasurable relief flooded through my body.

"All right," he said. "Whatever you need."

# CHAPTER THIRTY-SIX

The next day, I waited for Mrs Huxley to leave as she always did on a Sunday. I waited near the fountain, skulking like a sneak thief. As soon as she was gone, I sprang into action.

There would never be a perfect opportunity like this one. Lord Bertie had gone to visit one of his offices in York. Lottie hadn't come back after her night out. Margot was drinking martinis by the indoor pool. Alex was working in his office in the stables. I had Highwood Hall all to myself or at least close enough.

First I went to the north wing, but every way in was locked. Not surprising. Lord Bertie's office and Mrs Huxley's rooms were all locked. But then I remembered how Roisin had told me that she and Bertie would go down to the wine cellar together. I'd never been to the wine cellar—though Roisin and I had spent a lot of time in the laundry room below the kitchen—but the fact that Bertie used it as his secret meeting place made me think I should investigate. Highwood was full of surprises. What would Lord Bertie's secret rendezvous spot yield?

The entrance to the wine cellar wasn't far from the servants' quarters, close to the main staircase. A door in the adjacent corridor opened up to a narrow staircase that descended to the cellar. It was unlocked, thank goodness, and I made my way there, watching my step on the concrete stairs. I'm not sure what I expected but certainly not the modern room I stepped into. There were spotlights built into the plastered and cream-painted ceiling. Bottles of wine were arranged in temperature-controlled glass cabinets not dissimilar to the ones in the library. Hundreds of bottles lined the shelves, no doubt worth more than I'd ever made in a year. In between them was a cream sofa and a small bookcase, presumably to sit and enjoy a glass of wine as you read a book.

I cast a glance at the sofa, and my stomach flipped over. A mental image of Bertie charming Roisin flashed into my mind. *Have another drink, sweetie. This one is special, just like you.* A hand on her thigh or her back, that jovial smile always on his face. No matter how much she liked him, he was always the aggressor in my mind. I hated him. But then I'd always hated him. I'd tried to hide it as well as I could.

Time ticked on, and I had a job to do. I walked the perimeter of the cellar, testing the walls for possible secret panels. But the plaster was smooth. There was, however, an electric fireplace with candles on the lintel. I reached over and lifted each candle, expecting something out of an Indiana Jones movie. Sadly, nothing opened, and the candles were just candles. I ran a hand over the entire thing, but I couldn't find anything else that could unlock a secret door.

I pulled back the rug to check for a trap door. Nothing. I tried pulling books out of the bookshelves. Nothing. And then I ran my hands around the edge of the wine shelves themselves. I smiled. I'd found a button.

Tiny and inconsequential. An object with no sense of theatre to it at all. It simply opened the shelves when I pressed it. I laughed out loud. The shelves themselves were the door, and it opened up to yet another secret corridor. Perhaps I'd found Lord Bertie's apocalypse bunker, or perhaps it led to some sort of torture chamber.

I stepped in, pleased to find there were lights in the tunnel. Cold air tickled the back of my neck. Before I began following the corridor, I paused to ensure there was a button to open the shelves from the other side. I definitely didn't want to get stuck in this place when no one knew where I was. Lord Bertie would be the kind of man to let me rot rather than admit his secrets.

I walked quickly through the tunnel. An hour had already passed since I started searching, and I didn't want Mrs Huxley to know I'd been snooping.

The tunnel sloped steeply upwards, which meant I travelled up to the first floor. After what I thought must be a fair comparison to one flight of steps, I noticed a door to my left. It wasn't the end of the tunnel, however. Surprisingly, it kept going up, meaning a second location existed. Perhaps this was the reason for Mrs Huxley turning up when you least expected her. But which direction had she come from the day I tried to get into her office? Up or down?

When the door opened, I breathed a sigh of relief. To have come this far only to face a final hurdle would have been devastating. It creaked open to reveal Mrs Huxley's office. Now my heart was beating fast. This was the first time I'd ever been in here. My eyes ate the scene hungrily, desperate for clues. I sought out her personal diorama first, finding it on her desk. I opened it fast and examined the scene one more time. The sight of the ghostly faces painted at the window made my breath catch. They were small, almost translucent, their pale faces round and gloomy. I hadn't noticed in the kitchen but there were several faces, at least ten, all staring back at Mrs Huxley. All women. I shivered.

Then I rummaged through her drawers, but it was fruitless. Pens, papers, envelopes, ring binders full of cleaning contacts and vegetable suppliers, caterers and private hire cars, even a contact for a helicopter pilot. I placed the ring binder back. One document stood out to me: a bill from the Heather Grove care home in Wicklesworth. I opened it and managed to find the name of the person she'd visited. Charlie Huxley. Included in the document was a handwritten note from one of the carers. *Charlie is doing very well. We're so proud of him. He loves arts and crafts especially. He's well-liked by the other residents and is improving with his social skills.* I found a photograph of Charlie, who stood with his head slightly bent, a hesitant smile playing on his lips. The kind of innocent smile of someone who didn't quite understand the world but lived in it purely. He was in his early twenties, possibly the same age as me, which, I thought, must be about the same time she started working at Highwood. The resemblance between Charlie and Huxley was clear to me. They had the same bone structure, the same dark eyes. One thing I did notice was that Charlie's skin was a shade or two lighter than Mrs Huxley's, and his curls were looser. But he was her son; he had to be. I lifted the picture one more time, wondering if Mrs Huxley had been forced to make the same sort of difficult decisions as my own mother.

Then I placed it back down and found Charlie's diagnosis—he had autism.

Aware that I didn't have much time, I searched quickly through Mrs Huxley's files, fingers flying through the cabinets, eager to discover what I needed. I flicked through the years *2018, 2006, 2002*... Until... I grabbed a folder and shoved it under my tunic, tucking it into the waistband of my trousers. I didn't have enough time to read through it now. I had to find out where the rest of the tunnel went.

I left her office and walked through to her bedroom. Everything was tidy. The walls were papered in dark florals. I found a Bible on her bedside table. I couldn't bring myself to look through her belongings even though I wanted to. I left through the tunnel door and made my way up to the next floor. Where did Mrs Huxley go when she disappeared? I had my suspicions, and now I wanted them confirmed.

The corridor was so steep that my thighs began to ache. I tried imagining Mrs Huxley striding up and down the secret tunnel, her long, dancer's stride giving her a floating appearance as she walked. I pictured her face, tight and worried, running secret errands for the Howards. It took perhaps a minute or two to reach the door, though I believe it felt longer than that. I eased it open slowly, nervous to uncover what was on the other side. And then I found myself in Lord Bertie's office.

It confirmed my suspicion. Mrs Huxley and Lord Bertie were connected on a deeper level than anyone knew. This solved the mystery of how the housekeeper would appear randomly at different points and how she'd often beat me walking through the servants' hallway back to the kitchen. And now I was in Lord Bertie's office on my own and I could do whatever I wanted.

I sprang into action, rifling through drawers, checking documents, shelves and cabinets. I checked every nook and cranny of the fireplace on the opposite wall, moved every poker, pressed every tile. At one point, I got excited because I'd found a secret nook beneath the desk, but then I realised it was a dog bed for Leo.

What was I looking for? I sat down on Bertie's office chair and opened up the dioramas one by one. Mrs Huxley hadn't given hers to him, which made me wonder if he was even still investigating the strange gifts. I checked through his files one more time and found an invoice from an investigator. So, he had at least paid for someone. My gaze drifted to Bertie's laptop. Gently, I lifted the lid and waited for it to come to life. If it was password protected, as I suspected it would be, then I had no chance of uncovering any secrets. The screen unlocked, and I saw an eye icon searching my pupil. Quickly, I slammed the laptop shut before it took a record of someone trying to log in.

And then I heard a key in the lock.

Without thinking, I dived underneath the desk, tucking myself into the small nook. Feet shuffled into the office while I kept myself folded up tight amid the strong scent of wet dog. Whoever had just walked in headed towards the desk. I held my breath, my heart racing. A dog hair tickled at my nose, but I kept myself still as stone.

They sat down at the chair, and for the first time I saw a pair of brogues beneath the desk. I recognised those shoes. I remembered Alex wearing them, kicking up gravel as he took me to the north wing. Alex cleared his throat and tapped the keyboard. He was working on Bertie's laptop? That seemed odd. I heard him humming while he worked. The Chopin étude, I thought.

The padded dog bed soon heated up below my body. Sweat trickled down my temples and back. I bent my head and breathed softly into my knees, hoping he'd soon be done. Alex opened a desk drawer, reaching deep into the back. We were inches from each other. At any moment he could lean closer and see me, or reach a little further to the right with his foot and find me curled up in a ball. Silently, I tried to manoeuvre my head to get a better view. Curiosity kept getting the better of me. I heard a *clunk* and the gentle swish of a door opening somewhere else in the room. Alex closed the drawer, got to his feet and walked away. In the sweaty, stinky dog bed, adrenaline surged through me. What I wanted more than anything was to poke my head out to see what he was doing. Instead, I had to settle for sounds. I measured the sound of his footsteps. He moved across the room. The door swished softly against the carpet followed by a second clunk. Once I was sure the door was closed, I remained where I was for at least two minutes. Silence settled around me. Quietly, I unfolded myself from the nook and crawled out from the desk.

The room was empty. I had no time to figure out where Alex had gone. I needed to get out of there. I found the secret door, stepped back into the cold corridor and made my way back down towards the cellar.

# CHAPTER THIRTY-SEVEN

She stood in the kitchen, dark eyes deep inside her sharp face, watching me, as always. I saw the way they followed my movement as I walked through the kitchen on the way to my bedroom. It was clear she wanted to know where I'd been, and she wanted to know why I walked with one hand protecting my stomach. I nodded to her as I moved past, and then her nose turned up as she smelled the dog on me. In that moment, I was convinced that she could tell where I'd been and everything that had happened. But she said nothing. She turned away and got on with making a cup of tea. I continued on to my room, knees trembling beneath me.

When I closed and locked the door behind me, collapsed onto the bed and removed the file from under my top, a realisation hit me. Before Roisin died, I'd considered losing my job to be the worst thing that could happen to me. My lifeless body left swinging from a branch was the worst thing that could happen to me. I shivered, the sweat grown cold on my skin and the chill of the secret corridor buried deep in my bones. I pulled the covers around me, praying I was safe in my room and no one had any proof that I'd been snooping. The file lay on the cushion next to my head. I needed to build up the strength to open it.

It didn't take long. Curiosity chased away the fear. I reached for the file, pulled it open, and let my fingers flip the pages, searching for her. Huxley had kept written notes of the maids at that time. When they started, their CVs, their references, when they left, transcripts of their exit interviews if they had one—I read one interview that gushed about Bertie but complained about the food—and any details of misconduct. One maid had been accused of stealing. Some of them had come from troubled backgrounds just like I had, and they relapsed and left. Some of the girls had even spent time in prison for minor offences, usually drugs. It made the high turnover of maids inevitable, just like Mrs Huxley had warned me. I read every account of these young women trying to make a life for themselves, but she wasn't there. My mother was missing.

My heart sank, but I thought that perhaps I'd made a mistake. I quickly checked the dates on my mother's letters to my father and then checked the files again. When I matched up all the different maids within the timeline, I noticed a gap. One maid worked at Highwood between the 17th of January 1999, and the 20th of March 1999, whereas before there were always two. Why would my mother's records be removed?

In addition to the missing record for my mother, I noticed that another maid had left during that time, and the Howards hadn't found a replacement for over a week. Surely someone as meticulous as Mrs Huxley wouldn't have allowed the Howards to be without a maid for that long? There were always temps to hire, but the Howards were a demanding family, and Highwood Hall was massive in scope. I knew Mrs Huxley, and I knew she needed at least two maids.

I shoved the folder into my underwear drawer, covering it with pants and bras. All that sneaking around and hiding for such little information. I'd found nothing linking Bertie to Roisin's death, but I hadn't truly expected to. There'd be no convenient lengths of rope or CCTV footage of him killing her. I'm sure it happened in the dark, away from people, if he'd even killed her himself. Bertie was so rich that he could've had help from an outsider to cover it up.

I'd found nothing about the dioramas. If Lord Bertie had any additional information about that, he hadn't shared it with anyone, and I guessed it'd be on his private computer. If I even tried to guess Bertie's passcode, the computer would probably take a picture of me. No, I wouldn't be able to hack into his laptop, that was certain.

The mystery of the secret passage could be explained with logic. It made sense for the housekeeper's rooms to be connected to Lord Bertie's office. I'd heard about servants' rooms being linked via secret passageways to children's rooms in the past. That way the nanny could comfort a crying baby without having to walk through the house to get to the child. Perhaps Bertie and Huxley took advantage of that pre-built corridor. But why? And why wasn't it common knowledge amongst the staff? I had my suspicions, but I was a long way off confirming anything.

But what had I learned? I now knew that Alex had a key to Lord Bertie's office and that he disappeared through *another* door while in that room. I'd learned the name of Mrs Huxley's son and I'd seen that records connecting my mother as a maid here had been either lost or destroyed.

All those things added up to... what? My mind swam with the possibilities. I sat up in my bed, wrapped my arms around my legs, and felt true, all-consuming fear grip every one of my muscles. I didn't like where these nuggets of information were taking me. *There's something wrong with Highwood Hall.* Secrets, so many secrets to be uncovered. Now I wondered whether I'd be the one to expose them before those secrets consumed more innocents like Roisin. Or me.

FOR THE REST of that Sunday, I avoided Mrs Huxley and took a chunk of Pawel's freshly baked bread to eat in the garden. The grass was warm beneath my jeans, and I wished I'd put on shorts or a skirt. The aroma of the rose garden grew cloying in the late spring heat, especially when I thought of Roisin and heard her voice in my mind. Cross-legged, I waited, chewing on the bread, hardly tasting it despite Pawel's baking talents, until Ade walked over, blocking the bright sun from view. He sat down on the lawn next to me.

"I need to tell you something," I said.

"Funny way of saying hello." He flashed me some teeth and adjusted himself on the lawn. Then he noticed the expression on my face and his smile dissipated. "What is it?"

"I didn't just come to Highwood Hall because I needed a job and a place to stay. I came here because my mother used to work here a long time ago when I was a baby."

"Okay," he said. "Wow. That's a lot to take in."

"I know," I said. "Sorry, I should've told you sooner. But I didn't want Mrs Huxley to know. She worked here at the same time as my mother."

"They knew each other?"

"Maybe. My mum, she left me right after she stopped working here. Dumped me with my aunt and disappeared."

Ade shook his head. "I'm so sorry—"

"It's okay." I glanced at my fingernails and grimaced. "I have so many... so many conflicting thoughts, and I don't know how to arrange them..." To my horror, I began to cry, and then I couldn't stop. The tears burst from me, breaking through every barrier I'd ever constructed. I thought I'd built a sturdy wall, but it was little more than a delicate veil.

"Hey, come here." Ade pulled me into his arms, encasing me, covering me with warmth.

I blinked away tears, looking up at Highwood. Alex stood in the window. Watching.

I let Ade comfort me and then we carried on talking until the sun went down. About my mother, about Mrs Huxley, about Roisin, about everything. But all I could think about was Alex at the window. Watching.

# CHAPTER THIRTY-EIGHT

My sleep was light and frequently interrupted by bad dreams that I forgot as soon as my eyes opened. When I woke, I expected to see Roisin there, mussed hair spilling over her shoulders, waiting for me to tell her my dreams. But the bed was empty.

I sleepwalked through Monday, thoughts elsewhere. My hands worked while my mind made decisions. Going through the motions became life. I followed Huxley's orders to the letter. I swept, I polished, I served food.

Tuesday and Wednesday came and went in the same way. I ran some errands for Margot, helping her pack away items from her wardrobe that she wouldn't need for summer. Several moth-eaten Chanel dresses were thrown away completely. She'd placed a diamond necklace in my hand with a wink, but I put it back on her dressing table as I carried bags of old clothes out of the room. I could never accept a gift like that. For all I knew, Mrs Huxley or Lord Bertie would turn around and accuse me of theft and Margot would suddenly forget that she even gave me the necklace in the first place.

And then the second half of the week dragged me kicking and screaming out of my fog, forcing me to sit up and take notice. First, in the early hours of Thursday morning, I woke up convinced that I'd heard someone closing my bedroom door. It was like an echo, something I wasn't sure if I had dreamed, but I staggered out of bed and ran down to Mrs Huxley's rooms anyway. A terrible sense of déjà vu hit me as I pounded the door with my fists and waited. She never answered. I hurried through the kitchen, but it was empty. I went along to the stairs and checked there, but it was empty too. Quietly, I opened the door to the cupboard above the stairs so I could wait and watch to see if anything strange happened, something that could help me figure out what was going on at Highwood Hall, but instead a hand reached out, grabbed me by the throat and squeezed.

I panicked, clawing at the thin fingers around my neck until the attacker suddenly ceased his throttling and let go. Alex's striking blue eyes emerged from the darkness. He let out a long, breathy sigh.

"Sorry," he said. "I didn't realise it was you."

When he came out of the cupboard, I still took a cautionary step backwards, a hand resting on my neck. "Who did you think it was?"

He was dressed in silk pyjamas. Scarlet red, almost ridiculously bright but somehow threatening on his body. "I don't know. I was sleep-walking."

I glanced at the cupboard and back to Alex. "Do you do this often?"

"Yes. Odd, isn't it? I'm fixated with this place."

"Because you saw—" I caught myself before I said it out loud.

But he knew what I was going to say. His chin tilted down, and he took a step towards me. "Because I saw my mother die from here."

My cheeks flushed with heat. My throat ached. It made me think of Roisin with the rope around her neck. Lady Laura hanging from the chandelier.

"Women seem to have a habit of dying at Highwood," Alex said. "Sad, isn't it?"

"Disturbing," I said. "Were you in my room?"

I saw that his mind was elsewhere. Perhaps he was still half-asleep. He didn't seem focused on anything in particular, just lost to his own thoughts. He didn't answer me at first.

"Hey," I said, grabbing him by the arm. "Answer me. Were you in my room?"

"No," he said. "Don't be ridiculous. Why would I come into your room?"

I stepped away from him and staggered back to my bed, rubbing the part of my throat he'd gripped. When I reached my room, I tested the lock. It worked. I remembered specifically locking my room that night, and yet the sound had been clear as a bell in my mind. If someone had come into my room, then they needed a key. Who had a master key for the house? Mrs Huxley? Alex? Lord Bertie?

It took a long time to fall back to sleep, which remained restless until my alarm blared. When I pulled on my uniform and made my way back to the kitchen, I had a feeling Alex wouldn't even mention what had happened the night before.

Zombielike, I carried trays through the servants' corridor to the dining room, kicked open the hidden door and stacked up the pastries, eggs and bacon. Alex avoided my eye contact as usual, but I did see him stare at my neck. Luckily, his fingers hadn't left a bruise, and I think he was relieved about that as well. Even Mrs Huxley seemed distracted. I hadn't forgotten how I'd banged on her door in the middle of the night, and not only had she not answered, but she hadn't asked me about it this morning. When I caught her yawning, I knew she hadn't been in her room. So where was she? Perhaps she'd come into my room to find the stolen file and hidden in the corridor when I woke. I mulled on that for a while, but I didn't get much time for idle thought.

The second of the strange occurrences happened during breakfast. When the buzzer sounded for the front gate, Mrs Huxley disappeared and later re-emerged as I poured Margot's coffee. There, in her arms, lay yet another white gift box tied up with a red bow. I splashed hot coffee on the tablecloth when I saw it, swearing under my breath. But no one noticed because we were all staring at the box as Mrs Huxley placed it in the centre of the table.

"There's no card," she said, stepping back. "All the others had cards."

Lord Bertie slammed his newspaper down. I flinched as the porcelain clattered.

"Daddy," Lottie said. "Be careful."

I noticed Alex regard his sister with a sardonic expression on his face. "This should be over and done with by now. Why haven't we found the person sending these things?"

When Lord Bertie answered, it was as though he addressed the entire table rather than his son. "Because it wasn't who I originally thought, that's why. If we'd been right the first time, this matter would be over. But now we don't know who it is or what they want."

"You mean you can't pay them off," Lottie said with a scoff.

"Isn't anyone going to open it?" Margot snapped. "We'd may as well see what we're dealing with. Go on, Huxley. You fetched it; you can do the honours."

Mrs Huxley nodded, stepped forward, and gently pulled on the bow. As with the others, the front flap dropped, and it revealed the scene inside. I was standing straight in front of it, and I saw the contents first. I let out a little gasp that I tried to cover with my hand, then my eyes flew up to Alex, which he noticed right away.

"What is it?" Alex asked his grandmother.

"See for yourself," she said, turning the box around.

His eyes flicked up to mine, held them for half a second and then flicked back to the box. He didn't look at me again. He either stared at the diorama or the table, pointedly anywhere but me. Lottie shrugged and glanced away, seemingly disinterested, seeing as the scene didn't involve her. Lord Bertie frowned but said nothing.

This diorama showed nothing violent or disturbing like some of the others, but its scene shook me down to my bones. I saw the music room brought to life, with the floral mural and striped wallpaper garishly recreated. A miniature chandelier, again made out of tiny plastic jewels, hung from the box lid. Beneath the lights, curved cardboard mimicked the shape of the grand piano, painted a glossy black to match its counterpart. Tiny individual keys spread along the front like bared teeth. And about to play the instrument were two small figurines sitting on the stool. One, a man with dark hair cut neatly short wearing a smart shirt, sleeves rolled to the elbow. The other, a young woman in simple clothing. My maid uniform. Her brown hair was pulled back, but there were loose, wispy tendrils framing her face.

The box wasn't labelled, but it clearly showed me and Alex together in the music room. But why? And how did they know small details like the fact that I sat on the piano stool with Alex. Most page-turners stood next to the piano to turn the music, but Alex liked me to be close to him. How did they know that? I clasped my hands together behind my back and fought the urge to run from the room. I needed to know... I needed to be sure... that we hadn't been watched.

# Chapter Thirty-Nine

By that point, a fatigue had settled over Highwood Hall, and everyone in the room almost seemed bored of the latest diorama, as though it'd become such a common occurrence that no one cared. Margot asked what it meant, and Alex explained to her that he practised the piano with my help each Friday. Lottie then made a comment about how Alex liked spending time with the *help*, to which Alex stood up and walked out of the room. Shortly after, Lord Bertie took the diorama away, and breakfast was over.

Dusting the library could wait, and as soon as Lord Bertie and Mrs Huxley were out of the dining room, I sprinted all the way to the music room. My raw throat choked on air, feet scuffing the floorboards. When I grabbed the door handle, it didn't budge.

"Need a key?"

I spun on my heel to find Alex dangling the key between his thumb and forefinger.

"It seems I had the same idea," he said, reaching around me to unlock the door.

"Someone's been watching us," I whispered. "How else would they know?"

"Know what?"

"That I sit next to you, that you roll up your shirtsleeves? And why are they showing it to us? I don't understand the context. That's two dioramas with me in it now. Why am I being targeted more than anyone else? Do you think whoever it is will hurt me? Like how Roisin was hurt?" I loathed myself as I rambled on and finally snapped my jaw shut. I was saying too much, blabbing to a man I didn't trust.

He simply rolled his eyes as he pushed the door open. "I think you might be being a tad dramatic. But I also thought it might warrant a double check." He shrugged. "Like you said, this person knows some odd details."

"What's so interesting about you playing the piano and me turning the pages?" I stepped in, noticing that everything was in its usual position. The piano top had been closed over the keys. Sheet music for a Rachmaninoff prelude waited on the stand. A violin lingered in its usual position on the wall.

"God knows," Alex said, sounding almost bored. He closed the door behind us, blocking me from the exit.

As soon as the door clicked shut behind him, my hand rose to my throat. I thought of the dark, the pale fingers emerging from the secret cupboard, and my eyes drifted to his. I hadn't been afraid of him before, but I was now.

"Who do you think it is sending these boxes?" I asked, moving a few steps closer to him, defying the fear making my muscles tremble. "Do you think it's someone in your family? Whoever it is knows a lot about you all. Or is it Mrs Huxley? I've always thought so. At least I did until she received one herself."

"Not Huxley," he said, dismissing the thought as though it was preposterous. "She's far too loyal to Daddy. No, I could never see it. Lottie or Margot, however..." He ran a hand along the wall as though looking for a secret door. His eyes roamed up and down the length of the room.

I checked the corners for any secret cameras. I peered into the violin through the taut strings. "You'd expect this of your family more than you would an employee?"

Alex hesitated by the piano. "Yes, I would."

I let out a shuddering breath as I made my way around the room. "It feels strange being in here in the daytime. When we come in here on Friday evenings, I feel as though we're in a different time and space. Do you ever feel that way?"

"Yes," he said. He faced me now, and his expression was as impassive as ever, but his eyes were bright and burning. I could've sworn I saw longing illuminating the ice water of his irises. "I've felt like that from the very first week."

"I don't think there are any cameras or peepholes in here," I said, scanning the room one more time.

"No, neither do I," Alex said. "I think someone has speculated about what happens in this room." He rubbed his chin. "Unless you told someone about our Friday nights."

"I told Roisin almost everything."

One corner of his mouth twitched. "Almost."

"Almost."

"Do you think she could have told anyone else?"

I shrugged. "I suppose she could. Pawel maybe, or..." I froze. Alex saw the change in me immediately and circled in until he was close. He looked down at me as we stood there face to face.

"Or?"

"Your father."

Alex's already clenched jaw tightened, a ripple of tension working its way across his face, and then he let it go, exhaling and closing his eyes as though completely exasperated. "No matter how many times we tell him not to fuck the maids."

"And what about you?" I snapped. "How many times have you been told not to fuck the maids? I should go."

"No one is keeping you here," he replied.

"I'm aware of that." I wrenched the door open and left.

MY BLOOD BOILED. I'd reached the point where enough was enough and I was sick of the Howards and sick of holding my feelings in. I stopped at the dining room on my way back to the servants' quarters, and I stared at the portraits there for a long time. Those strange, ethereal women and their serene expressions, passively gazing back at me. I sought out the woman I'd noticed on my first day, then I looked at Lady Laura for a moment before ducking through the secret door.

Tomorrow I'd have to spend yet another evening in the music room with Alex. I wasn't sure whether I could bear it anymore. But of course, I would go anyway. I'd stay pliable, submissive, the good girl he wanted.

But what did I want?

What did I want to do?

I'D DECIDED it was time to stop playing pretend, and later that day, after eating dinner with Pawel and Ade, I went to Mrs Huxley. Someone needed to tell me why my mother had been erased from the files. She knew. I was sure of it. She'd been here for decades, she had to know. But would she tell me what went on here? And if there truly was something wrong with Highwood Hall, was Mrs Huxley in on it? This one woman held my fate in the palm of her hand, and she'd either close her fist and crush me or she'd guide me through what I needed to do next. Everything I'd learned about her so far suggested that she would close her fist, *except* for Charlie. I needed to take a chance. I couldn't take down Lord Bertie on my own. I stood outside her door and took a deep breath.

She let me in, closed the door and walked over to her desk. She stood behind the diorama and placed her hands on the surface. She said nothing. She waited.

"I think you know why I'm here," I said.

To my surprise, she picked up a remote control and pressed a button. The room filled with the orchestral sounds of chamber music. Then she walked over to the secret door and began to drag a filing cabinet in front of it. When she strained against the cabinet, I instinctively went to help her until the door was blocked. After that, she opened a desk drawer, produced a large bottle of whisky and two stainless steel tumblers.

"I'm clean and sober," I said.

"You were addicted to drugs. Painkillers, tranquilisers..."

"Yeah, but—"

"Look," she said, "I think you're going to need this. I *know* you will, and I sure as hell do."

"So you do know why I'm here." I reached for the tumbler.

"I do."

"Are you going to tell me everything?"

"Yes," she said.

"There's something very wrong at Highwood Hall, isn't there?"

Huxley downed her whisky, and her body crumpled over. I thought for one awful moment that she was going to collapse, but she sucked in a long breath and composed herself. I sat down in a chair next to her desk and listened to every word, a sense of dread running deeper and deeper through my body until she'd finished her story.

# THE MUSIC ROOM

I was anxious to go in, afraid to see him. Too many times I'd dismissed the strangeness at Highwood Hall, and now I had to face up to the fact that I didn't trust the Howard family anymore. But at the same time, what I felt for *him* was more complicated than that. *Inside the music room we are me and him and the rest of the world doesn't matter. We are something else, and time stands still. Whatever I am afraid of, I have to ignore it.*

He walked up to me, smiling, and I thought to myself that perhaps I could talk to him and ask him questions about his father and the things that frightened me about Highwood. But that smile faded as he approached because he noticed my mood right away.

"What's the matter?" he asked. "You seem nervous."

"I'm not nervous." To hide the lack of conviction in my voice, I plastered a large grin across my face. But I saw from his frown that it didn't convince him.

We went into the room, and he closed the door and leaned against the wall. "Things have been weird around here, haven't they? Look, I know you're feeling a bit spooked, but I promise you that things are going to get better. Do you trust me?"

I nodded.

He held his hand out to me. "Listen, I don't feel like playing tonight." He opened the door again. "Why don't we go for a walk instead?"

*In the music room time stands still.* "I don't know. I like hearing you play."

"Please," he said. "I'd love to walk with you. Sometimes I feel like you learn so much about me in this room, but I never learn anything about you. Come with me. I'll give you another tour of the house if you like."

I reached out to take his hand but then hesitated. "What if someone sees us holding hands?"

He smiled, closing the distance between us, and ran his fingers through my hair. "I don't care. Do you care?"

At first I leaned into him, and when our lips touched, longing stirred within my body, circulating through my bloodstream. He smelled like the glossy wood of the grand piano, but with the earthiness of the wood was an undertone of sweetness edged with sourness, like a ripe pear about to turn. He was gentle, for a change, until he wasn't. I felt the pressure on the back of my head, and I wanted it to stop. I pressed both palms against his chest and pushed him away.

"That wasn't very nice," he said.

"You were hurting me."

"You've never complained before."

"Well, I am now," I replied. "I don't think I want to go for that walk after all."

But he grabbed me by the elbow and spun me around. "I want to go for the walk. Come on."

My heart pounded then, driving the blood so fast that I heard it whooshing in my ears. He was playing one of his games. If I played along, I'd have to do whatever he wanted, just like I had several times already. Despite everything, I felt guilty because I'd been doing it to keep my job here and because I hoped that just maybe it would lead to more. Not because we were meant for each other. This whole time, all I kept thinking about was the financial security someone like him could offer me and all the choices it would give me in life. But then I realised, nothing was worth the kind of pain he inflicted on me. I was wrong about whether I could handle it. I couldn't. It was time to drop the ruse, to stop leading him on.

"I should go back to my room. Mrs Huxley—"

"Isn't expecting you for an hour," he pointed out. His smile was unpleasantly toothy, with eyes that flashed underneath the chandelier. He reminded me of a cat about to pounce. "Come on. I'm not taking no for an answer."

Common sense fought with the instinct to flee. Violence happened to other people and not at the hands of someone you trust. Didn't it? I wasn't walking down an alleyway at night; I was with my boss's son. So why did I feel afraid? The problem with people is we don't imagine danger around the corner. We never expect to be the person targeted by a terrorist or a violent criminal or to be hit by a car. That's what we see on the news, and it always happens to *them*. We have such narrow views of what peril is and who experiences it. Drunk women alone at night. Gang members dealing drugs. The unfortunate people born into a turbulent, war-torn country.

Even though I was afraid of him in that moment, I still walked with him because—despite the warning signs—I didn't expect anything bad to happen to me. I should've ran.

He took me to the north wing. He'd taken me there before and told me about how he and his wife would live there together once it was renovated. I'd often wondered if his honeyed words were a ploy to keep me expecting him to fall in love with me. Perhaps I thought I could win him around in that moment and somehow end up being that wife in the north wing with all the money in the world.

I noticed that the sky was cloudless as he walked me through the great hallway. Craning my neck, I saw the tint of dark blue turning day into night. He walked so quickly that I almost tripped two or three times, and on occasion, he put his hand on my elbow to steady me. A firm hand.

Why was he walking so fast? Why was he so eager? It seemed as though he had something planned for me in the north wing, but he'd also opened the music room door as normal, ready to start his practice. Had the walk been part of his plan all along? Or was this truly a spontaneous decision? Several times I opened my mouth to ask, but fear stopped me. And then my mind would try to reassure my heart by telling it there was a rational explanation for his erratic behaviour. Then my spine would come into play, trying to get me to speak up. I finally did as he unlocked the door.

"Why have we come here?" I asked.

"I want to show you something."

"You know," I said, "I'm not sure I want to go in there tonight."

"Why's that?"

"I'm feeling a bit off it. I think I'm coming down with a cold. Maybe I should head back now and get an aspirin from Mrs Huxley."

He took my face in both his hands. "Five minutes. I promise. It's worth it. Will you stop being so nervous? This is a nice surprise. I promise."

Some of the tension worked its way out of my taut muscles. He was smiling now. A proper smile that reached his eyes. I nodded my head and followed him through. At first he seemed as though he was going to close the door behind us, but I hesitated long enough to force him to go ahead. I'd had a horrible feeling he was going to lock us in at first, and I wanted to make sure he didn't.

When we turned the corner into the large rooms, the sound of music took me by surprise. Debussy played in the background. My favourite. He saw my head lift and he laughed.

"I told you it was going to be a nice surprise."

"You did," I said. "I'm sorry."

"Will you relax now?"

I threaded my arm through his, leaning into his side. "Yes."

"Good girl."

We walked like that, arm in arm, through the north wing while he recited some of the same things to me as last time. About which rooms will be for children, where he'd entertain, which would be the kitchen, and so on.

"I want to be more self-sufficient than Daddy. I want to be able to cook for myself and for my wife."

Suddenly I couldn't listen to him anymore. I stopped, withdrew my arm and sighed. "Please stop this. Please stop teasing me. We both know that I'm never going to be your wife. You'll marry some young woman with a double-barrelled name who drives a Porsche and went to a private school. Your children will go to Eton and then Oxford and probably run the country someday. My children..." My voice cracked. "Well, they won't do those things. Look, I probably should... Maybe I should just go. I can get a reference from your father and move on. This has been—"

"No," he said. "You're not leaving." He glanced at the final door, and then he grabbed my hand.

When my eyes followed his to the door, a strange sense of coldness washed over my skin, like a wet rag being pulled over the flesh. It took my eyes a moment to understand what I was looking at and why it seemed so out of place. The door was nothing like the others in the north wing. And now everything seemed so obvious. All his chattering about the home he'd build for his family was nothing more than a distraction for what was lying ahead inside that room.

It had a keypad. The door in this abandoned wing of an old house had a keypad. I couldn't think of any decent explanation for why that was possible. And then I saw him watching me, and I saw the mask slip from his face. He knew then that I was no longer able to distract.

"Daddy," he called.

I tried to wrench my arm from his grip. He held me tight with his strong fingers. My jaw dropped. I stared at him, no doubt an incredulous expression on my face, but he didn't relent his grip. My eyes widened, the pain taking me by surprise. Yes, he had been forceful and inflicted some pain here and there as part of his games, but this was different. This vice he had me in was cruel.

And then the door opened. In the doorway stood his father, Lord Howard, tall and imposing, with soft greying hair and those bright blue eyes, filling the space leading into the next room. He glanced coldly at me before turning his hooded eyes to his son.

"Get her in here," he snapped.

"No," I said. "No, I want to go." There were tears in my eyes. I should've listened to my instinct. I should've run away when I had the chance. But now I had a choice. I couldn't let him drag me into that room. God knows what existed behind that door. I didn't know for sure, but I suspected I'd never come back out.

"Stop fighting me, you fool!" He bared his teeth at me. All his pretences faded away, leaving the fundamental essence of him on show. I saw it now, finally. He was a monster.

It was time to fight. I kicked him hard in the crotch, leaned over and bit his wrist, and then spun on my heel to run in the opposite direction. Neither he nor his father reacted quickly enough to grab me.

I careened through the rooms—the nursery, the kitchen, the space for entertaining guests—feeling like a newborn foal not in control of her legs. And yet somehow the momentum, the fear and instinct to flee, got me through to the door I'd made sure stayed open. I heard the clattering footsteps of their pursuit. As fast as I could, I slammed the door behind me and ran back through the hall. What were they going to do to me in there? I thought of the high turnover of maids. Had anyone heard from the maid I replaced? *What did they do to them?* And then the realisation hit me.

I'd been hired for a reason.

I had a troubled background and very few family members who actually gave a shit. They'd chosen me because I was less likely to be noticed if I suddenly disappeared. They could do whatever they wanted here in this enormous house with as much money as they needed at their disposal. I was nothing to them and nothing to the world. *What were they going to do with me?*

I sprinted down the great hallway, past the long stretch of wooden panels and paintings. I wanted to shout for help, but could I trust the rest of the family? What did the women know about their men? Could I trust the staff? My safest option was to get out as fast as I could, run down to Paxby and call the police from there. Though what I would do without any evidence, I didn't know.

When I turned the corner towards the door, I ran so hard into Mrs Huxley that I almost knocked her clean over. However, the tall woman was solid enough to take the blow. Even though she was barely a few years older than me, she had this worldly air about her, and I was relieved to see her. Huxley would know what to do.

She grabbed me by the upper arms and steadied me. By now, I had tears streaming down my cheeks and snot coming from my nose. I struggled to breathe in enough air to tell her what happened.

"They... The north wing."

"Come with me," she said, taking me by the shoulders.

It was a relief to have help. I wanted more than anything to have someone make me feel safe. I smiled at her, but she was so intently focused she didn't return the smile. Then she gripped my shoulders hard and spun me around. With her hands still on me, she walked me back the way I'd come.

"What are you doing?" I twisted my body out of her grip, but she took hold of both elbows, bony fingers digging in hard.

"It'd be easier for you if you didn't fight it," she said. Her eyes dropped to the floor. "Come on."

I made a run for it. I'd hesitated too many times before. But she was between me and the way out, which sent me towards the kitchen. To my surprise, when I tried the door, it was locked. The servants' quarters were never locked. Heavy footsteps thudded behind me. All I could do was sprint up the main staircase. Breathless, I passed the long line of portraits into the first-floor corridor and groped the walls until I found the secret door to the servants' corridor and ran inside.

My heart was a piston, the thumping so loud it frightened me. A tremor vibrated through every muscle in my body as I ran towards the spiral stairs. I could get out through the servants' door as long as it wasn't locked. If it was, I'd break a window. I'd do whatever I needed to do. Behind me, a deep voice yelled at me to stop. Oh, I was a fool. I hadn't believed that I'd be the lady of the house and that I'd give birth to privileged children and buy them horses and watch them grow up in the grounds of a stately home, but I hadn't expected what I should have known—that my life meant so little to them I was the prey in a game they'd honed together. Now I saw what I should've seen before—I could only lose. My heart ached for those who'd gone before me and the ones who would come after. The clues had all been there, and I'd missed each one.

I still wouldn't give up.

Never.

I had someone to fight for.

But he was faster.

He reached me at the top of the stairs, his face flushed bright red. I'd never seen my own fearful expression reflected in someone's eyes before, but there it was. He wrapped his hands around my neck, and when he strained, his face reddened to a deep scarlet and his hair fell forward across the bridge of his nose.

"You couldn't let us have our fun, could you? You just had to wake up the whole house with your antics."

"Please... B—"

"Give up, Emily," he said.

I struggled against his iron grip, but it was worthless. Even with my fingernails digging into his knuckles, he never budged an inch. And as life left my body, he threw me down the stairs.

My body was bruised and broken by the time I landed. I closed my eyes, opened them, saw all three of them looking down at me: Mrs Huxley, Lord Howard... and him. Bertie. Seawater eyes watching me die.

It's funny. I'd thought that I'd see my life flash through my eyes as I died, and some of it did. I saw the people I loved. I saw the beautiful moments that I treasured.

I saw my sister.

I wished she still loved me.

I saw my baby girl. Such a beautiful baby girl.

But then the loudest thought in my head was my name, because I was sure it would soon be forgotten, not just by the people standing over me, but by the world.

Emily.

*Emily.*

*Emi—*

*Em—*

# PART TWO

"Hell is empty, and all the devils are here."
William Shakespeare, *The Tempest*

# CHAPTER FORTY

I read in one of my mother's letters that ghost is another word for maid. No matter how close you believe you are to your family, one day you will mean nothing to them. They will forget your name, forget that you are a person, forget that you have the same wants and needs as everyone else. Sometimes they'll tell you all about themselves, but they won't want to know about you. And when they're done taking from you, you'll be nothing but a husk. An outline against the wall. A ghost in the hallway.

He was already in the music room when I got there. I watched him for a while, standing in the shadows against the wall. He sat down at the long piano stool as always. Him on the left, waiting for me to sit to his right. Those strong fingers lifted the lid and caressed the keys. But he didn't play, not yet.

He had no idea I was there. I thought of what he'd said to me in the cupboard above the stairs, about the power of observation, of voyeurism. I enjoyed it too. But then I breathed in quickly, and he turned to face me. I saw some sort of emotion traverse the glassy surface of his eyes. Not happiness. Desire maybe?

"Ruby," Alex said. "What are you doing lurking over there? Come here and sit with me. I want to teach you."

I did as I was told, as I always did. I sat down, and I allowed him to move my hands over the keys. It was just like every other time with

Alex's strict tutoring and my compliance, only now I was pretending, just like him.

"You know, I don't think I ever told you this, but my father is an excellent pianist," he said.

"Not as good as you though, I bet." I flashed him a grin that I knew would excite him. The kind laced with wickedness that would make him want to play one of his games.

"Yes," he said faintly. "I am better actually. Daddy's too obsessed with Debussy to learn the most challenging pieces. Though I never saw him play when he was young. Maybe he was better then. Anyway, all the men in my family learn some sort of instrument, usually the piano. It's a tradition. My grandfather learned the violin."

"What about the women?" I asked.

He launched softly into my favourite, a delicate Chopin étude. "No traditions there as far as I know. Not many women either. My father had a sister I think, but she died when she was ten."

"What happened?"

"She fell down the stairs."

"Like your mother."

He retracted his fingers from the keys and turned to face me. "Yes. Like her."

"Is there a portrait of her in the dining room?"

"Daddy's little sister?" Alex shrugged. "Maybe."

"When your father played the piano, did he have a page turner like you?"

Alex smiled. "Yes, I remember that the maid would help sometimes."

"Which maid?"

He shook his head. "Oh, many over the years." He reached out and took my hand in his. "Listen, Ruby, I want to take you for a walk."

"I thought you wanted to teach me some more notes." When I caressed the ivory keys, he slapped my hand away. It made me smile, seeing him react. I'd been waiting for that side of him to come out again.

"I've changed my mind. Come on. Let's walk around the grounds."

"All right," I said.

Despite the silence that followed us from room to room, Highwood Hall was not empty. Far from it. The place fermented from its own history. Pale-faced men and women loomed down at me from within their frames on the walls. Ghosts everywhere. As we made our way through the grand hall, past the rooms the Howards used for their living quarters and through to the north wing, I thought of Margot enjoying her last cigarette before bed and Lottie on her phone texting or using TikTok.

The more we moved through the house, the tighter Alex's grip became. I did not remove my hand from his, despite how odd it would have looked to other members of the staff or the household. No, I allowed him to squeeze my fingers as we walked. I knew what I was doing.

But when we approached the dining room, I stopped in my tracks, breathing hard with a fluttering of nerves in my stomach. "I want to see the mural again."

Alex tugged on my hand. "Later."

"Just for a moment," I begged.

He sighed. This was an inconvenience for him, a roadblock to where he wanted to go and what he wanted to do. A man like Alex didn't like to be inconvenienced because he wasn't used to it. And yet, he relented.

"Your aunt might be in here," I said, stepping into the room. He let go of my hand, and I moved both of them behind my back, rubbing the parts that ached from his grip. My heart raced as I paced the perimeter of the room, taking in each of the faces I saw before me.

"One of the cherubs maybe," he said, his voice flat, disinterested. But I noticed his eyes move across to his mother's portrait.

I, however, was drawn to another face on the wall. She had brown hair and brown eyes. She had not been painted large on the wall; she was tucked behind a blond angel and peacock in flight. But her eyes drew me in. Even though I wanted to, I didn't linger. As soon as I was done, I signalled for us to leave. If Alex was suspicious of anything, he didn't show it. But he did take my hand, applying that same pressure to my fingers.

"I love working here, you know," I said. "I've been a maid in many other households, but this is my favourite. The house is so beautiful."

He grunted. He wasn't listening to me at all. I wanted to say more. My mouth longed to open, for words to come tumbling out, for secrets held deep within to finally be released, but I snapped my jaw shut. I watched him walk. I almost stumbled into a door jamb as we approached the north wing from inside Highwood. Even as he reached into his pocket and retrieved his swipe card, he didn't let go of my hand. Instead, he fumbled with it until the door opened, and once we were inside, he manoeuvred around me so he could close the door. Only then did he let me go, and at that point he locked the door behind us.

"What are you doing?" I asked. "Why did you just lock the door?"

"Quiet now." He placed a finger to his lips.

Fear rushed over me like a bucket of freezing cold water. He saw the intention in my eyes before I'd even decided to run. As soon as I tried to spring away from him, he lurched forward, grabbing my waist. I screamed, but he clamped a strong hand over my mouth. Like that, he half dragged me through the rooms he'd promised would be left for his wife. I struggled and squirmed and kicked, and he panted and swore and whispered threats in my ear.

"Listen here, you little cunt." His hot breath hissed against the nape of my neck. "If you don't stop struggling, I'll shut you up for good."

I bit his finger, and he retracted it with a cry. It gave me about a second to try to make a run for it, but before I managed a few paces forward, he grasped hold of my hair and wrenched me back, shoving me as hard as he could so that I went flying, landing in a heap on the cold, hard floor. From there, he took hold of the neck of my tunic and dragged me like a sack of potatoes across the room to a final door.

Once again, he fumbled to open the door one-handed, this time with a keypad. I tried to sink my teeth into his ankle, but he kicked me away. A heel caught me in the mouth. Blood exploded from my mashed lips along with the sudden bloom of pain.

And then the door opened.

In the pitch black, Alex hauled me through the door, swinging it shut and locking it. I was quiet now, and still. I waited, hearing nothing but the panting of my breath. I could tell Alex bided his time. Perhaps he enjoyed these moments of complete control, or perhaps he was waiting for me to lose it, to start screaming for help. Both, I decided. But after a few moments of silence, he switched on a light.

We were in a room as red as the pyjamas I'd seen him wearing the night he was sleepwalking. It was almost an empty room, aside from one bed, a chair, a sink and a toilet. The smell of blood and sweat lingered sourly in the air, but I couldn't be certain whether that came from me.

A chain hung from the centre of the room, and from that chain was a harness. I repressed a shudder, knowing exactly where that harness was going to go.

"Mrs Huxley has cleaned it for you," Alex said. "We're all set for your arrival. I checked it over myself not long ago." He took a tiny remote control and pressed a button. All around us, Chopin played from tiny speakers in the walls. My favourite étude.

"Who am I replacing?" I asked, raising my voice above the music. "Were you coming here when you went through the secret door in your father's office?"

He turned the music down a few bars. "Those are your first questions?" He laughed. "I think you might be my favourite, Ruby. During these past few weeks, I've enjoyed playing with you. I truly believe you actually thrived on our games." He stepped closer to me and forced me to my feet, using one hand on my throat. The sudden pressure made me gasp. "Don't fight me." Then he pulled me into the centre of the room, strapped the harness quickly around my waist, and staggered back, laughter playing on his lips.

No, I hadn't fought him because there was no point now. I was trapped. I was the mouse with its tail caught. The fly in the web. Alex had done this before, and he knew exactly how to manoeuvre me quickly so that I couldn't escape. This was his game after all.

Once I was secured, he frisked me, searching for a mobile phone, but it was back in my room anyway. Then he removed his own phone from the inside of his blazer pocket and made a call.

"It's done. You can come now."

I tested the extent of the chain. It dangled from a rig on the ceiling with the harness around my waist and chest. I couldn't reach the side of the room with Alex and the door. Above me, the ceiling was covered in spotlights, making the room almost unbearably bright, turning the walls into slick blood-coloured rectangles. But my arms were free at least.

"Who did you call?" I asked. My eyes roamed the walls, checking every inch. They were so bare it was hard to look at them. I tried not to think about what might've happened in those rooms. Part of me wanted to sit down at least, and the bed looked inviting, but yet again, I couldn't bring myself to look at it, let alone touch it. "What are you going to do with me?"

Alex removed his blazer and tidily arranged it over the back of the chair. Then he pulled the chair into the corner of the room and sat down. He had the appearance of a man at a business meeting, waiting to negotiate a deal.

"Whatever we want to do with you," he said.

I nodded my head. "I thought so."

"Are you afraid?" His head cocked to one side as he tried to figure me out.

I answered honestly. "I have been for a while."

"And yet you didn't leave."

"Who killed Roisin, Alex? Did she learn too much? Was she too close? Why didn't she end up in here?"

"Roisin killed herself," he said. His response made my blood boil. Even now, after allowing his mask to slip, he couldn't tell me the truth.

There were footsteps in the distance. Someone had entered the wing. I wasn't stupid. I knew who it would be.

"Alex," I said. "Can you turn the music off please?"

He grinned. "Fine."

"And then will you look under the bed?"

He scoffed. "I'm not falling for that. What are you going to do? Try to choke me?"

"No," I said gently. "I promise I won't."

His eyebrows bunched together, and his head turned slightly towards the bed. Mine did too so that I could see the edge of the box peeking out below the hanging duvet. He frowned and clicked a button on the remote. I could tell he hadn't expected to see anything beneath the bed. He'd thought I was bluffing, but I wasn't.

"Maybe you should see what it is," I said. "It might be of interest to you."

His expression said *what the fuck*, and a delicious smile of satisfaction spread across my lips. He hurried over to the bed, one eye on me at all times. *He's afraid of me*, I thought. Then he dropped to his knees, grabbed the box, and took it back to his chair.

When he pulled on the bow, the front flap opened to reveal the diorama inside. It had been perfectly arranged with blood-red walls and a chain hanging down from the centre of the room. A man stood slightly off centre, wearing a shirt and jeans, the shirtsleeves rolled to the elbows. In the corner of the room a younger man lounged in an armchair with one leg crossed over the other. His arms dangled nonchalantly over the arm of the chair. Two small, piercing blue eyes, the colour of the deepest ocean, had been expertly painted on the doll's face.

"You like to watch, Alex, don't you?" I asked.

The door opened.

# CHAPTER FORTY-TWO

D*ear David,*

*THIS MUST BE strange for you to hear from me. We didn't end things on great terms, did we? And look, I want you to know that when you're clean, I'll let you see Ruby again, I promise. But right now I can't allow it to happen. She needs stability in her life. Why do you think I left her with Josephine? I can't provide her that stability, and I know you can't either. It's for the best. At least that's what I keep telling myself. That everything will work out fine.*

*I miss Ruby so much. I miss her smell and the way she wraps her tiny fist around my finger. I can't stand working here and not being able to see her, but it's so much more money than working in York. If I can just stick it out for at least six months, I'll be able to save up a deposit for a flat and move back. Have you been able to save anything? Look, I don't want to pressure you, but Ruby is your daughter too. If you can get your act together and find a job, please, David, I want Ruby to have the best start in life, and right now we're failing her.*

*Josephine is so mad at me for leaving. She hangs up the phone when I call and won't reply to my letters. I can't call very often because I never have credit on my phone and the housekeeper here only lets me call twice a* week. She says that outside distractions are bad for you. What does she know? She has no life. She's barely older than me, but she acts like she's fifty. And she calls herself Mrs Huxley when I'm convinced there's no Mr Huxley. It's some weird affectation.

You know, I think there's something wrong with Highwood Hall. Things are strange here. All the staff say the north wing is haunted, and sometimes I could honestly swear that I hear noises coming from that part of the house. But it's impossible, isn't it? The place gives me the creeps. I've never known anyone so stern as Mrs Huxley. Last night I went to the kitchen to get a glass of water, and I think I heard her crying in her room. God, this place... I can't wait to leave.

I feel like a ghost stalking the walls. When I'm in a room, the Howards ignore me as though I'm a piece of furniture. We shouldn't be known as maids; we should be called ghosts because that's what we are.

At least the boss's son likes me. Bertie's kind to me, and we spend a lot of time together. Maybe... maybe if we fell in love, he'd be able to provide for me. Someone needs to, David. I know you won't like hearing that, but it's true.

Anyway, sorry, I'm rambling. I just wanted to write to you and let you know that I won't be staying here forever. I want to build a new life for me and Ruby, and I hope you might be part of that too. It's nice to write to someone. Please reply. This place can make you feel so alone at times.

Tell Josephine I'll call her, and she can't hang up next time. I know she's mad about looking after the baby, but she can afford childcare and I can't. I'll be back soon. I promise.

And, David, if you can spare some child support... please. I don't want to stay here. I want to be with my Ruby.


EMILY


𝄞


DAVID,


.   .   .

*Well, you never wrote to me. I waited for weeks and heard nothing. That's nearly three months without hearing from anyone I know. Not Josephine, not you. I haven't heard my baby gurgle or cry, and I haven't smelled her beautiful head for so long. At night I cry myself to sleep and then I dream about her.*

*This place still doesn't feel right. I don't like the way Lord Howard looks at me, like I'm a prize, or something to hunt. I want to leave, but if I can stick it out just a couple more months, I'll have the deposit I need and then I can take Ruby back. I wish Josephine would talk to me.*

*Remember what I said in my last letter? About Bertie and how he could provide for us? Well, I don't think that's going to happen. He's a user. He just wants me to play these little sadistic games of his. He always asks me "Do you trust me" and I say yes, but I wouldn't trust him as far as I could throw him. I'm losing my resolve, David; every day I feel it slipping away. I want to run away from everything, my whole life. Maybe I should. I don't know. And then I start thinking that Ruby is better off without me, and then I slip into this fog that I can't explain. If it wasn't for Mrs Huxley and this job, I don't know if I'd get out of bed in the morning. I feel terrible, like there's no point in me existing.*

*Write to me. I'm so mad at you and Josephine for cutting me off. Don't leave me out here on my own. Please. I need someone, or I think I might end up being lost. Please. I'm so alone. This house scares me, and I'm so alone.*

*Oh God, those awful thoughts. How could I think about leaving my baby? But I want to run away from Highwood and I have nowhere to go. Maybe I could start a new life, be a different person. Find a husband and have a planned child instead. Maybe then I'd be a good mother, not like now.*

*Fuck, I didn't mean that. I swear, I didn't. I love Ruby more than life. I wouldn't leave her.*

*But I dream about it too, you know. I do.*

*Write to me or I'll never speak to you again.*

*Emily*

# CHAPTER FORTY-THREE

I'd had my suspicions for a long time, but now it was time to confirm them. Unfortunately, I hadn't found anything incriminating in Lord Bertie's office, and I knew I needed to know the full truth before I did anything about it. Women had a habit of dying at Highwood Hall, and it was time to break that cycle.

You see, it had all started a few years ago when I went to visit my father. I went because I wanted to know him but also because I wanted answers. My mother hadn't been seen by anyone since I was six months old. That was when she came to Highwood Hall to work as a maid. She was here for just over three months, and then she left a note saying she couldn't cope with her responsibilities any longer and vanished.

Dad filled in the gaps Aunt Josephine had left out over the years. He gave me Mum's letters from when she worked here, and I'd read them so many times that I sometimes felt like I'd become her, walking these halls, cleaning these rooms.

She worked here before Lord Bertie became a lord, and in her letters, she said they spent time together. I'd speculated that they'd had a relationship. My mother also mentioned that Highwood Hall frightened her. What had happened to her here? The very first letter she sent sounded as though she was building a future for herself, not preparing to abandon it altogether. And why did history keep repeating itself? Maids had a habit of leaving suddenly, like Chloe.

The Howards hired parentless, rudderless young women for a

reason. They chose girls who would not be missed, who could be considered flighty. This was a pattern. An awful, disgusting pattern. I was sure it involved Lord Bertie, that his misconduct forced those girls out of a job, and I knew one person to ask. Mrs Huxley.

"I think you know why I'm here," I said.

After the first whisky, she poured herself a second and shook her head. "You don't want to know. Trust me. If you have anything between your ears, you'll get out now and never look back. You should've left the first day after that box arrived."

"No," I said. "I'm not leaving until I have all the answers. I know about your son in the care home. I think Lord Bertie killed Roisin. And I don't think it's the first time he's killed someone, is it?" I gazed at the empty tumbler on the desk. My heart raced as quickly as the tempo of the music. This was a risk, going to her. She was an agent for him—I was sure of it—and yet, I had a feeling... a misguided one, but nonetheless it was a feeling that I could appeal to her humanity. I knew it was in there even if it was buried deep. "The box you sent to yourself threw me off at first, but then I realised what you were doing. You sent that diorama to me to frighten me away, didn't you? If you're threatening them, you're sick of whatever it is they make you do. But you're also stuck. That care home must be expensive. Is Lord Bertie paying for it in exchange for your silence?"

Her eyes widened, expanding until two saucers stared at me in the low light of the room. Her jaw hung loose for a second, but every other muscle in her body appeared to be drawn tight. She downed the last dregs of her drink.

"Don't say another word," she said, turning the music up a few more bars.

"Has he bugged your room? Are they listening?" I kept my voice low.

"I don't know." She frowned and stood. Her eyes trailed the corners. I saw them flick over to the secret door. She paced the room with her arms folded across her chest.

"He uses the corridor to come and visit you," I said.

She nodded.

"Your son. Is he also Lord Bertie's son?"

She stopped pacing. Her sharp face turned to me.

Of course he was. That was just one of the reasons why Mrs Huxley had remained so loyal all these years. But I wondered when their relationship had turned sour. If Lord Bertie was anything like his son, domination and control excited him, not love and compassion.

"Did he kill his wife?" I asked, again keeping my voice low.

Mrs Huxley's face screwed up for a moment. And then she nodded slightly.

Tears flooded my eyes. "Roisin?"

This time when she looked at me, her face had softened. "I don't know. It's possible."

"They were in a relationship."

"I know they were," Huxley replied.

I walked over to her, taking her by the arms. She recoiled for a moment, and I felt her rigid body beneath my grip. "Tell me everything."

"I can't." Her eyes were wet. She shook her head so quickly, it had a manic quality. "I can't tell anyone."

"But you want to. I *know* you do. You've had enough of working for them. Haven't you? You're sick of doing their dirty work and letting them get away with whatever they want. I can help you stop them."

She pulled herself out of my grip. "I knew you were trouble as soon as you arrived here. Bertie couldn't see it, but I did. Your surname is different, isn't it? But you are the spitting image of her."

"You remember her?"

"Of course I do," she snapped. "All their faces are imprinted on my mind. I can't forget even if I wanted to."

*All their faces.* I stared over at the diorama, and a chill spread over my body. "How many?"

She closed her eyes, letting out a shaky breath. "I'm tired. I'm so tired."

"The women on the dining room wall." My stomach lurched. I wanted to throw up on the carpet. "That face, the one I thought looked like me. It's my mother, isn't it?"

"Yes."

"We have to stop them. You need to tell me. Tell me everything!"

She slumped back into her chair. "What you're asking me to do is turn myself in. You have no idea what I've done. You have no idea. Your mother, she was one of the first ones they... It was the last Lord Howard who controlled everything back then. Bertie was in his late twenties and... Well, let's just say he was already a monster. I think he came out of the womb like that. I swear I didn't know the extent of what was happening, but even if I did... I don't know if I could've stopped it." Her eyes glazed over; she was lost to the past. "I was pregnant, and I loved him. I helped him. And then... Suddenly I was part of it. When Charlie came along, I tried to get out. I even lived with him in the village for a time, but Bertie wanted me back. Charlie needed special care that I couldn't afford and it *trapped* me here."

"Tell me what happened to my mother. Please. I need to know. I grew up believing that she'd abandoned me."

"She used to talk about her baby all the time. She showed me pictures. I fell pregnant with Charlie not long after she arrived so I enjoyed seeing them." She sniffed. "Bertie told me that she'd been telling lies about him and that she was unhinged. He told me she'd try to run away, and if she did, I was supposed to make sure she went back to him. And I did. I saw her running away, saying crazy things about him trying to hurt her, and I led her straight back to him."

"Then what happened?"

"She fell down the stairs," the housekeeper said. "Which is half-true. I believed it at first. By the time I reached her, she was at the bottom of the staircase and Bertie was at the top. He told me she'd tripped and fallen."

"Which staircase?"

"The spiral staircase."

"So that's why you sent me that diorama. It wasn't me after all; it was my mother." My stomach and chest cramped with a sudden, intense ache. I leaned forward, placing my head in my hands. "You're as sick as them."

She shook her head slowly. "You don't know how sick they are yet."

I paused. I needed a moment to breathe. "Do you make them? The boxes?"

She shook her head. "Bertie chose you from the beginning you know. Providence sent over your details. I saw a photograph of you included in the file, and I knew then who you were. I made a choice. For the first time, I didn't warn him. And then I took the photograph to someone..." She drifted off.

"Why didn't you warn him?"

She poured another whisky. I worried she'd pass out before I got the whole truth out of her. "I kept more from him than the dioramas. A diagnosis." She slugged the shot of liquor. "I don't have much time left. All I can do is salvage the mess I've made. And yet... Well. I've already made a mess of *that* too. I thought to myself if I could save one, *just one*, then I'd done something good. But then I thought, what if I scared all of them? Margot and that brat, Lottie, and... him."

"Lord Bertie?"

"Yes. I've come to hate them quite a lot."

"So, the boxes were your revenge?"

She shrugged. "I suppose you could call it that. I sent the first one and... Well, I got a little power back that day. Have you ever felt completely powerless?"

I sighed in frustration, confused and disappointed by her ramblings. "Mrs Huxley, please tell me what they've done. Tell me how to stop it."

"You have to make a promise to me first." I noticed a little of the old steel coming back into her dark eyes. She lifted her chin, an unsmiling face regarding me coldly.

"What is it?"

"I've managed to save money for my son. You see, I've thought about it a lot, what will happen when I die or go to prison, whichever comes first. He won't understand. One day I'll just stop going to visit him, and he won't understand why." The tears finally fell from her eyes. She had a heart. I wondered what her life would've been without the Howards in it. "I have enough money saved for Charlie to stay in Heather Grove for another few years, but after that, it dries up. His needs are complex. He could maybe live outside the home, but I worry it wouldn't be what's best for him. He's *happy* there. It's his home and I can't stand the thought of him losing it. If I do as you ask and tell the police everything, then Bertie will go to prison. I need another source."

"Who?"

"She has a soft spot for you. It happens on occasion. She's as stuck as I am, you see. She knows who Bertie is, and she knows what he did to her daughter, but she's too old and frail to do anything about it. She stays to make sure nothing happens to Lottie."

"Margot."

"You have to promise me that you'll go to her."

"I will."

"And you have to promise that you'll visit Charlie every Sunday."

"I will."

Her chin wobbled as she continued. "And you have to promise me we'll finish this once and for all. I can't start anything that will fail. I've brought you in now. I've trusted you. It's time for you to take this... this weight from my hands and make sure it ends." She closed and unclosed her fists in front of her body, as though handing the metaphorical weight to me.

"I promise."

I saw her swallow the rest of her tears, controlling the spasm working its way across her face, and I saw the determination flood back into her. "All right then. I'll tell you everything I know. But I don't think we can do this alone."

"That's okay," I said. "I know someone who will help us."

She nodded. "Well then. The first thing you need to know is that Lord Bertie is a serial killer, and Alex isn't much better."

# CHAPTER FORTY-FOUR

L ord Bertie entered the red room first, but Ade was close behind
him, a shotgun jammed into Bertie's lower back. I'd never seen
such rage on another person's face before, but it was there, red
and ugly like a screaming newborn. The man once in control of everything at Highwood Hall had finally lost his grip on it all.

"Alex, restrain this idiot behind me, won't you?" Bertie
commanded.

But Alex was still too distracted by the diorama. Ade retracted the
gun, turned it over in his hands and hit the lord squarely in the spine
using the butt of the rifle. Bertie crumpled to the floor with a gasp,
suddenly appearing his age for once.

"Have you any idea what you're doing? All of you?" The smooth-
talking, controlling and formerly powerful man writhed on the floor.
He'd been reduced to complaining like a spoilt brat at a disappointing
birthday party.

"Yes," I replied. "We know exactly what we're doing."

Bertie rubbed his back and positioned himself upright. He stared up
at Ade, who had the gun trained on him. I felt terrible for Ade because
I'd sprung my plan on him just a week ago. He wasn't someone used to
fighting, and he certainly had little practice with a shotgun, but he'd
done this for me. I saw the tremor running up and down his arms, and I
hoped he wouldn't have to pull the trigger.

"How the hell did this gardener jump me in my own office or know about the tunnels I expressly keep to myself? And the code to the damn door too. What the fuck is going on?" Bertie sat at an odd angle, one hand on his injury.

I answered for Ade. "I found the entrance to one of the secret corridors in the wine cellar. And then, when I hid under your desk, I heard Alex use another secret door in your office. The rest we had help for. Oh, and the code for the door is 1603, the date you killed my mother."

That brought Bertie's attention back to me. His eyes widened in surprise, and for the first time, recognition swept over him.

"That's right," I said. "Emily Ferguson. I took my aunt's married name as a child. I was worried you might recognise me when I came for the job interview, but you never did. You groomed her, like Alex has been grooming me, playing piano for her, building up her trust. And then you tried to bring her here. She was supposed to be killed in this room, wasn't she? But she ran away, and you pushed her down the stairs. That was the day you decided never to slip up again. And from then on, you never have. Who built this place? Was it your father?"

Alex dropped the diorama to the floor. His arms and jaw appeared slack, but he turned to me, and I recognised the same glint in his eyes that I'd seen when we played our games. That day cramped up in the cupboard together when I'd met his challenge. When I'd backed into the priest hole. The way I always answered no when he asked *Do you trust me?*

When Bertie refused to answer, I addressed Alex instead. "Who built this place?"

Alex simply shrugged. "Perhaps we found it. And maybe, just maybe, you lost your marbles, tried to kill us, and had to be detained here while we called the police. Or maybe you and the gardener are trying to steal from us. I managed to lock you in here, but then he came in with a gun and we had to shoot him. It was self-defence."

I ignored his fabrications. "How many girls have you kept in here? What do you do to them?"

Neither of the men answered.

"You're rich, Lord Howard," I said. "You had a beautiful wife, and I'm sure you, Alex, have had many beautiful girlfriends. But that wasn't enough for either of you. You need complete control. Both of you. You need to *know* you can get away with whatever you want. Right? Otherwise, what's the point?"

"You have no proof of anything," Bertie said. "You'd may as well give up now before either of you get in trouble. I tell you what, I'll even unchain you right now and let you both go. There'll be no contacting the police. You both get to live. Perhaps we'll give you... a severance package for your hard work at Highwood Hall. As a thank you."

His smile was sardonic, and for a moment, jarring. I'd known Bertie as the attractive older boss who cracked a dad joke every now and then, petting his Labrador as he chit-chatted. But here he was, in his true form. Here he was, the serial killer.

"No," I said.

"No?" He laughed. "You do realise that I know the chief of police, not just in Yorkshire, but in England. We went to school together. What do you think will happen next, maid? Do you think you'll win? Are you that delusional, girl?"

"I think you'll go to prison for murdering not just my mother but for killing your wife, probably your sister, Roisin, and what, a dozen maids? How many have you killed, Lord Howard?"

"That's a very imaginative story," he said. Slowly Bertie climbed to his feet. He stepped closer to me, somewhat unsteadily.

Ade's eyes widened in fear, but I nodded to say I'd be okay.

"You have no proof," he repeated. "I already told you that."

"I have Mrs Huxley."

For the first time I saw him falter. He stopped, an arm's length away from me, and then the anger rippled across his face. He grimaced, grabbing me by the jaw, those strong fingers digging into my flesh.

Ade raised the gun. "Let her go."

Bertie tugged me higher and higher until I had to stand on my tiptoes. My neck stretched, my eyes watered, and I emitted a high-pitched squeal of pain. But inside, I prayed Ade didn't shoot. It wasn't time. We needed them to stay alive so they'd pay for their crimes. After a long few seconds, he finally released me. My heels hit the floor and I whimpered.

"Stupid child," Bertie muttered, shaking his head. He saw the diorama lying on the ground, lifted his foot and smashed it.

"I'm not stupid," I said. "And I do have proof. Mrs Huxley is at the police station right now."

"Doesn't matter," he said. "They won't believe you. By the time they get a warrant, we'll have you both gone and this place will be transformed. No one will ever know, and they certainly won't believe a freak like her."

"But they won't just have to believe her," I said. "There's more evidence than that."

Alex and Bertie exchanged glances. I saw the cogs of their minds working. What did I know? What had they forgotten?

"The dining room," I said. "You were brazen enough to paint the faces of your victims on the walls. I saw my mother's face on there the first day I arrived."

Bertie started to laugh. "That can easily be denied. Most of the paintings aren't even a decent likeness."

"That's true," I said. "Seeing as you didn't even recognise me when I came for my interview. But there's more."

He rolled his eyes. "This is getting ridiculous." When Bertie lunged towards the door, Ade quickly caught him on the jaw with the butt of his gun. The lord staggered back, almost falling on top of his son.

I was afraid of them both attacking Ade at once, but Alex seemed to be stuck in some sort of trance.

"More evidence in my favour," Bertie said. "Showing what a savage animal your gardener is."

I kept an eye on Ade, trying to show through my face to keep him calm. This was almost over. Almost.

"What other evidence do you have?" Alex said, breaking his silence.

I lifted my head to the ceiling. "There are ten webcams hidden in the lights above our heads. All of them are live-streaming everything happening in this room. Ade is using his YouTube channel and Facebook page to host the stream. They are motion detected. As soon as Alex pushed me into this room and chained me up, it went live. There are also microphones hidden all over. There's one by the chair, one in the bed, and one above the door. You can't get away with this, because everything you've done and said has been seen by thousands of people on the internet."

The blood drained from Bertie's face, leaving him ashen. "We'll say you doctored the videos."

"Fine," I said. "But Mrs Huxley's testimony backs up our claims."

"This is just a play. It's a movie." Bertie clapped his hands and laughed. "It's a fake. It's all fake."

"The photographs you took of the girls you murdered have been delivered to the police," I said. "Mrs Huxley has them in her possession."

I saw him turn towards me, eyes ferocious, spittle flying from his mouth, but Alex moved faster. The Howard heir sped from his chair, punched in a number on the keypad, and sprinted away while Ade was preoccupied with Bertie's attempt to hurt me. By the time Ade had wrestled Bertie away from me, Alex was gone.

# CHAPTER FORTY-FIVE

A de had Bertie on the ground, but Bertie's hands were on the gun. He was a strong man for his age, not someone easily beaten in a fight. I yanked the chains, unable to do anything but watch. My chest tightened, stomach clenched, heart pounded, my whole body consumed by the unbearable grip of terror. Oh God, we were going to lose this. I pulled against my chain, stretching it to the max, fingers reaching as far as I could. I was going to lose Ade. This couldn't be happening.

When Bertie snatched the gun to the right, Ade clung on, but it tugged him sideways, giving Bertie some space to wiggle out of Ade's grip. On his way out, he kicked Ade hard in the side and I heard Ade grunt in pain. The gun fell from his grasp, and I held my breath. Both men charged for it. Ade was closer, but he was unbalanced. I heard him collide with the hard floor, his shoulder crunching. Ade's fingers were a hair's breadth from the weapon with Bertie landing on his knees, throwing his weight forwards. He grabbed Ade by the forehead, trying to yank him away. My knuckles turned white as I clenched the chains inside my fists, fingers tightening harder and harder. I imagined them wrapped around the barrel of the gun, having the power within my grasp. But everything rested on Ade now. I prayed for Ade to reach it first, but Bertie snatched it from his grasp, Bertie had the determination and speed.

I couldn't let that happen.

"I know about your son," I yelled. "I know Mrs Huxley had your baby and that he's stuck in a care home."

It didn't work. He didn't care enough for it to surprise him. Lord Bertie reached the gun first. He lifted it. And yet Ade was the one who delivered the next blow, the one that caught Bertie off guard. Ade rammed his thumbs into Bertie's eyes, and when the man cried out in pain as he fell backwards, Ade grasped hold of the weapon, wrestled it from Bertie's grip, and stumbled back. I saw him wince in pain as he rested the butt against his shoulder.

"Ade, don't!" I cried as the air exploded from the *crack*.

Ade staggered back from the recoil, his face wide open with shock. Slowly, he lifted his gaze from the bleeding man on the ground, to me in the centre of the room. Beneath him, Lord Bertie slithered and twisted in a pool of his own blood. Ade had shot him in the knee, leaving a gaping, throbbing gash through his ripped jeans. Bertie turned to us with the whites of his eyes gleaming, a look of pathetic desperation on his face. He shrieked, clutching the wound, his voice thin and high-pitched.

I ignored his cries of pain and looked at Ade. "See if he has keys for the chain. No, wait, give me the gun first."

Ade nodded his head. He needed both his hands to find the keys. I glanced over at Lord Bertie one more time, but the sight of his bloody, malformed leg made me dry heave. Ade passed me the heavy, cumbersome weapon. With it in my grasp, I convinced myself that all I needed to do was look like I could fire the gun if I needed to.

While Ade rummaged through Bertie's pockets, I listened, waiting for sirens. I couldn't be sure, but it was possible the room had been soundproofed. Some of the staff had heard things coming from the north wing, but not enough noise for any of them to suspect women were murdered in here.

We needed the police now, and that part of the plan hinged on Mrs Huxley holding her end of the bargain. I'd woken up that morning with a belly full of nerves, but I'd been sure that she'd help us. She was dying no matter what, and there was Charlie to consider. But she had to come through for us. Alex was loose, and we were in danger.

When Mrs Huxley told me what happened to the maids, she'd told me the date Alex had chosen to introduce me to the north wing. From there, we'd planned the entire operation. From buying the cameras with Ade to hiding Mrs Huxley's last diorama. Mrs Huxley knew the code to the door because when the girls were trapped in this room, she was the one who brought them meals.

We'd agreed that as soon as I went to the music room, Mrs Huxley would get in a taxi and go to the police station. Meanwhile, I'd allow myself to be chained up and try to make Alex confess. Then Ade surprised Bertie with the shotgun when he was in his office, forcing him to take them through the secret door tunnel to the north wing.

But what if the police refused to believe Mrs Huxley? What if the live stream failed? We'd tested the room. We knew the signal was strong enough, but sometimes those things lost connection anyway. I'd prepared myself to be chained up, but I hadn't expected how terrifying it'd been in reality, and yes, it had felt strong and powerful to deliver the diorama to Alex, but part of me had worried that he'd turn around and kill me right then and there.

We'd tried to think of a way to make this watertight. To hold them accountable at the highest level, and the best solution we could think of was trial by public opinion. Not being believed by the police was my main concern. Huxley had taken the photographs in case they didn't believe her, but it was still a crazy story, and the Howards were rich and powerful enough to give your average police officer pause.

Ade stepped away from the screeching Bertie. "I can't find any keys."

"Try the table over there," I said.

I held my breath as Ade opened the top table drawer. If Alex had taken them with him, we were in trouble. Losing Alex was an issue. We'd thought the gun would be enough to keep them both under control until the police arrived, but we hadn't banked on Bertie's pure rage or Alex being quick enough to sprint out of the room.

"I've got them," Ade said.

Relief flooded through me. "Have you checked the stream? Is it working? Have we done it?"

"I checked it when you got here with Alex." He fumbled with the keys as he unlocked me. We were both running on adrenaline. I could feel it. "Everything was fine then."

"Okay." Finally free, the chains clattered to the floor. I stepped over to Bertie with the gun raised. "What did you do to Roisin?"

He was close to passing out. His skin had taken on that sickly, waxy appearance of someone in the throes of sickness, and his eyes glazed over. Perhaps he was dying. His blood pooled beneath my feet, but I couldn't bring myself to help him.

"She killed herself."

"You're lying," I said. "Tell me."

But he simply stared at the ground.

"He won't admit it," Ade said. "He'd rather die. Come on, we need to get out of here."

"We need to find Alex," I said.

Ade paused before he nodded. I could tell by Ade's hesitation that he wanted us to get to safety, but I wanted Alex to face up to his crimes too. I needed to find him.

We hurried through the north wing and out of the main house. I was convinced Alex would head to the garage, get in his Ferrari and drive to an airport. For all we knew, they had a contingency plan in place for the day they were caught. A stash of money hidden in a safe, fake passports and a private plane waiting to take them to South America or Russia or a distant Caribbean Island. I couldn't stand the thought of it, the injustice.

Perhaps I should call this what it was. Revenge. Slipping from my fingers.

I handed Ade the gun, seeing as he could actually fire it, whereas I wasn't so sure, and together we circumnavigated the perimeter of the hall. I left bloody marks on the gravel path while Ade's jeans were splattered with the gristle of Bertie's knee. With each step, I prayed for the sound of sirens. The world stayed silent.

We walked towards the Howards' garage, both quiet, both aware that things weren't going well.

Sitting on a sun lounger in the middle of the lawn was Margot. She had a cigarette between her fingers and a bright pink turban covering her hair. She wore a cashmere wrap around her shoulders and didn't appear to give two hoots that the sun had set. When she saw me, she waved a hand.

"Could I have a martini please, dear?"

"Not right now, Margot," I called back.

And then I held my breath. Would she notice the gun, my dishevelled appearance, the blood trailing my footsteps, Ade's slight hunch from where he hurt his shoulder? The sky darkened around us. Margot's eyesight might not have been the best, but there were security lights above us. Sure enough, she slipped her reading glasses down her nose, and then she dropped her cigarette on the grass. I noticed her sit up straight and stare at us as we walked away from her.

"She's going to call the police," I said.

"Fine," Ade replied. "Let them come. We have the upper hand here. We're not weirdo serial killers."

"You're right," I said, exhaling slowly.

"Are they dead?" Margot called after us.

I turned to her then. "Alex got away." There was a chance Bertie had died by then, but I didn't say that out loud.

She nodded. "You'd better find him before he finds you, dear." And then she picked up her cigarette and took a long drag.

# CHAPTER FORTY-SIX

By the time we reached the garage, Alex's Ferrari was gone. My fears had been realised, and some of the air left my lungs. We turned around and started walking back to the hall, when the sirens finally screeched in the distance. Silently, I let us back into the hall, pressing the button on the intercom system to open the gate. We walked back out onto the drive to greet them, exhausted yet glad it was over. But my relief was short-lived when three police officers forced Ade down onto the tarmac.

"Are you kidding me? He's not the one you're looking for!" I shouted. "Didn't you listen? It's Lord Bertie you want. Let him go!"

"He was carrying a weapon." Some gruff, square-jawed officer grunted at me. The shotgun was on the ground, and yet they placed cuffs on Ade's wrists. Somehow I stopped myself from flinging my body at them. "It's just procedure. Calm down please, ma'am."

"I can show you where the actual culprit is," I said through gritted teeth.

Wasting precious minutes, one of the officers stayed with Ade in a police car while I led two uniformed police officers back into the hall.

"Mrs Huxley gave you the evidence you needed?" I asked, holding open a door.

"We can't discuss the case."

"She must have, or you wouldn't be here," I muttered to myself.

I breathed a little lighter after that. Despite everything, which included her part in my mother's murder, I didn't see Mrs Huxley as a psychopath like Bertie. She was a normal human being who'd been stuck in a cycle of terrible, psychological abuse. She was his prisoner just as much as the maids he'd killed. It'd taken a lot for her to break through his control, but she'd done it at last.

"Wait," I said as we passed the dining room. I beckoned the officers inside. "I don't know where they buried the bodies, but these are their trophies." I gestured to the wooden panels, the many angelic faces of the women Bertie and his son—and probably his father too—had murdered over the decades. Who knew how long this tradition had gone on? I thought about what Alex had once said about the men in the family learning an instrument. It was *tradition*. In reality, they used it as a way to groom the maids. And how many generations of Howard men had participated?

I closed my eyes for a couple of breaths, allowing myself a moment to feel the disappointment and disgust that had been building. No, I'd never thought Alex was a decent man, but I had been attracted to him. I'd been *addicted* to him, fascinated even. But he was a monster.

I opened my eyes. There she was. She had brown eyes, a wide nose, deep-set eyes and wavy brown hair. She had a serene, peaceful expression on her face, but her death had not been peaceful. My mother. She'd come here six months after giving birth to me, hoping to build a better life for us, but she had never left, and now she was trapped here. The ghost of her, just an outline on a wall.

"When this is over, can I take part of this wall?" I asked, but the officers simply stared at me with a quizzical expression on their faces. "I can't stand to think of her stuck here."

I pictured the diorama Mrs Huxley had sent to herself. The one where she stood outside the hall looking in at all the ghostly faces in the windows. She'd commissioned the diorama herself, and yet it had still shaken her as the package had been delivered. She was the keeper of these souls, and she felt it.

Silently, we left the dining room and continued on to the north wing, making our way through the building site to the hidden red room. Bertie lay unconscious in a pool of his own blood.

Finally the officers saw the room, and they began to understand what was happening. The youngest even turned bright white.

"We need backup," Square Jaw said into his walkie-talkie.

I sat down on the chair Alex had been sitting in and watched as a team of paramedics took Bertie to an ambulance. Other officers started to filter in too. Someone took pictures. Others dusted for prints. At one point, Lottie stood in the doorway, her features frozen, as though she'd donned a tight Halloween mask of her own face. Margot moved out of the shadows and placed an arm around her shoulders, watching as a stretcher moved Lord Bertie out of the forgotten wing.

Everything after happened in a blur. Officers bustled around me. They took pictures of the bruises on my wrists, removed the cameras from the places we'd hidden them in order to examine the footage, and asked me to give a witness statement. Towards the end, Lottie and Margot hovered in the periphery of my vision. Margot's taut face revealed cold rage, but Lottie crumpled inwards, tears running down her nose. She turned away when a police officer pointed out old bloodstains and scuff marks in the corner of the room. For some reason I smiled at Margot, but she walked away.

$\flat$

LATER, in the hospital, I was checked over for any real damage. There were bruises on my wrists and neck. I'd split my lip too, or rather Alex had split it for me. Aside from that, I'd come away lucky. Ade wasn't quite so lucky—he'd fractured his shoulder—but we made jokes together as the nurse put his arm into a sling.

"You know, you're going to have to water the plants for me now," he said. "This is my watering can arm."

"I didn't realise arms had a watering can preference."

"There's a lot to learn about gardening, young grasshopper."

I laughed. "Okay. When are you going to teach me?"

"How about tomorrow?"

"I guess it's better than sleeping at Highwood Hall." As soon as the words escaped my lips, the laughter between us stopped. The world felt very surreal in those moments.

"I can't believe Highwood Hall was my home," I said, shaking my head.

"You can stay with me," he said. "Seriously. For as long as you like. But I'll understand if you want to go and stay with your aunt."

I shrugged. "But then who'd water the plants?"

He smiled. "That's a great point, Rubes."

I'd never much liked it when someone tried to shorten my name and turn it into a nickname, but with him, it was different. I leaned back on the hospital bed, staring up at the lights. But when they reminded me of those bright spotlights in the red room, I shuddered.

"I can't believe I got cuffed," Ade said quietly.

I reached over and held his hand. "I'm sorry. It's not much consolation—or maybe it is, I don't know—but soon the world will know that you're a hero."

He laughed. "Yeah right."

"I mean it," I said. But he shook his head.

I knew what it had taken for Ade to fire that gun. Unlike Bertie or Alex, Ade wasn't the kind of man who sought out violence. But he'd fought for me.

"I just wish we'd forced a confession out of them," Ade said. "For Roisin."

"Me too. And I wish Alex hadn't escaped."

We looked at each other, and he nodded. An unspoken agreement passed between us. I think we both realised at that point we wouldn't be able to stop until Alex was behind bars along with his father. Ade squeezed my hand. We sat there for a moment, dirty, broken and exhausted, until a nurse interrupted us to say we could leave.

"I think we're stronger together," I said after the nurse left. "I think we're safer together."

"I think so too," he said.

Neither of us said anything more, but we both thought it. Alex was still out there, and he had a game to finish.

$\int$

BACK IN PAXBY, in Ade's cottage, I pulled the spare bedding out of his storage cupboard and tucked the sheets around the air mattress. Ade stuffed pillows into the pillowcases. We took turns showering with one of us standing guard outside the door. Ade had insisted on taking the airbed on the floor of his bedroom. He had a spare room, but we wanted to stay in the same room together. I was almost positive that Alex would have left the country by now, because that would be the sensible thing to do, and yet, I still couldn't settle.

Surely a rich sociopath like Alex would value self-preservation above everything else. But perhaps that way of thinking came from a motherless child who knew little more than how to survive her entire life. Another part of me wondered if he'd come back for us. And for as long as those thoughts were on my mind, I would be looking over my shoulder, unable to relax, unable to rest.

I surprised myself by calling Aunty Josephine that night. It was late, and I hadn't expected her to answer. But she had, and she'd listened and cried and apologised as I told her all about what had happened.

"I never knew," she said. "She went early one morning and left a note for me. It didn't say where she was going, but it said not to look for her. And I believed it. I thought... I thought she ran away. Ruby, why didn't you *tell* me you were going to Highwood Hall?"

"I don't know. I guess I didn't want you to stop me doing what I needed to do." I tapped my forefinger against the phone case. There was so much to say, I needed time to collect my thoughts. "I read the letters she sent to Dad. You kept hanging up on her every time she called you. Why wouldn't you speak to her?"

"I was so mad at her," she said. "She'd left me with a baby to take care of. I hadn't finished grieving for my husband, and then I had you to worry about." She sighed. "I'm sorry. I didn't mean it like that, but it was a hard time. I didn't know what I was doing. I was stressed and mad, and I couldn't speak to her. I thought if I refused to talk, she'd come home sooner. Which is... well, stupid. I know that now. We were young, Ruby. I'm so sorry. Not searching for her will forever be the biggest regret of my life. I'm so sorry. I wish your dad had contacted me while she was still at the hall. I didn't know she was in trouble."

"He was in the middle of his addiction at the time," I said. "When I went to see him, he told me that he read the letters again a few years later and barely remembered reading them the first time." We cried together then. Tears dripped down my chin as I thought about poor Emily, my mother, living life as though she'd been forgotten by everyone around her.

"Ruby," Josephine said. "I just searched for your name online, and I think I might have found the video."

"Don't watch it," I warned. "It's... It's not nice."

"Okay," she said. "What's going to happen tomorrow? Your life isn't going to be the same again is it?"

"I know."

Despite feeling the exhaustion right down to the marrow of my bones, Ade and I stayed up late, setting up a website to track potential sightings of Alex. The police had checked airports and put out an alert on his passport. Margot had already told the police that the family didn't own a private plane. They occasionally shared one with the owner of a Premiership football club, but his plane had been in the air at the time without Alex in it.

He was out there somewhere. As we finally gave in to sleep, I thought of him shutting me in the priest's hole. I thought of us pressed up close in the cupboard above the stairs. I'd had no idea then how depraved he and his father were. I thought of him sitting back and watching as his father tortured a young woman.

That night in Huxley's private office, she hadn't held back from the details. I'd reached for a second glass of whisky when she explained to me how Bertie tended to keep the girl locked up a week or longer, depending on whether anyone cared that she'd disappeared. He would take two or three a year, depending on his desires at the time. Chloe had been the last to die in the red room. I made sure of that.

Roisin had never been destined for the red room because she had a family who cared about her. She had parents and friends in Sligo. I still didn't know what had happened to her. But it had to be Bertie. Mrs Huxley suspected that Roisin either became too needy, and he lost his temper, accidentally killing her. Or she uncovered his secret and needed to be killed. Either way, Roisin died because Bertie was a psychopath.

I missed her. My biggest regret was not uncovering what Bertie was doing before she died. Should I have told her that my mother never came home from Highwood Hall? I'd grown so used to keeping my own secrets that I'd failed to let her in. She'd deserved more. From me, from life, from the Howards. I fell asleep, crying softly into Ade's pillow, hoping to at least dream of nothing.

# CHAPTER FORTY-SEVEN

I found a photograph on an online news site of Margot and Lottie walking down the street. Margot in full protective mode, her arm slung over Lottie's shoulder. Typical, right? There were two male serial killers, but the mother-in-law, sister, daughter or whatever gets the attention. I scanned through the article for any mention of Alex. Given his wanted status, several celebrities had come out and condemned Alex and Bertie's crimes, expressing shock that two monsters lived beside them in polite society. To me, it wasn't surprising; to them, their bubble of safety had been burst.

"There are a ton of messages on here," Ade said. "Not many sightings, but I'll forward what we have to that detective from the police station."

I nodded, my body numb. Weirdly, I wanted to go back to Highwood to be where my mother was. Where did they bury her? They had to bury their bodies somewhere. Mrs Huxley hadn't told me that. She said they had a system, and she didn't know what it was.

Would Bertie talk? No. He'd be Ian Brady, always hinting that he knows where the bodies are buried, ensuring a television crew go with him to the moors—or woods or river or wherever they took the maids—to point at different areas, none of which would be right. Maybe he'd use it as a bargaining tool to get a better cell. I paused for a moment to dwell on my bizarre thoughts because they didn't feel real.

Ade came downstairs at that moment and filled up the kettle. On his way past the table, he flicked on the television, and to both our surprise, Pawel's face appeared. In his thick, Eastern European accent, he told them about Roisin and her suspicious death.

"They're reopening the case," Ade said, tapping the volume button. "That's great!"

I nodded. "Yeah, it is."

"You okay?"

I watched the tears glisten in Pawel's eyes and wondered how Roisin's parents were coping. I decided to call them once I'd pulled myself together.

"Yeah. Still processing things. How's your shoulder?"

Ade tapped the top of his sling. "It's actually not that bad. What do you want to eat?"

"I should make it—"

"Hell no." He grinned at me. "You have no idea what kind of magic I can perform one-handed." He tilted his head. "That sounded dirty."

I shook my head, amazed that he could make me laugh despite everything going on and watched him pour oats into a bowl with his healthy arm. He made porridge with honey and two cups of strong tea. But I couldn't finish it. I was... not quite there. Almost, but not quite, and I think Ade saw that.

After breakfast he chatted to me as he tended to the houseplants, telling me which plants needed the most sunlight and water. Every now and then, I helped him spritz palm fronds with water. But I was so distracted that they either ended up soaked or I moved on to the next plant before finishing.

We went into the garden where the sky was blue and the sun was warm, and we watered, deadheaded and pruned. In a baking greenhouse, Ade picked tomatoes for lunch while I held a basket for him, staring out into space and nodding along as he talked. I tried to listen. I tried to keep my eyes focused on him, but my gaze roamed around the garden, searching for danger. For Alex.

He fried up the fresh tomatoes with some bacon and hash browns for lunch, smiling broadly as he handed me my plate. It was piled high with delicious food, but I didn't find any of it appetising at all.

After Ade finished his meal, his dark, sad eyes rested on my hands.

I'd pushed my food around the plate for about ten minutes, hoping he wouldn't notice. "Come on. Eat as much as you can."

"I can't." I leaned my head against a fist, a fork hanging loosely from my fingers. "My stomach's in knots."

"I know," he said. "I don't feel much better."

"He's still out there."

His voice was soft. "I know. Hey, you're in shock. Take it steady. This will take some time to get over, but you will, and I will. You saved a lot of people's lives." He put his fork down, squirming in his chair. "Look, this is sappy as all hell, but you should know how fucking brave it was to do what you did."

I shook my head and made a scoffing sound. "No way. You were the brave one."

"Ruby, you offered yourself up as bait. To a serial killer."

Alex's face appeared on the television and I flinched. He stood proudly in his cap and gown, Bertie smiling next to him. The ivy-clad walls of a university behind them. He was so handsome with those perfect white teeth and piercing blue eyes.

"You were right about his smile," I said. "It doesn't reach his eyes."

"I'll turn it off." Ade adjusted himself to stand, but I stopped him.

"No, we should keep it on so that we know when he's found."

"Okay."

The report mentioned finding Alex's Ferrari dumped in Edinburgh, just outside the city. We watched in silence, both of us stiff as two boards, bated breath trapped in our lungs. But there were no other leads. Alex hadn't been sighted near his car. No one had been found with it.

"Christ, he must've floored that thing all night," Ade said. "You reckon he's trying to leave the country?"

"I guess I would if I were him."

Ade nodded. Once the report was over, he turned the TV off. "I'm surprised they found it. I thought the Howards would have some sort of apocalypse bunker nearby. You know, with a garage for sports cars and a decade's worth of tinned food. Guns lining the walls and hazmat suits."

"Rich people." I smiled before reality hit me again. "I still can't believe what we did. I can't believe it worked."

"It did."

"Except for Alex." I sighed, deciding to force down some food. I jabbed a tomato and popped it into my mouth, chewing quickly, afraid I'd spit it out. "Please tell me they won't win. They can't win this time, right?"

"They can't." Ade reached over and took my free hand in his. "They *can't*."

But I experienced the portentous sense of a tide turning. I felt our advantage slipping away, like Alex slipping through the door in the north wing. A fundamental element, a part of the puzzle, remained elusive, but I couldn't figure out what it was.

# Chapter Forty-Eight

I waited until the evening, and then I told Ade what I needed to do. He said exactly what I thought he'd say: that I was crazy, that I was making a mistake and that it wouldn't achieve anything. But he also insisted on coming with me, which I agreed to because we needed to stick together.

The press had been on top of Lottie and Margot like flies on shit, and yes, I sympathised with them to a point. However, the line had been drawn in the sand when it came to Margot. I knew for certain that Margot understood who Bertie was. Lottie, I wasn't sure about.

With all the attention on the two women, the name of their hotel had been mentioned several times on the internet. Neither woman had been arrested, though I believed they'd been questioned individually. That wasn't enough for me. I needed to see them.

Ade's shoulder still hurt, and I hadn't driven for a long time, so we took a taxi to the hotel. The driver frowned at us from the rear-view mirror as he saw the bustle of the paparazzi on the streets.

"Do you want to stop here?" he asked.

"Take us a bit further up the road, would you?" Ade said. He sensed me tense up and flashed a look of concern my way. We didn't need to say it, but I knew he was worried. I nodded, hoping to ease his worries even though I felt like I was about to walk into the lion's den.

"Deep breaths," he said as we paid the driver and got out.

The photographers already knew who we were. Though we'd

managed to avoid a lot of the scrutiny from the press, our identities had already been leaked. Never had I been so glad that I kept my social media accounts private, meaning no drunken or drugged-out pictures made it into their news articles. But now they had a photo of us walking, our heads down, hands shielding our faces. The unflattering camera flash drawing out every flaw in the drizzling rain. It didn't matter, but I still felt like a deer, cold and shivering in the centre of an empty road, one car coming straight for me.

Inside, the open foyer shone like gold with a grand chandelier glittering over our heads. The hotel was beautiful, opulent even. I didn't know there were any that looked like this outside London. It made my resolve weaken. My damp shoes slid across the marble floor, squeaking with each step. When heads turned, blood rushed to my face. We hurried over to the front desk to get away from those judgemental faces.

"I'd like to speak to Margot Pemberton. Is it possible for you to call her room?" I asked. Call it an instinct, but I had a feeling she'd want to talk to me. "Tell her it's Ruby Dean."

The concierge nodded his head and did as I asked. If he knew who I was, he was excellent at hiding it. I craned my neck, gaping at the moulded plaster on the ceiling, feeling almost exactly like I had the first day I arrived at Highwood Hall. Did it matter? Truly? A home was a home. All this was extra. All this was unnecessary. And yet I kept staring.

"She's in the penthouse," he said. "I'll take you up there."

I glanced at Ade with a slight eye-roll. *Of course* she's in the penthouse. Why would I expect anything less?

Trainers still squeaking, we made our way to the lift, and the concierge used a swipe card to access the top floor. I hadn't eaten since lunch, not even bothering with dinner, and yet my stomach still managed to churn. Margot and I had once shared a sensitive moment together, but it was possible she'd see me close up and turn defensive. I needed her to be open with me. I needed to relate to her again.

The lift opened up inside the penthouse, next to a small entryway. I'd certainly never stayed in a hotel room with its own entryway before. Then again, I could count the number of hotel rooms I'd stayed in on one hand. The concierge pointed us in the direction we needed to go before closing the lift doors. Ade and I glanced at each other. I wondered if we should tip the man, but I didn't have much cash on me, and he seemed to disappear before we had the chance.

"He'll spit in our soup later," Ade whispered, thinking along the same lines.

I tried to smile at the joke, but it faded quickly. We walked deeper into the apartment and then stopped, unsure.

They were waiting for us. Margot with a martini in one hand and a cigarette in the other. Lottie stood with her shoulders hunched. A baggy woollen cardigan covered her hands. She ran at me, and for half a second, I thought she was going to kill me. Instead, she wrapped her arms around my neck.

"Rita!" she exclaimed. "I'm so glad you're okay. I can't believe Daddy..."

Gently I extracted her arms. "It's Ruby."

Her eyes were empty when she gazed at me. "It is? Oh, sorry."

I turned my attention to Margot, who frowned. The elder woman sighed and waved me through to the next room, cigarette smoke trailing her.

"Would either of you like a drink?" she asked. "I had room service bring up a pitcher of martinis. It's going to be a long night." She gestured for us to sit down on a white sofa, pointing towards the glass pitcher resting in a bucket of ice. "Don't mind Lottie. She's on her third." She smiled. Her red lipstick bled into the cracks.

"No, thank you. I'm clean and sober, remember?"

"Oh yes," she said. "My apologies." She sipped her cocktail. "And what about you?" She raised her eyebrows towards Ade.

"No, thank you, ma'am."

"Ma'am. Dear Lord. Who am I, the queen?" Margot leaned back. "Oh, let's just get to it, shall we? I didn't know as much as you think I knew. Lottie knew nothing."

My eyes flicked over to Lottie, who was chewing on a thumbnail, staring hard at the windows. She hadn't sat down; instead, she sort of hovered over by Margot's chair.

"That's not why I'm here," I said. "But I am interested in what you knew. What did you think was happening when all the maids kept disappearing?"

Margot's usually steely expression crumpled momentarily. She took a long drag of her cigarette. "I know you'll think I'm lying, but I honestly thought he harassed them and they ran off. I thought that was the end of it."

"You never went in the north wing?"

"No."

"You're lying," I said. It was obvious to me then. I didn't say the words in order to start an argument or to aggravate her. I just knew.

She closed her eyes tightly.

"How dare you say that?" Lottie said on the edge of tears. "Mo-mo wouldn't lie."

"Lottie, honey. You need to get some rest. Why don't you have a lie-down?"

"But—"

"Please, darling."

Sulkily, and with one cardigan-wrapped hand over her mouth, she stumbled away to one of the bedrooms. We waited until the door clicked, the silence dragging. Finally she was gone and the truth could come out.

"You've no idea how many lies I've been told over the years," Margot spat out. "As far as I understood back then, my daughter was due to marry an upstanding citizen. A mild-mannered man who had no known vices. He wasn't known as a drinker. He was kind enough to the people around him. There'd been no complaints, not even in business, which is where the claws usually come out and the masks are removed. And then about a year after they married, my daughter started turning up to our house in tears. He was having affairs, she said. With the maids. They could never keep a maid for longer than a few months because Bertie couldn't keep his hands off them. A few weeks before, she'd gushed about how kind he was for hiring troubled young women." Margot paused to pour herself a second martini. When her hand trembled, Ade reached over and helped her. She thanked him and continued. "I didn't know he was hitting my daughter until several years after that. That's what it's like in these kinds of marriages. She hid the marks he left. And he was careful not to beat her face." She closed her eyes for a heartbeat, then opened them and carried on. "The maid turnover remained high, but I didn't know things had gone that far." Her lips pursed together. "I didn't know he killed them. My daughter was sad. She was my priority back then. You see, Laura would never leave him even though I implored her to. She was far more religious than I ever was and felt it against her beliefs to leave her husband."

"Did she ever find out what Bertie was doing?"

"Bertie and his father," Margot said. "They lived together at the time. Of course, Bertie's mother was dead by then."

"Let me guess," I said. "Another accident."

"Car crash."

I nodded slowly.

Margot's chin wobbled. "I'm sure you think I'm stupid for not seeing all the signs, but the mind never goes to *serial killer* does it? I suppose even Ted Bundy had a mother-in-law."

"When did you first find out?"

"After Laura died," Margot said. She let out a small gasp, clamping a hand over her mouth. I saw her working hard to fight back her tears. "Though I should've picked up on it sooner. The children did. When Lottie was a child, she once told me that Daddy kept disappearing into the north wing. Alex would talk about women like... like they were less than him. Even as a child. They were to be told what to do, he said. It was disturbing. But still, I didn't think *serial killer*. Would you?" She fumbled with the stem of her martini glass, and her eyes dropped to the carpet. "Laura sent me a note on the day she died..."

"What did the note say?"

"It said, 'I can't call, Mummy, because he'll know. He listens. I married a monster. He takes the maids.'" She leaned forward, still struggling with her tears, spilling some of her drink on the carpet. I removed the glass from her hand.

"Why didn't you go to the police?"

"I don't know," she said.

Again, I knew she was lying. "Yes, you do."

"My husband had died of a heart attack the year before, and I was living alone," she said slowly. "And... I'd run out of money. The note struck me as something an unhinged person would write, and I was concerned my daughter had become increasingly unstable over time."

"That's because she was married to a serial killer," I said coldly.

"Yes," Margot admitted. "I know that now. I... I think deep down it made sense to me, but I pushed it away. The thought. I buried it deep down. I still moved in with him because I wanted to make sure Lottie would be safe. By then I..." She stared up at the wall with unfocused eyes.

"Say it," I demanded. "Whatever it is you're about to admit, say it."

"I realised there was something very wrong with the men in that family. I thought that if I lived there, I could keep Lottie safe and perhaps try to stop it happening to Alex, though it turns out I was too late. Every time a maid left, I thought to myself, *at least it wasn't Lottie.*"

"You stayed for the money," I said. I got to my feet, so angry that I needed to move. I needed to pace the length of that room to stop myself from hitting her and never stop hitting her until she was a crimson puddle on the beautiful white carpet.

"No," she gasped. "That isn't true."

"Yes, it is, and you should admit it to yourself." I walked back and forth near the huge flat-screen television on the wall. I wanted to smash it into smithereens, but I didn't.

"It was for my *family.* I didn't want them to know what their father was."

"Yeah, because who cares about maids. Who cares about those drug-addled little sluts who bring you martinis and organise your wardrobe? You were kind to me, but it was all an act to distract me from the sacrificial offering you were providing him. Fuck you."

Margot nodded her head. Mascara smeared in the corners of her eyes as tears ran down her face. Her bottom lip wobbled. She melted before my eyes, turning into a pool of her own misery. The Wicked Witch of the West unspooling onto the floor.

"How can I make things right?" she begged.

"If Bertie and Alex go to prison, will you be put in charge of Bertie's estate?" I asked. "You and Lottie?"

"I'd imagine so," Margot said.

I sighed. "Well, you could tell the police that you knew all along and pay for your crime in a prison cell. But you won't do that. Instead, you're going to write me a list of all the places you think Alex might be, and then you're going to pay for Mrs Huxley's son's care home fees for the rest of his life and make sure he lives a life of luxury. Is that clear?"

"Yes," she said.

"And if this trial goes badly... If there's any glimmer of hope for

Bertie Howard, well then you'll come forward and you'll tell the police everything you knew, and you'll provide the note from your daughter because there's zero percent chance you destroyed it. And you'll make sure justice is served."

"All right," she said. "And you? What do you both want? Money?"

"I want my mother back," I snapped. "I want twenty-one years with her."

Margot's eyes fell to the floor.

# CHAPTER FORTY-NINE

There was a fundamental shift in my world—in the air around me—as we made our way out of the hotel. Like oxygen had been replaced by soup. It hit me all at once. The grief, the fear, the mother I missed whom I'd never known. Was it possible to miss a person you'd never met? I longed to feel better, to press fast-forward and skip ahead to waking up peacefully rested, my life ahead of me and full of opportunity. Always the addict, I longed for the convenient methods of reaching that peaceful feeling, and my mind raced with possibilities.

"Are you all right?" Ade asked. He helped me away from the photographers, gently guiding me with a hand on my lower back.

All warmth fled my body. It was impossible to breathe, and I hyperventilated with the tight bud of panic ready to blossom inside my chest. I tried to stay calm as I had my first anxiety attack since coming off drugs. But instead, my body fought against it, making everything harder. Every breath, every unsteady step, every tear dribbling down the bridge of my nose. Ade guided my hunched body down the rest of the street. The slick pavement reflected streetlights and headlights that danced beneath my feet. I couldn't lift my gaze from the ground.

"Keep breathing," he said. "One breath at a time."

I leaned on him, forgetting his bad shoulder, thinking only of my greedy need for human warmth and strength. But Ade never complained. A little down the street we found a restaurant, and I managed to pull myself together enough not to make a scene. It was late, and I wasn't hungry, but we still went in, sat at the bar and ordered Diet Cokes.

"Sorry," I said.

"Don't say sorry. Are you all right?"

"Better now, thank you." I lifted my glass, cocking it slightly as though toasting to us. The cold, sweet fizz was just what I needed to calm down.

"That was intense," Ade said. "And hugely impressive. I can't believe you said that to her."

"Me neither."

"But it needed to be said." He shook his head. "She won't be punished, will she?"

"Nope." I sipped my Coke. "I wonder how many girls she could have saved but didn't." Then I sighed. "I wonder what it's like to live with a monster like that. Would you keep pushing down your suspicions? Would you freeze up in terror? Jesus, Ade, I came to Highwood Hall because of my mum's letters, but I also worked there and made friends. I started some sort of strange romantic relationship with the son of the man I thought might've hurt my mother. I mean, I didn't know. I knew she'd had a relationship with Bertie and that she'd been afraid at times, but I didn't know he'd killed anyone. Not until Roisin died. I certainly didn't know he'd been doing this for *decades*. I didn't even suspect it until Mrs Huxley sat me down, and told me everything she knew. And..." I glanced up at Ade before looking away.

"What?"

"I was connected to him. Alex. It wasn't love, or even like, but I was drawn to him. What does that say about me?"

Ade laughed. "It says you can be charmed by an attractive, rich man. Big whoop."

"No, it's more than that," I said. "I was attracted to his games, not him. What if there's something wrong with me?"

"There isn't. You went to Highwood to solve a mystery, and you got pulled into another mystery."

I drained half my Coke. "The dioramas messed with my head."

"It's understandable," Ade said. "Come on. Let's finish these and go home." He gulped down his drink. "Damn, I wish I had my truck with me. Not that I can drive, I guess."

"Your truck's still at the hall. I completely forgot."

He shrugged. "The police searched and released it yesterday. They said I could collect it as long as I didn't go inside the house."

"My mum's letters are there too. And her portrait." I couldn't stand thinking of her on that dining room wall.

We walked together out into the drizzle. Ade turned up his jacket collar and hunched his shoulders, eyes roaming the street. I did the same, shivering against the sudden cool air, searching for taxi lights. Across the street, I thought I saw someone watching us. Someone tall, broad-shoul-dered. A photographer? But then the taxi pulled up, obscuring the view. Once I was inside, I glanced out of the window and the figure was gone.

Ade gave his address to the driver, and we set off for Paxby, but the whole time I thought about that figure watching us from across the street.

I'D THOUGHT CONFRONTING Margot and Lottie would bring me the peace I needed to go on, but it didn't. Ade made sweet, warm porridge again that morning, but I still had no appetite. I couldn't stop thinking about the Howards and what they'd been able to get away with. I was sure that Alex had left the country and would never see justice. The Highwood Hall search was still ongoing, but so far, no bodies had been found. Someone had made a meme based on the live stream of me in the red room. *When you spent $150 on dinner and your girl won't put out. Take her to the red room.* "Take her to the red room" was trending on Twitter. Torturing girls is funny now apparently.

On the other end of the scale, someone had set up a GoFundMe for me and Ade, which had already passed one hundred thousand pounds. I was floored. But neither I nor Ade had talked about it. I didn't think we could face the surrealness of our own situation. Every hour someone tried to call me to get a comment on Alex's disappearance or Margot Pemberton in the penthouse or the GoFundMe money. Networks wanted us on television. Newspapers wanted an interview. There were online debates about the live-stream video. One expert said it was doctored, another said it wasn't. The "comments" section had exploded with vitriol from people on both sides.

An online petition for Mrs Huxley's freedom had ten thousand signatures. They claimed she was a victim, and because she was ill, she should be released. A counter online petition claiming Mrs Huxley should never see daylight again also reached ten thousand signatures. All I knew was that she'd been arrested for accessory to murder. In the madness it was impossible to process how I felt about that.

I was exhausted. I scrolled, and I watched, and I read. The day passed by, and I remained in pyjamas, unclean, without focus, thinking of what it might take to stop my mind from spiralling out of control. Sometimes I sat on Ade's sofa, imagining I walked down the grand hall at Highwood with the wood panels on either side, the grinning Cavaliers staring down at me. Mrs Huxley gliding along with her burgundy dress swooshing. At least then I felt connected to my mother. I saw her picture on the wall. I knew she'd been there, knew she'd once breathed and lived, however short that time might've been.

"Ruby." Ade placed a gentle hand on my shoulder. "Let's go out, shall we? It's stuffy in here. You need fresh air." He pushed me, just enough, to get me up. To force me to shower and change.

It was a bright day. A sunglasses day, but I didn't have any at Ade's house. I realised, as we left the house, that I didn't know what day it was. And then I wondered whether Mrs Huxley knew too. I didn't even know where she was detained, whether she was in a prison cell somewhere. I felt completely left out in the dark, despite the bright sunshine.

We walked to a pub in Paxby and ordered fish and chips even though I still wasn't particularly hungry. If I'd been slim before, I was skeletal now.

"Rubes." Ade hooked a finger underneath my chin. "Talk to me."

Were we more than friends? Through all this stress, I couldn't quite decide.

"I'm not doing well," I admitted. "I can't stop thinking about her. My mother. She's still stuck in the hall. They painted her on the walls and left her there as a trophy for everyone to see, and I can't... I can't stand it. Their sick, sadistic secret. I recognised her on the first day, and I didn't understand then. I don't know how I worked in that place, setting up the table, serving food, and all the while she was there, looking at me. It's sick. I can't... I can't *stand* it. I feel like they've won. Don't you feel like they've won?"

"No," he said. "We won't let them win."

"Alex is gone. He's probably on some beach somewhere." Bitterness slipped into my voice, drops of vinegar in water. "I wish he was dead."

"I know it's hard, but we have to believe the police will find him."

"You mean the same police who handcuffed you after Huxley told them about two white serial killers?" I shook my head.

He grimaced. "Yeah, well... They have to find him. The world is watching them."

"And us too," I said. "I'm so tired."

A teenage waitress served us two huge plates of fish and chips. My mouth should've watered, but instead my stomach cramped. I picked up a fork, ready to force down some chips.

"Let's get her back," Ade said. "I need to collect my truck from the house. There are tools in there that should be able to take a wood panel off the wall. You can get your mum's letters too."

I sighed. "We can't. It could compromise the evidence."

He shook his head. "I think you need this. Don't you? To move on?"

"Yes," I said. "But the court case—"

He shrugged. "I don't see what harm it would do. It's not like we're outsiders. Your DNA, my DNA, it's all there anyway."

"I'll be the first suspect. They'll come for us both."

"Who cares?" Ade said. "We didn't murder anyone. Fuck the Howards and fuck the police. Let's do something for us."

"No," I said. "We can't. I can wait. I don't want anything messing up the evidence." I put down my fork. "I wish we could though."

"The police will be done soon." He reached across the table, placing his hand on my forearm. "Then we'll get her back. I promise."

The warmth of his hand, the gentleness in his brown eyes, it released the cramp in my stomach. I nodded, picking up my fork. I needed to believe him. I longed to. And finally, I allowed myself to believe everything would be okay.

# Chapter Fifty

A couple of days after our pub dinner, Ade woke me up excited. He placed a cup of tea down on the bedside table and clapped his hands together like he had big news.

"The detective dude just called. There's been a sighting of Alex."

I sat bolt upright in the bed. "Where?"

"Spain."

"Spain?"

He nodded. "They're working with Spanish police to find him." Ade rubbed his palms together again. "They're going to get the bastard. I can feel it."

I reached for my tea, waiting for that release to come. That unfurling of the tight coil inside my abdomen. Maybe when they had him in custody. Or after the court case when he's behind bars.

Ade noticed my subdued expression and sat down on the edge of the bed. "It's a great development. It feels legit. The police are following through on this."

"You're right. It does." My fingers tightened around the hot mug. "I just need him to be locked away. I won't be able to relax until then."

He nodded. A tentative smile played across his lips. "I swear, Ruby Dean, as soon as Lord Psycho and Mini Psycho are behind bars, we're going to the nicest restaurant in Paxby, which is... Well, it's Gino's Italian restaurant near the brook. But we're going to order lobster or caviar or whatever fancy food posh people eat and the best, biggest bottle of champagne you've ever seen."

I laughed. "Ade Bello, that's rather forward of you."

He shrugged. "I'm sick of wasting time."

"Me too."

When he shook his head and bit his bottom lip, I thought it was the cutest thing I'd ever seen. And I realised there was no other person on Earth I'd rather go through hell with except for maybe Roisin. Our eyes met, a question in his expression. I saw him wrestle with the decision of whether to kiss me or not. But as soon as I realised what he was thinking, I tensed slightly, and it broke the spell. He returned to his feet, and I considered blurting out an explanation about how I didn't mean it. I *did* want Ade to kiss me, just maybe not first thing in the morning after finding out Alex Howard was in Spain.

He paused by the door. "It's nearly over, Rubes. We're through the worst."

I nodded my head.

"Hey, I almost forgot. Pawel wanted to meet me for a drink later. He's struggling, poor lad. Do you mind if I meet him for a beer?"

"No, of course not."

"I know we've not been apart..."

"Yeah, no, that's fine," I said, desperately trying not to let fear creep into my voice.

"He's in Spain. He can't hurt us."

"I know. Seriously, I'm fine."

"Okay," he said. "I'm making eggy bread, so get your arse downstairs pronto. I'm not exaggerating when I say that my eggy bread is the best bloody eggy bread in the entire world."

"No exaggeration? Well, all right then." I forced the smile to stretch across my face to hide the sharp edge of fear I lived with every second of every day.

He left the room with a wink, and I sank back down into the pillow. The thought of being alone even scared the daylights out of me, but I couldn't admit that to Ade. It was irrational and stupid. The man who terrorised me was across a sea, far away. I was safe. And yet my hands trembled.

ADE LEFT the house just after seven p.m. and walked around to the Crossed Scythes to meet Pawel. He'd requested Ade alone, presumably for some man talk. I found myself wandering around Ade's home, running my fingers across plant leaves, hovering next to the drawers and wondering what was inside. But in the end, I didn't snoop. I settled on the sofa and watched old episodes of *Friends* and *Frasier*. Anything with a friendly laugh track to make it feel as though I wasn't alone. The house shivered with emptiness. I pulled a blanket around my shoulders and eventually fell asleep to Rachel and Ross arguing.

I woke to the sound of my phone ringing. The soundbar on the television had turned itself off, and now an episode of *Sex and the City* played on mute. I rubbed sleep from my eyes and answered the phone, expecting it to be Ade telling me he was coming home or staying out late. In my sleepiness, I hadn't noticed the number on the screen.

"Hi, Ruby."

I dropped the phone.

A scream lodged in my throat as I scrambled off the sofa, falling heavily on my knees. The blanket tangled around me as I sat on the floor, staring at the illuminated screen of my mobile phone. A thin, tinny voice came out of the speaker.

"Ruby? Answer me, Ruby. You're going to need to listen to me."

I snatched it from the sofa cushion. "How did you get my number?"

"You've always asked such fascinating questions," Alex said. "But this time you might want to know *why* I'm calling you and why it's after midnight and your gardener hasn't turned up to your little love shack yet."

A dull punch of despair spread through my body. "What have you done to Ade?"

"Why don't you come and see?"

I shook my head in disbelief. I didn't want this to be real. A squeaky voice emitted from my throat. "But you're in Spain."

Alex laughed. "Oh, Ruby. You sound so different. So meek. Where's the manipulation now? Where are your silly cameras and little doll house?"

"Have you been following me?" I thought of the shadowy figure I saw across the street near Margot's hotel. "Did Margot help you escape?"

"That's more like it," Alex said. "There's that curiosity I know and love. If you come to find your lover, perhaps I'll answer some of those questions."

"Where are you?"

"Where it all began," he said.

I pulled in a deep breath, steadying myself, steadying the fear. "I'm coming."

"Good girl. Now, there's one stipulation, Ruby."

"What is it?"

"If you call the police, I'll slit his throat."

I pulled the phone away from my ear for a moment, allowing the rage to bubble up inside me. Then I placed it back. "How do I know you haven't killed him already?"

"One moment," Alex said in the exact same tone a person would use when putting someone on hold.

I waited.

"Ruby, don't come. He'll kill us both. Go to the police—"

"Ade!"

My hand gripped the phone so tightly that I felt the blood drain from my fingertips. A rush of tears hit my eyes. He'd never sounded so panicked, so afraid. I seethed and burned.

"There you go—"

"I'm going to kill you," I blurted out. "I'm going to. I swear it."

He chuckled slightly. It wasn't the evil villain laugh from a super-hero movie, but the kind of titter a person lets out when told a mediocre joke. Somehow, that was even more terrifying.

I was about to hang up when I heard him say one more thing. "Do you trust me?"

"Never," I replied.

The sound of his laughter continued in my mind long after I'd hung up the phone.

# CHAPTER FIFTY-ONE

I followed the edge of the woods where the boughs of the trees were crooked and the roots poked up through the earth. It was a warm night, and I sweated through my T-shirt and cardigan. My palm felt slick against the hilt of the kitchen knife I carried, and every now and then I swapped hands. Pins and needles worked their way up my arms. Dozens of thoughts flashed through my mind. How did Alex get past the police guard? How would I?

The wrought iron gates loomed up ahead with the turrets of the house poking above. I walked over to the control panel and used the code to open the gates. As far as I could see, the place was empty. The mechanical whirring made me start, and the hand holding the knife flew up in defence.

"Stupid," I whispered, watching the gate judder open. I lowered my arm.

A couple of security lights flashed on as I stepped onto the drive. Yellow police tape fluttered around the place, some tied to the gate, some loose, flapping along the breeze. Part of the lawns had been dug out, destroying Ade's hard work. I found I couldn't look at the excavation site; it made my chest constrict.

Aside from a couple of lights on inside the house, Highwood seemed still and quiet. I made my way to the main entrance, pausing to control my breathing. I hadn't called the police. I couldn't risk it. No matter how much I wanted justice for my mother, Ade's life was worth more than that. If the only way to save him was coming here alone, then so be it. But this time I had no tricks up my sleeve. No hidden cameras and microphones. No Mrs Huxley with her keys to the locked rooms. No Ade with the shotgun stolen from Bertie's hunting collection.

All I had was me and the knife in my hand.

I opened the door. Perhaps that was enough. I'd made it this far, hadn't I?

As soon as I stepped inside, I heard the music. Chopin. The dreamy étude floated through the hallways. I knew the sound of that piano and the unmistakable touch of Alex's playing. It froze my blood now, chilled the marrow of my bones. And yet, I walked towards it. Alex had to be in the music room, which meant I couldn't surprise him by using the servant corridors. None of them connected to that part of the house.

I turned the knife in my hand as I strode through the grand hall, noticing something amiss. Highwood smelled *wrong*. It smelled like petrol. The air reeked of it all around me.

My heartbeat quickened. Of course I'd entered a trap. I'd expected nothing less. But still, that odour released primal, terrible fear. And yet I carried on until I reached the music room door. Inside this room, Alex and I had felt like we were in another world. But that had been the point, hadn't it? To break down my defences, to groom me, make me like him. Make it fun for him.

I saw the security guard first. So that was how Alex had got through the surveillance. He'd either knocked out or killed the poor man employed to watch the estate. He lay in a heap on the ground by the music room door. I bent down to check his pulse before noticing anything else.

"He's dead. Put the knife on the floor, Ruby."

I leapt away from the body on the ground. Shock ran through me, quick as an electrical current. The piano stool remained empty. The playing I'd heard was a recording, and Alex was nowhere to be seen. Instead, Pawel lounged in an armchair with a remote control in one hand and a smaller object in the other. A petrol can sat at his feet. He smiled at me. I couldn't believe what I saw.

"Put the knife down or I'll set everything on fire. I swear I will."

I dropped the knife to the carpet.

"Well done."

A muffled sound pulled me out of my shock. Ade was tied to a chair on the other side of the room. I ran over and removed his gag as Pawel used the remote control to turn off the music.

"You shouldn't have come," Ade said. "It isn't safe." His eyes drifted over to the piano where I noticed the portrait of my mother, resting against the piano stool. Half of the wood panel had been ripped from the dining room wall. The sight of her severed body made me nauseous. "This is all a trap for you."

"How did this happen?"

Ade's eyes flicked over to the cook.

Pawel grinned as he fiddled with a small, square object, and a tiny flame manifested between his knuckles. "Your boyfriend here was too stupid to suspect anything. When he got in my car, Alex and I restrained him. We took out the guard, disabled any surveillance equipment and tied him to that chair."

I stared at him in disbelief. "But why? Why are you here?"

"Destroying evidence before it's too late. Which includes you."

"Where's Alex?"

He shrugged.

"Why are you working for him?"

"He's good to me." The tone of his voice brought out the alarm bells in my mind. I knew danger when I heard it. I'd been around enough drug dealers and bad boyfriends to recognise a man about to snap. He was drunk. I saw that in his red eyes. His hair was greasy and pulled forward. "Everything worked. Until *you* and *Roisin* came along. You two women managed to screw everything up."

"Did you kill maids too? Were you helping the Howards all this time?"

"I didn't murder those women. I just..."

"What?" I snapped. "Raped them?"

"No!"

"Oh, you were one of their lackeys then. A pathetic bootlicker paid to do what they asked of you. Including burning evidence. Why are you doing that, Pawel? Is it because you murdered Roisin?" The realisation hit me hard. Now everything clicked into place. I hadn't seen it before. Even Ade let out a gasp.

Pawel's eyes were dark and dangerous. "She wasn't supposed to be with him. She was supposed to be with me."

"So you strangled her?"

He flicked the lighter, and another flame licked his fingertips. Orange light reflected in his glassy eyes, bringing them to life. "It was an accident."

"She fell into your hands, and you squeezed the life out of her by accident?" While Pawel was preoccupied by his thoughts, I backed up closer to Ade. Keeping my hands behind my back, I reached towards the ropes around his arms. "How did you get away with it? There was an autopsy."

"Bertie knows people," Pawel said. "Besides, I used... I used an apron string. The marks... on her neck... they were similar to that..." He cleared his throat. How dare he be upset? "Bertie helped me get her into the tree. We waited until night."

I thought of Roisin's lovers stringing up her lifeless body. But despite the vomit-inducing story, I managed to work through the knotted rope behind my back. Soon Ade had one arm free. I positioned myself between Pawel and Ade to block him from Pawel's view. Behind me, I sensed Ade's movement as he worked on his second arm.

"How did Alex get rid of his car? Why was there a sighting of him in Spain?" I kept talking, biding time for Ade.

"There was a kitchen boy who worked here for a while. He lives in Leeds. When he got caught dealing drugs, Lord Bertie paid for his lawyer. He stayed loyal."

"So Alex drove the car to this kid who then drove it all the way to Edinburgh?"

Pawel nodded. "They're about the same height, same hair colour. You know, for any CCTV footage. As for the tip in Spain, all I needed to do was email in some convincing sightings from a few different email accounts."

"Clever," I said, lacing my voice with sarcasm. "Where is he, Pawel? He called me. I know he's here."

But the cook nonchalantly shrugged as though he couldn't care less. I glanced behind me to check that Ade was free. Then I directed my eyes to the wood panel resting against the piano stool. It was the closest we had to a weapon that I could reach out and grab.

Pawel played with the lighter, bringing the flame to life and then making it disappear, then bringing it to life again. I grabbed one end of my mother's portrait, lifted it and rammed the wood panel against Pawel's jaw, tipping back the chair. The lighter dropped from Pawel's hand and hit the carpet with a bounce.

The flames came to life.

# CHAPTER FIFTY-TWO

I couldn't let it go. Even at half the size, the panel was heavy, and it pulled my arm down with its weight. Behind me, flames latched onto everything in its path. Every curtain, every ornate piece of furniture, every portrait. It did not discriminate. But where was Alex?

Ade looped his uninjured arm over the back end of the wood panel to help me move faster. We outpaced the flames, but barely. By the time we came to the entrance to the house, the hall had been consumed, but to our surprise, so had the kitchen. Someone else had started a fire here too. Alex?

Heat emanated from the open kitchen door. Tiny, delicate flames licked the doorjamb, growing and expanding with each moment. On the other side, Pawel stood between us and the exit. He must've slipped out of the music room and used the servants' corridor. I kicked myself for not doing the same.

"Ade in three," I said, hoping he'd catch on. I counted us down and thrust the wood panel forwards as hard as I could. I felt Ade's weight behind it too, knocking into Pawel's chest. It sent him flying back towards the door.

But Pawel was merely winded, able to shake off the blow with ease. I swung my gaze back towards the kitchen where the fire was building in intensity, the heat piling out of the room, waves of it hitting my face. And then my blood turned ice cold because I'd just seen two blue eyes staring at me from the shadows.

He was crouched, halfway down the stairs, slithering low like a snake, his hands on a lower step than his body. He'd tried to creep up on us like a cat, but the fire had illuminated his features in the dark. I knew exactly where he'd come from. Alex had been hiding upstairs. He probably ran into the cupboard when he heard us walking through the home. And now, he smiled at me. He smiled, and his lips stretched, and his teeth came out.

He straightened himself to full height.

"I believe that belongs to me," Alex said, nodding at the wooden panel.

"The place is about to burn, Alex," I said. "Just let us go. Don't do anything stupid." I'd turned to face Alex, and now I checked on Ade behind me. Pawel was back on his feet, blocking the exit. His arms folded. My mind screamed at me to stay calm and think rationally, but the heat from the fire and the pounding of my heart made it almost impossible. Meanwhile, Alex walked leisurely down the stairs like it was Sunday morning and all he had to do that day was read a newspaper and smoke a cigar.

"I want my property back," he said, his eyes lingering on me.

That's right. I had been next on their murder list, and that meant he owned me. I dropped my half of the panel, and Ade did the same. At least it freed up our hands. I racked my brain, trying to think of a way out of this. But we were surrounded by fire. I checked Alex for weapons, but I didn't see anything. No obvious knife or gun.

"Take it then," I said.

He kept coming. I saw no hesitation in his eyes whatsoever. He walked towards me until we were face to face.

"That's not the property I was referring to," he said.

So swift it almost blurred at the edges, Ade was by my side, shoving a hand against Alex's chest. "Run, Ruby."

But I saw Pawel moving out of the corner of my eye, and I knew Ade was in danger. Ade managed to push Alex back towards the fire while Pawel lumbered up behind, his arms stretching. I had to act fast, so I dropped to a crouch, took hold of the panel with both hands and spun it until it hit Pawel on the back of his knees. He flinched, but it wasn't enough to knock him down. When he stumbled and caught himself, I dropped the wood and ran to the door, praying it was open. It was.

"Ade!" I yelled, but he was tussling with Alex on the floor, the two of them dangerously close to the fire. It raged now; it had a rumbling sound all of its own with golden-red flames covering the walls. I saw them spread into the entryway and felt the thick smoke hit the back of my throat. "Ade! We need to go!"

I leaned out the entrance, desperately gulping in the cool night air, when a pair of hands wrapped around my throat. Gasping, struggling in the midst of the curling smoke, I dug my nails into my attacker's flesh, clawing, fighting for my life. A gurgled shrieking sound burst from my body. He was strong. Somehow I knew it was Alex and not Pawel. I recognised those fingers without even seeing them.

As suddenly as the hands clasped my throat, they let go. When I spun on my heel, I had to bring my sleeve up to shield myself from the boiling-hot flames, and then I saw Alex step out through the smoke. His face was set into an expression of tight determination. He grabbed me by the shoulders and forced me out of the house. Never had I felt terror as I did then. Alex had zeroed in on me with all his psychopathic resolve, and now I had no idea if Ade was alive or dead inside that house. But when I tried to rush back in, Alex shoved me down so that I landed on my backside, hands scrabbling in the gravel. And he kept coming. Even as I scrambled away, he kept coming.

This wasn't supposed to happen. When I'd used myself as bait, I'd had a plan. I'd organised it so that I knew what I was doing at every moment. Yes, it had been dangerous and scary, but I'd felt in control, knowing that each element of our attack had been meticulously planned. Now I had no tricks up my sleeve, no sleight of hand whatso-ever, except...

I grabbed a handful of stones and threw them as hard as I could, aiming up towards his face. At least half hit the target and his arms flew up to protect himself. While he clutched his injured face, I climbed to my feet and ran back towards Highwood. I couldn't leave Ade in there even with the tall flames licking the ceiling. The windows were lit up from the fire, which meant it was only a matter of time before someone in Paxby called the police.

"Ade!" I covered my mouth with my hand, squinted through the hot smoke, eyes searching for him.

He was lying on his back near the stairs, legs and arms limp and lifeless. I had no idea how I'd get him out of there, but I still ran in, trying not to listen to the tiny explosions popping and hissing through the house. I grabbed his foot, and I pulled and pulled. But just as I managed to yank him almost to the door, Alex's arms wrapped around my waist. He dragged me outside, threw me down on the lawn and climbed on top of me, pinning me to the grass. He glowed orange from the fire, his usually perfect skin marred by the tiny cuts across his nose. Cuts I'd caused with the stones. I noticed one bright red spot on his eyeball.

"Stop making this harder than it needs to be!" Alex demanded.

I spat at him and he roared back at me.

"If I didn't make it hard, it'd be boring for you," I said, taunting him. "Or am I wrong? After all, you're the voyeur, aren't you? You just like to watch. This is new to you, this violence. You're pampered and spoilt. Daddy's little boy. Or is it Daddy's little disappointment? Aren't you sadistic enough for him? Not enough of a killer?"

His sour, laboured breath hit my damp skin. Above me, his skin burned bright red with either rage or shame or both. His fingers tightened around my wrists, and yet he still hesitated. He pinned me, but he didn't try to hurt me.

"I'm sorry your plan didn't work. You thought Pawel would kill me, didn't you? Set the place on fire and let me die slowly and painfully. But now you're faced with doing the job yourself and you can't do it." I watched his lip twitch and enjoyed it. "How old were you when he first made you watch? Were you just a boy? Did he tell you all about the traditions in the family, about how the powerful Howard men take what they want when they want it?"

Alex said nothing, but the pressure of his hands on my wrists was almost unbearable. I squirmed beneath him. He remained solid.

"He always made you watch. Training his boy to be a miniature psycho version of himself. You're a victim, Alex. He doesn't understand you. He just wanted to dominate you."

"Shut up."

"Let me go. Let me go and run. You're not Bertie's lapdog anymore. You don't need to stay here and destroy the evidence. Let me go so I can help Ade and then get out of here. Let your survival instinct kick in."

But Alex shook his head.

"Why did you come back here?"

He smiled. He wanted to talk. "There was an agreement I had to keep."

"How did you even manage all this?" The longer he talked, the longer I stayed alive.

"There's a way to get into the house unnoticed. Under the stables."

"You could've just gone to Spain."

He shook his head. "Daddy and I always agreed someone would destroy it. Them. That we'd destroy them."

"Who?"

"Who do you think?" he said through gritted teeth.

"The bodies." A chill passed over me. "My mother."

"Yes," he said. "I had to burn them and the room and everything else."

"Why bother? The police will have enough evidence anyway."

Alex shrugged. "It was our arrangement."

"Whatever helps you get away with it." Of course, I thought. Men like Alex and Bertie never saw the end in sight; they saw what they could still cling to. They would fight until the bitter end. I should've considered that.

"Tell me where you put her," I said. "Please."

To my surprise, Alex pulled me up to a sitting position and rolled off me. He still had his back to the house, but his weight was no longer on top of me. He pointed over to the stables to the west of the sprawling estate, away from the gates. I hadn't even noticed that it was on fire.

"Underneath," he said. "A cellar of sorts."

"Every day you go to work and take calls and you sit at your desk and have meetings on top of the bones of the women your father murdered."

His blue eyes held mine. There was no remorse in them, but I saw intrigue. He saw things from my point of view as not only a maid, but the daughter of a victim. I saw his mouth open and close as though he wanted to talk. I smiled then, and he paused. He didn't know. He didn't see what I saw.

"Goodbye, Alex," I said softly, and Ade brought the remains of my mother's portrait down onto his head.

Alex fell onto me first, until I pushed him off me. Ade turned the panel on its side and rammed it down three more times until we were sure. Then he threw the panel away, grabbed his hurt shoulder, and collapsed onto his knees. I hurried to his side, and we huddled there together. The wail of sirens sounded out in the distance.

# CHAPTER FIFTY-THREE

Ade struggled to breathe. I helped him loosen the clothes around his throat and pulled the sling into place around his hurt shoulder. I couldn't even imagine the pain it'd taken to lift the wood panel and bring it down on Alex.

"Can you breathe?"

He wheezed in and out. I tried to help him find a rhythm with his breath. But as he strained, tears gathered in my eyes. I saw him losing consciousness and rubbed his chest, not knowing what to do. In front of us, the hall blazed, its structure crumpled. I saw Margot's curtains tumble from the window as a fire engine roared onto the driveway.

I waved my arms, and several men came running out of the vehicle. Two of them carried Ade over to the engine while another stayed with me on the lawn.

"Are you all right?" he asked. His face paled when he saw Alex's smashed face.

I nodded, and he reached down to help me up.

"Let's get you checked over."

But I paused. There she was, on the grass. The wood panel. My hand stretched out once, but I changed my mind and left the portrait where it was. Nothing would bring her back. Yes, her body would be tied to Highwood Hall forever, especially after Alex's cruel final act, but it didn't matter. It was just her body, not her essence. Whatever had made her Emily Ferguson no longer existed.

I could never go back and meet her. I had to make peace with that. Taking a piece of wood with her face on it wasn't going to change anything. I let the fire fighter walk me over to Ade.

"I told them about Pawel," Ade said, doubled over, a blanket around his shoulders.

I nodded, suspecting that Pawel was probably dead by now. I struggled to feel sympathy for him. He'd murdered my friend and then had the gall to pretend he was heartbroken.

And as we waited for the ambulance, I watched the great hose unspool. I heard the thunderous gusts of water that spewed onto the remains of Highwood Hall. Above our heads, ashes floated into the night. Tiny burning flecks of gold. They danced.

No doubt, in time Lord Bertie would speak about the heinous acts executed here—he'd want the attention—but for now, I wouldn't know what prompted Pawel to turn over to their side. I'd been so sure that he'd loved Roisin. Maybe he'd simply wanted to possess her.

Lord Bertie and Alex Howard didn't just use their power to do what they wanted; they corrupted the people around them. Margot, Mrs Huxley, Pawel and others. I had to believe they were as capable of good as they had been bad. I needed to believe they would've remained good if they'd never met Bertie. But in the same breath, I had to believe that I wouldn't have been corrupted so easily. And there it was, the fairy tale I told myself. *What happened to them would never happen to me because I'm better than that.*

Ade received oxygen in the ambulance, and soon we were on our way out of Highwood. I tried to wipe away the residue of smoke and grime from my face, but it wouldn't come off. Instead, I leaned back inside the ambulance and imagined the dark branches of the woods that slanted towards the house. Highwood crumbled, but the nature below would survive. Perhaps it would even flourish.

$\flat$

A WEEK AFTER THE FIRE, I went to Heather Grove to visit Charlie. It was my promise to Mrs Huxley, and I intended to keep it. Ade had left the hospital the day before, and I'd stayed in his house until I got back on my feet. Margot had, however, paid me one month's wages along with the money for Charlie's care. At least I had some spending money now. The GoFundMe was still in progress, and Alex's last stunt had ended with Ade and I receiving over half a million pounds in donations. We were overwhelmed to say the least. I hadn't even thought about what we might do with the money. Not yet.

I'd heard news that Mrs Huxley had been admitted to hospital and was receiving chemotherapy for advanced lung cancer. She'd been allowed one visit to see Charlie and say goodbye. I was still deciding if I wanted to visit her or not. I had a lot to process.

The sun shone down on Heather Grove, turning the lush vines emerald green against the limestone walls. Pink and purple flowers bloomed through the garden, heavy with paper-soft petals. Ade would know the names of them all, but I didn't. I gazed at a rose bush, remembering Mrs Huxley taking a flower and smiling at her son. She was indirectly responsible for my mother's death, and yet, I couldn't hate her. Not even close.

"Hi," I said to the young woman behind the reception desk. "Ruby Dean. I'm here to visit Charlie Huxley."

"Oh yes," she said. "One of the nurses will take you."

"Thanks."

I waited for a few moments, casually browsing the internet on my phone. The Howards were all over the news. The paparazzi had caught a photograph of Lottie crying on the street. *Heiress grieves over monster brother.* I thought that was unfair.

Lord Bertie's mugshot had been plastered onto every news article. He had such piercing blue eyes and handsome features that, apparently, he received fan mail in prison. Nothing surprised me anymore.

"Are you ready?" A smiling nurse beckoned me over.

I nodded, placing my phone back in my bag.

"He's so excited to meet someone new. He wants to show you his art," she said.

"Oh lovely! Did you receive the money?"

"Yes," she said. "Everything's sorted."

"Great." My chest loosened as we made our way through many white corridors towards the room.

"I'm sorry for everything you've been through," the nurse said. "I mean... I hope you don't mind me saying that."

"Thanks." I wrapped my arms around my body as we reached a brightly painted open area. Some of the residents played board games or read a book or watched television. They were loud, rambunctious, giggling and singing. Life went on, and here was the evidence.

"I'm so shocked by Vera," the nurse said.

"Who?"

"Vera Huxley."

I laughed, and the nurse gave me a bemused look. "Sorry, it's just I never knew her first name. I don't know how I never learned it even now. She was always Mrs Huxley to me." Even in the news reports, Mrs Huxley had been referred to as "the housekeeper" or "middle-aged woman" not by her actual name.

"Oh, I see. You know she was such a nice lady. I can't believe she did those things."

We left the communal area, and the nurse stood outside a room with a blue door and a nameplate on the outside.

"For what it's worth, I don't think she would've done it if it wasn't for her son. She felt trapped, I think."

"Still," the nurse said, her eyes moving towards the door. "Anyway. Charlie is a lovely boy, but you should know that at times he doesn't communicate too well. If he doesn't talk to you, don't take it personally. Sometimes Charlie goes through non-verbal phases. But don't think that you can't talk to him. He loves the sound of voices. It brightens him up so much. I'll leave the door open in case you get overwhelmed, but I think you'll be just fine. I'll be right outside."

"Thanks."

She opened the door and I stepped in. I immediately understood why Mrs Huxley had wanted her son to live here. The room was lovely. Bright and airy with high windows that let in sunshine. It overlooked the roses and beyond to the sprawling meadows that lay like patchwork. I allowed my eyes to roam over the rest of the room, to the boy—no, man—sitting at the desk by a window. An open face lifted to see me. He was so like Mrs Huxley and yet, so different at the same time. He had her high cheekbones, but I saw a softness too. His eyes were deep hazel, but they were the same shape as Bertie's. He waved to me, and I responded.

Then I saw what he had in his hands. It was a small lump of plasticine that he moulded between finger and thumb. I found a chair over by the wall and dragged it closer to his desk.

"Are you working on your art?" I asked.

He nodded.

He reached forward, showing me a box. It was cut open, and inside he'd painted his room. The artistry was perfect. Every detail had been re-created, from the tall windows to the desk—fashioned out of cardboard —to the paintbrushes lined up along the wall and a figure hunched in a chair. He'd used a little doll that he'd customised to look just like him. He'd placed an empty chair next to the desk in almost the exact position I'd moved the chair for the visit.

"Are you making me?"

He glanced up at me and lifted the lump of plasticine. I saw that he was moulding it into the shape of a person's face.

"Did you run out of dolls?"

He nodded his head.

"But you remembered what I look like because your mum showed you a picture?"

He nodded again. And then he held up a finger as though asking me to wait. He pushed his chair back and reached under his desk. There he lifted up another box, this one opened in the same way. Inside, he'd reproduced the communal area in the care home with tiny dolls and plasticine figures occupying sofas and chairs. He'd even painted a television on the wall with actors on the screen.

"These are beautiful," I said. "Did your mum ask you to make special ones?"

He smiled and nodded his head again. I had to wonder whether he'd understood some of the scenes he'd made. I now knew that the first diorama had been of my mother, laid flat on the floor by the stairs, blood coming from her broken skull. Lady Laura hanging from the chandelier. But he was so happy to be making them regardless of their dark themes.

"Shall I sit still for you so that you can make me into a doll?" I asked.

He nodded enthusiastically and picked up his plasticine. When I pulled a funny face, he laughed. I laughed too. It was over, I thought. The nightmare was finally over.

THE HOUR with Charlie went by in a flash. He'd promised to finish up my diorama by the time I went back next week. And as I walked out of the home, a weight lifted from my shoulders. I'd never experienced this lightness before. This bountiful sense of possibilities. For so long I'd had a single purpose in my mind that I wasn't sure what to do next. I couldn't stay at Ade's indefinitely. Our relationship had gradually evolved to more than friends, but it was new and fragile, and we couldn't just move in together without building a foundation first. Both of us had come out of Highwood with hidden bumps and bruises. We needed space to heal separately.

Which meant I needed a job. I'd had offers from journalists and publishers. *Tell your story*, they said. I heard *Make us money*, and I felt nauseous.

I caught the bus back to Paxby, walked around the village for a while, bought a coffee and browsed the ads in the window of the newsagent. Then I made my way back to Ade's cottage. He still used his YouTube channel as a platform to talk about gardening, though it had exploded since the live stream in the red room. But now he had to deal with a constant barrage of questions about the monster of Highwood Hall rather than horticultural matters. He'd even had calls from TV producers asking him if he wanted to be on *Gardener's World*.

Ade had a future. He was skilled and he knew what he wanted. I didn't. I hadn't trained in anything, and aside from managing to catch a serial killer, I'd done nothing with my life. What was I going to do?

For a week I floated around, sleeping in until noon, staying up until the early hours of the morning, trying not to remember Alex Howard's eyes appearing in the dark shadows of Highwood Hall. For that entire week, I thought of Heather Grove. The bright walls, the smiles, the giggles and loud voices. Perhaps that was what I needed after so many years of quietude at my aunt's home.

It called to me. I'd finally figured out the ending—no, beginning—to my story.

The morning of the next visit I woke up excited for the first time, and I didn't even need a vat of coffee to energise me for the day. In fact, I left early, and I dressed in my smartest clothes. When the same nurse started talking to me, I decided to take a chance.

"Could you tell me how you trained for your job? I think I'd like to do it too."

"I'd love to," she said. "Why don't we meet for a coffee after my shift? I finish at four today. You can still get the bus back to Paxby until six."

That afternoon, Charlie finished my doll. I asked him if we could have her wearing a nurse's uniform. He agreed, and we started making it together.

# AUTHOR NOTE

Thank you for reading THE HOUSEMAID. This book was the most enjoyable challenge to write, and I hope you loved Ruby's story as much as I did.

If you enjoyed this book, you'll love My Perfect Daughter. Zoe adopts the child who lures her to her serial killer father... Ten years later, there's another body.

# ABOUT THE AUTHOR

Sarah A. Denzil is a British suspense writer from Derbyshire. Her books include SILENT CHILD, which has topped Kindle charts in the UK, US, and Australia. SAVING APRIL and THE BROKEN ONES are both top thirty bestsellers in the US and UK Amazon charts.

Combined, her self-published and published books, along with audiobooks and foreign translations, have sold over one million copies worldwide.

Sarah lives in Yorkshire with her husband, enjoying the scenic countryside and rather unpredictable weather. She loves to write moody, psychological books with plenty of twists and turns.

Writing as Sarah Dalton - http://www.sarahdaltonbooks.com/

CPSIA information can be obtained
at www.ICGtesting.com
Printed in the USA
LVHW090540170822
726095LV00002B/219